Michaelbrent Collings

Written Insomnia Press
WrittenInsomnia.com
"Stories That Keep You Up All Night"

Sign up for Michaelbrent's Minions
And get FREE books.

Sign up for the no-spam newsletter
(affectionately known as Michaelbrent's Minions)
and **you'll get several books FREE**.
Details are at the end of this book.

Contents

DEDICATION

To...

My readers, who make this continuing journey possible…

And to Laura, FTAAE.

PROLOGUE: watcher

The terminal.

An appropriate name for the place, which is a squat, concrete box that hunches just this side of Hell and just the other side of Nowhere.

A Shit County Sheriff's Dept. squad car sits near the terminal. It does not occupy any of the spots closest to the front door, or even to the small exit that leads to the sheriff's satellite station in the terminal itself. The sign of an officer who wishes others to have the better placing. Or the sign of an officer who wants to get a few extra steps of exercise. Or, last of all, the sign of an officer who is incompetent and who doesn't want anyone looking when he sneaks out to take a nap during his "rounds."

The Watcher notes all this. That is the Watcher's job.

There are other Watchers, of course, but this one is here *now*. This Watcher has been charged to take note of these things. To prepare the way for what will come next.

As though bidden – for bidden it was, and is, and shall continue to be – a thick fog rolls in. It eats the night as it crawls forward, otherworldly and strange.

That is as it should be. That is as it was *designed* to be.

This fog is thicker than any fog that has ever been seen in this part of the world. It catches the light cast by the metal-halide bulbs that jut from the cracked asphalt like iron sprouts trying to survive in a concrete jungle. It swallows most of the illumination cast by the bulbs, but that does not matter, because the fog itself gleams with a wan, sickly light. The glow is disquieting for most who look upon it. The Watcher knows this, for that, too, is part of the fog's design.

Every moment that has come to pass has been part of the design.

Every Cycle has played out as expected.

But an expectation met does not necessarily equate to boredom. Every Cycle has played out as expected, but the myriad routes the players have taken to reach their destinations has thrilled the Watcher.

A Watcher who does not love its job – its purpose – should not be a Watcher.

The fog engulfs the Watcher. But the Watcher still sees. Three eyes are better than the two. The Watcher's three eyes glow, and the glow casts strange shadows in the mist – but also allow the Watcher to see through the fog as though it has disappeared.

The Watcher sees the people in the concrete box.

Most of them will never leave.

The Watcher has seen the outcome. The expectation of the one who will survive.

Lights blink around the Watcher as more Watchers arrive. All of them gaze on the old bus terminal, which has now been converted to a new prison, though the people inside do not know this.

Not *yet*.

One side of the terminal is a featureless wall of cinder block and concrete. The other side consists of long, tall panes of glass that allow travelers to view the bus parking spaces, as well as the general-use parking lot beyond. A pair of automatic doors, also glass, sit in the middle, ready to allow entry and exit for those who will use this place.

The bus slips are empty. They jut out from the curb at forty-five-degree angles, long yellow lines that seem to glow with their own light. The glow fades as the fog encroaches.

The Watchers gaze upon the box through the bright green, triple light of their eyes.

And still the fog thickens. It pushes toward the terminal, the leading edges forming an almost perfectly vertical wall.

Perpendicular to the ground, rising high enough that the top of it – if there is a top, which the Watcher does not know because it is not a Watcher's job to know such things – disappears into the night.

The fog stops moving, halting fifty feet away from the terminal. It has eaten the squad car and all but one of the parking lot light poles. It does not consume the terminal, because the order has not been given. The last Cycle has ended, but the bridge between the one that ended and the one about to begin has not yet completed his passage.

The Watcher waits. They all wait.

The people inside wait, too. They wait for work shifts to end or for the next leg of their journeys to begin. They wait for things that will never come.

That is part of the Cycle.

That is part of the *fun*.

Inside the terminal, hard metal benches shine dully under the migraine-inducing fluorescent lights, one-third of which do not work. Soon, none of the lights will work.

That, too, is part of the Cycle.

The Watcher can see it all. Even the electronic sign to one side of the terminal lobby, next to the ticket counter. The sign reads:

Current Time: 1:22 A.M.

LA to SLC arrive 1:38 – ON TIME

BOISE to LOS ANG. arrive 3:20 A.M.

The current time is correct as listed. The rest of the sign is a lie. Co-opted by the Cycle.

To the back of the lobby is a small locker area, a vestibule with an open door frame. A row of lockers in the middle, and a few more affixed to the back wall, are more than enough to service the needs of the passengers who wait here, or who choose for some unknowable reason to stay for a while in this place. The light in this tiny space is even worse than in the rest of the terminal: a pair of fluorescent bars hanging on the wall in the very back cast a grim, grimy kind of glow that makes the vestibule a thing more of shadow than light.

The Watcher presses a control, and one of the bulbs in the locker room sputters and dies, pushing the vestibule into twilight. Soon darkness will fall.

Beside the lockers, a small baggage carousel waits, motionless, for bags to be slung through a plastic-sheeted door on the outer wall. That door, the Watcher knows, is sealed from the inside. The Watcher knows, too, that other Watchers will soon seal the small egress from the outside, as well – in ways far more permanent than the simple lock and key that now shut the baggage claim area off from the rest of the world.

Baggage claim. Lockers. Two bathrooms. The ticket window and office. The sheriff's satellite station.

A small terminal. But large enough for a Cycle. Large enough indeed. In fact, the terminal contains six passengers, two employees, a prisoner, and a hidden child. Ten in all: the largest group of any Cycle so far.

The Engineers begin to arrive. The Watchers do not turn to look. They have all seen this before. And the fun part is not what happens out here, but what is about to happen *inside.*

The fog pushes forward again. The final light pole disappears in the mist. The parking lot lights extinguish. The mist, however, continues to glow.

A moment later, the lights of the bus terminal flicker. Off, on.

Off.

On.

They stay on. For now.

The Watchers move forward with the fog. The Engineers remain behind.

It is time to begin.

Soon, it will be time to end. The watched will bleed, and die. And that will be the most fun of all.

PART ONE: Six Hours Left

1. Monitors

Meriweather "Mary to my friends" Holiday rarely hated her life. It was a hard life, sure, but what life wasn't? She was working a low-pay job in a low-traffic bus terminal, pretty much the least exciting job in existence. But it came with benefits for the family, and she got enough extra shifts that the double-time added up to a tidy sum. She didn't like it that she often doubled as the janitorial staff, and her one regular coworker was a creep, but even with all that… nothing to hate.

Not really.

It beat dark alleys and the constant threat of gang rapes whenever she had to go get cigarettes for her dad. He wanted cigarettes, he *got* cigarettes; that was a lesson that Mary had learned early, and learned hard.

She could not remember the first time he shook her awake, the first time she looked up at his unshaven face, his wild eyes, and heard him whisper, "Out of smokes." It had been part of her life since she was old enough to walk, to hold the bills he shoved into her small hands, and to make the three-block trip to the nearest place that would serve a child because that child was "Big J's kid."

That was all she ever had to say: "I'm Big J's kid." The man behind the counter – always a man in that place – took the money. He never gave back change. He would instead fill her palms with a carton of the Kools that were all her daddy would smoke, and she'd walk back home where Big J himself would be waiting. Often, he waited asleep since the reason he sent her was generally because he was having trouble walking any distance longer than the ones from couch to toilet to fridge and back again.

When he was asleep it was better. She could put the Kools on the floor beside him, and creep back to play, or perhaps even dare to sleep a bit herself.

When Big J was awake, he insisted she "smoke" with him. That meant she had to sit on the floor beside him while he smoked and yelled at sports on TV. If she fell asleep, he beat her.

If she *didn't* fall asleep... he usually beat her then, too. For looking bored. For staring at him. For *not* staring at him. For making a sound that his booze-sodden brain would somehow convince him had led to a bad snap by the quarterback, or a fumble caused by the overly-loud breathing of a five-year-old girl in a Compton hood hundreds of miles away from the game.

Big J died when Mary was twelve. A twofer, because after the autopsy one of the less-than-sympathetic social workers who processed her let her know that if the lead poisoning occasioned by the drive-by hadn't killed him, the golf ball-sized tumor in his lungs would have done him in within the year anyway.

Mary thought, for about ten seconds, that Big J's death would get her out of the hood. She was going into The System, which she had heard terrible things about, but even The System couldn't be as bad as home, could it?

Yeah. It could.

She made it through, though. Eventually, she got out. She *escaped*. She worked one low-paying job after another, but each paid a few pennies more than the last. Each was a little better, a little farther from danger, than the one before.

Each was a step up. And that was all she wanted: to step up a bit each day. That, she determined, was the secret to happiness. You couldn't control the universe, but you could constantly try to step a bit higher, and make a bit more of yourself no matter where you landed.

So she was happy, by and large. No more Big J, no more late-night smokeathons. After she fled the last foster home – six months shy of eighteen years old, so though she was technically a minor on the run, no one looked too hard for her – no more beatings, no more rapes. Just her. Just stepping up.

Those facts were enough to keep her happy. Usually.

But once in a while, there still came a day when she hated the universe. Since she was a part of that universe, it meant she hated herself as well.

Today was one of those days. Yet another absence notification popped up on her phone, which she'd only seen five minutes ago because her carrier stank and the message popped up well into her shift, rather than during school hours as it was supposed to do.

Then she *still* didn't see it for a good long time, because of the no phones policy in place for terminal employees. She'd already been written up twice for personal calls during work hours, and a third might mean the end of this job. So she'd stopped keeping her phone anywhere but the small locker she had in the back of the ticket office.

She pulled it out at the end of her last break, and by the time it processed – *really* processed – what the message waiting for her meant, she was already through her break and supposed to be back at the desk.

The other girl who worked nights with her occasionally was out tonight, "sick," which meant she was probably banging away at whatever poor sap she'd recently met at the low-rent bar she frequented. Mary was the only employee of the bus line on duty, so there was technically no one to report on her should she get back to her station a few minutes late. But there was still Sheriff's Deputy Paul Kingsley to deal with. He didn't work for the bus company, but that didn't mean he wouldn't rat her out given the chance.

He had never actually done that, to her knowledge, but… no, she wouldn't put it past him at all.

She glanced into the terminal. The passengers waiting for the next bus were still waiting, and still mostly looked half-bored or half-asleep. The two exceptions to that rule were the guy playing some kind of handheld – too intense to sleep – and the creepy guy with the tats. They both looked fully awake and aware, but neither was looking her way, and she doubted either would care if she did *anything* short of setting herself on fire and then asking for hugs.

She glanced at her phone. Still in her hand, which by itself violated the no-phones policy – cells were to be left in the lockers at the back of the ticket office unless on break or off duty.

She looked at the passengers again. Still half-bored, half-asleep, or otherwise uninterested in her.

She looked around for Kingsley. Old bastard was nowhere to be seen.

She hunched over. There was nowhere to hide in the ticket office – a few file cabinets, the lockers, a desk and circa-1980 computer at each of the ticket windows, and another desk with a quartet of security monitors cycling through the closed-circuit feeds that showed everything inside and outside the terminal. Hunching over just meant she looked like a whale that had somehow beached itself in the middle of Idaho, but she couldn't help doing it.

Part of it was that she didn't want anyone to see what she was doing. She didn't want to lose her job. That was what she told herself.

But she knew, too, that part of it was her hiding not just from the possibility of someone reporting her cell usage, but someone seeing her shame. She had worked so hard to get herself out of a certain kind of life. And now the person she loved most of all in the world seemed determined to run right back into that world as fast as possible.

Mary dialed her phone. The line rang a few times, then her daughter's voice spoke. "This is Taylor. And if you're leaving a message instead of a text like a normal person, it means you're either a telemarketer or my mom. Either way, please go –"

Beeeep.

Mary felt her mouth stretch into a thin line at the message. It was a new one, but always the same motif: *Hi, I'm Taylor. I'm so cynical and worldly. Now I'm going to end with what should be a cuss word so you know how edgy and cool I am.*

"Ha, ha," said Mary. "I just got a message from the school. You and I have to talk."

She said more, but the words felt like bees buzzing around her head. And as with bees, the noise sounded irritable, angry, but mostly incomprehensible even to her ears. The opening salvo in an argument that would play out when she got home in the morning, but would resolve nothing. She and Taylor would fight, and there would be a new level of hurt feelings and emotional scar tissue to deal with, but other than that nothing would change.

Buzz, buzz, buzz.

She droned on for several seconds, making all the right angry noises to prove she was a good mother, tamping back the despair in her heart that whispered the truth:

You're a failure.

Just a used-up old woman who failed her way out of one world, and now is failing her daughter back into that same horrible place.

For a moment, she thought she smelled the Kools again. The feeling made her sick as it always did, but now it was worse because the image in her mind wasn't that of Big J. It was

Taylor, sitting in the easy chair, pulling the belt out one-handed, ready to inflict pain on someone.

Mary shook her head. Tried to clear it. It didn't work.

The buzzing noises kept coming from her mouth, and she found herself staring at the security monitors. Still hunched over, still a whale beached in the middle of a landlocked place. Still desperately out of her element, and looking for something to take her mind away from that reality.

The sight on the monitors didn't help. The top two cycled through the interiors of the terminal – the lobby, the locker area, the baggage area. The bottom two were devoted to views of outside.

They showed only gray. Fog had come.

Buzz, buzz, buzz.

Fog outside, fog inside her mind.

"Hello? He*lllooooo*?"

The rapping of knuckles on the bulletproof acrylic that separated her from the fares was what brought Mary back to the moment, back to the terminal.

She looked up to see one of the passengers glaring at her. He was shortish, with a hairline that was receding toward the bald spot in the back of his head, as though his scalp were fighting to break free. The recession was uneven in front, making the man's features all look vaguely off center. The effect was highlighted by his eyes, which continually narrowed and widened to show various stages of displeasure.

"Hello? Earth to bus lady?" He snapped his fingers in front of the window.

Mary stifled a sigh. She knew this guy's type: just successful enough to rub shoulders with people he wished he was but knew he would never be. Perpetually hurried, harried, bitter. The kind of guy who always had Big Plans but never quite got around to setting them in motion – or if he did, it was because the Big Plan in question was a get rich quick scheme that was supposed to work in one step or less. When it didn't, that Big Plan was abandoned (to the sound of much complaining about the unfairness of it all), and a new one dreamed up.

Always on the move. Never going anywhere at all.

"May I help you, sir?" Mary asked, pleased that she had managed to keep the irritation from her own voice.

"I don't know. Are you done with your little phone call?"

Mary felt herself squeeze her phone so hard it was a wonder it didn't break. Through gritted teeth she said, "I *am* sorry, sir. How can I help you?"

The man's eyes went squinty as he said, "How does your phone even work?" He raised his and waggled it, eyes going from squinty-angry to wide-how-is-this-always-happening-to-*me*? "Mine keeps turning on and off. You have a jammer in here or something?"

Some of Mary's irritation drained, replaced by amusement at the idiocy of that question. "Why would we have a cell phone jammer at a bus station, sir?"

The man's eyes went squinty again. He peered at her as though aware how hard she was trying not to laugh at the question, and deeply offended at that fact. "Are you laughing at me?"

That killed some of her mirth. She didn't need a complaint in her file. "No, sir. It's an honest question. But to answer *yours*: no, we don't have a jammer in here."

"Then why does my phone keep turning off?"

"I suppose that's a question you would have to ask your phone company."

"How, when I can't call them?"

"It is a dilemma."

The man waited. Seeing no more answers coming, he opened his mouth as though to say something further, then exhaled angrily, threw his hands up in the air like a baseball player protesting a bad call by the umpire, then stalked away. He shook his phone as he went.

Mary looked at her own phone again. One more peek around to see if Kingsley was anywhere to be seen. He wasn't. Probably in his office "working" – which was code for napping or boozing, so far as she could tell.

She called her daughter again. One more time.

She got shunted to voice mail. Her daughter's voice clicked strangely toward the end, as though she had been in a Tilt-a-Whirl ride as she recorded it.

It ended the same as before, though. "… either a telemarketer or my mom. Either way, please go –"

Beeeep.

Mary left a message, but when she ended the call she could not for the life of her remember anything she had said. She stared at the security monitors. The fog had taken everything away. She felt as though it were in her mind as well, cloaking the past she had tried to flee but had instead only carried with her, to pass down to her child.

2. BOLO

"... a rare total inversion, traveling through the United States, following a pattern that both baffles scientists and –"

"Oh, Katie, come clean: you caused the fog because you didn't want anyone seeing you driving drunk this morning."

"Oh, Paul, you're so funny! No, I don't start drinking until at least ten in the morning. Hahaha!"

Deputy Paul Kingsley turned off the television before Overly Tan Male Anchor could make another annoying joke that Overly Big-Hair Female Anchor would then take in stride with a smile that reminded Paul of the way people tended to look right before they pulled a trigger.

He wouldn't have been surprised to see it on air: Big-Hair getting hit with a vaguely sexist remark from Too-Tan, smiling one of those frozen smiles, then pulling out a .357 and blowing a Dirty Harry-style hole right through Too-Tan's botoxed forehead.

Then again, not much would surprise Paul. Not these days, and not for the better part of the last decade. He'd seen it all, and done far too much of it himself – wasn't that the reason he was here?

For a second he heard the gunshot again. Saw the twin bores of the shotgun that had ended his time as a real cop. That had ended so much of *him*.

He stared at the small TV. It was a holdover from the last poor sap to hold this job – a dinosaur named Coot of all things, like his mother had looked at him, declared, "That is the *oldest* baby I've ever seen; let's just name him Coot and save people the effort of doing it later on!" Coot had cleaned out his desk, top to bottom, but left the TV like a silent indicator of all the boredom set to befall whatever human-shaped sack of desperation took over his job.

Enter Paul Kingsley: human-shaped sack of desperation. Extra desperation packed in the ever-growing gut, no extra charge.

Paul knew that was as apt a description of him as any. He had other physical traits, of course – a face that used to come in one version of clean-shaven but now cycled through various levels of scruff, gray hair with only a few militant strands of black jutting out around his sideburns, and blue eyes that had once shone bright but now gazed dully out at the world.

But anyone describing him wouldn't spend time on those. They'd spend time on that desperation. The dejected, raw, pained expression that he wore like a coat he was always just a bit too tired to take off.

That bothered him sometimes. But less and less each day. Like the gut in front of him was driving its mass into the space where he cared about things, shoving that caring right out into nothing.

So Paul watched a television full of people who smiled smiles that he'd seen on husbands who beat their wives, on wives who stabbed their husbands; on kids who grinned until they finally had enough and shot the bully or the adult or the simply-unlucky-asshole who crossed their path on the day when they snapped... and kept grinning as they pulled the trigger until the hammer clicked dry. Those smiles were all the same. The smiles of someone in the process of losing their minds.

The smile on a little girl holding a gun.

The smiles were the worst. Because they were the smiles Paul felt on his own face. They were the reason he had chosen – asked, *pleaded* to be stationed out here at the terminal.

Coot had been sent here because he was a bad enough deputy that he was useless on the street, but good enough they hadn't quite been able to fire him. So he got stationed at the terminal, where everyone figured nothing much happened... and even Coot couldn't mess up *nothing*.

That was the funny part, of course: Coot had presided over nothing, *been* nothing – until the day he finally retired. Then he cleaned out his desk – leaving only the TV full of angry newscasters droning into the night – and went home. Slept a full twelve hours.

Then returned to the terminal and shot three people before killing himself.

He had spent a life as nothing, sure. But he went out as something worse than nothing, and took three other people with him on that terrible trip.

Maybe that was why Paul never threw out the portable TV. Maybe it wasn't a reminder just of desperate boredom, but of the fact that it was all too easy to let boredom become despair, to fan despair into rage, and after that...

Madness.

Following the triple murder, there was talk of closing the satellite office. There was never a breath of closing the terminal itself; not with it being the only connector between BFE and Nowhere In Particular. But there was a lot of chatter about turning the County Sheriff's Office at Bliss Terminal (and no, the irony of *that* name wasn't lost on Paul, either) into a sandwich shop or a souvenir store. That lasted only until someone with a pair of brain cells pointed out that any shop or store would go broke inside of ten minutes, given the number and excitement levels of the few people who traveled through here. The terminal existed as a connection to a few actually *profitable* hubs that petered out before quite reaching each other, but that was its only redeeming feature. Not enough people for anything else.

So, no shop here.

But they still might have shut the satellite office down had Paul not asked to be transferred to the place.

It had seemed to Paul like a good idea at the time. Before he realized, ten years too late, that it was exactly the opposite of what he'd hoped to find.

Well, almost. There was still Mary and her daughter.

He thought of them sometimes. Thought of them a *lot* of the time. This time, though, his impending daydreams were interrupted by the overhead lights. They flickered, and Paul cursed. They'd been doing that all night. The bus terminal, laughably, was cited as "critical infrastructure" on some FEMA/Homeland Security list, so it was supposed to have backup generators and battery-powered emergency lighting that would keep everything up and running in a crisis. But apparently whoever was in charge of that stuff hadn't paid the light bill, because the power had been acting wonky all night.

Paul's computer beeped and he looked away from the now-silent television, glancing instead at the desktop computer that had been old when Y2K was still a concern. The desktop image – Sports Illustrated's Model of the Year, 2007, which he'd never quite managed to figure out how to change – was marred by a department alert marching across it.

"BOLO… MULTIPLE MISSING PERSONS… Descript –"

The banner stopped its slide across the screen before paul could see how the message ended. The white letters leaned suddenly, green and blue and red peeking from their edges like an old color TV about to give up the ghost. A glitch.

Paul frowned and leaned closer to the computer. He had never seen it act this way before. He pressed a half-dozen keys on the keyboard, but nothing happened. The screen remained frozen, and even the reliable workhorse Control-Alt-Delete had no effect.

A crackle of interference took the place of SI's buxom model, making the entire desktop flicker, disappear, then reappear again.

The half-finished BOLO – a "be on the lookout" alert – was no longer there. Miss 2007 remained, her body scarred by desktop icons for email, trash, and various other programs… but no BOLO message.

Paul opened his email. The computer froze as the program opened, the window half-open on his screen. Paul whacked the side of the computer. It didn't help. He quelled the urge to rip the thing off the desk and toss it across the room, instead leaning down to the surge protector that hung from the side of his desk. He flicked the red-glowing switch. It went dark. Paul counted to ten. Flicked it back on again.

The computer remained inert. Silent.

Dead.

It stared at him with its gray eye, and the sight of it disquieted him in a way he couldn't quite describe even to himself. Maybe it was the sight of his own distorted image in the curved glass of the screen. Maybe it was the gray of it all.

Whatever it was, Paul shivered and turned away, fixing his gaze instead on the large, one-way glass window that allowed him to see the western half of the parking lot. From the outside, the window was just a dark mirror. From the inside, it gave him an angle on whatever buses were approaching, and any passengers getting on or off said buses. The view was smoky and dim in the bright light of day, and in the middle of the night, it was almost useless to look out there. Just a murky gray punctuated by spots of hazy glows where the parking lot lights hung.

But he looked now, to see if the lights outside were working. They were supposed to be on their own system, separate even from the terminal's interior controls.

The lights outside were off. No dim bulbs of haze hanging in the dimmer haze of night. Just…

"What the hell is that?" he muttered to himself.

He approached the glass, not quite touching it but leaning so close that he could feel the coldness of it on the tip of his nose. Leaning close didn't change the fact of the mist, though.

Idaho got its share of fog, sure, but Paul had never seen a fog bank like this. The strange thing wasn't the thickness of it – though it *was* thick; so much so that he couldn't see even a dim shape to mark where he had parked his squad car at the beginning of the shift. No, the strangeness of the fog was... was...

Paul's mind tried to process what it was observing; tried to cough up some expression or some comparison that would make the fog into something sensible. The only thing he managed was a single word:

Alive.

The word was crazy, and for a moment Paul glanced at Coot's old TV, half expecting it to come alive and start whispering madness to him. It was silent. Gray. Dead.

He turned back to the fog... and *it* was not dead. Paul decided the word "alive" wasn't insane at all. No, it was the only word that could possibly fit.

The fog hung thickly over anything in the parking lot, but it had not touched the sidewalk that ran around the outside of the entire terminal. It hung in a perfectly-vertical wall of white, just a few inches off the curb. The interior lights of the terminal shone upon it, infusing it with a strange glow that writhed as the fog turned and twisted upon itself.

Paul blinked. Now he *did* press his nose up to the cold glass.

There it was again: that strange, twisting motion as the fog curved around inside itself, a snake coiling into its own body, burrowing into its own guts and consuming itself from the inside out. But that was impossible, wasn't it? Because if there was that much air movement, then how could the mist possibly have stopped like that? How could it simply *end* the way it did?

As though to tease him, a single, tentacular whisp edged out of the fog. It writhed closer, almost seeming to wave before drawing back into the larger bulk of itself.

The wall, Paul realized, was so perfect that – other than that single, probing strand – it looked almost like it was contained behind a transparent barrier that stretched into the sky. Glancing left and right, Paul saw that the wall of mist continued as far as his angle would permit him to see. And somehow he knew – *knew* – that if he went out to the lobby and stared at the big glass windows that comprised the outer wall, he would just see more mist. More perfectly-contained fog, hovering exactly at the curb that marked the end of the terminal's sidewalk and the beginning of the parking areas.

He turned away from it. His back muscles clenched as he did, his shoulders drawing tightly together as though he had turned his back not on a bit of nature, but on a cornered perp holding a gun in his hand and madness in his heart.

Paul went to his desk. Considered turning the TV back on. No.

He unlocked the bottom right drawer instead. Drew out the small bottle of caramel-colored liquid. He rarely drank on duty – he was a bad cop, he knew that, but he liked to think he hadn't descended to outright, on-the-job alcoholism – but the fog had him severely creeped out.

He twisted off the cap. Swigged. Not much –

(Bad cop, not terrible *cop. Not yet, anyway.)*

– just enough to feel it burn pleasantly in his throat, and for that burn to singe away a bit of the fear that still had his back knotted up.

"I *seeeee* you."

Paul didn't have to turn to see who had spoken; who had drawn out the middle syllable into a sing-song bit of mockery.

Bella Ricci was what her ID – now tucked in another locked drawer of his desk – had said. Paul had no reason to believe it was a false ID, though if it was it wouldn't be the first time one had passed through here.

Certainly "Bella" was a good enough name. Paul had a Latino partner for a while when he was in the Idaho State Police, and that guy was constantly calling every single woman they pulled over "*una bella*": a beauty. So yeah… Bella worked for this gal, because she was definitely a knock-out.

She wore the clothing to prove it, too – or the lack thereof. Paul noticed those things like any other heterosexual male, though he had changed over time from admiring them to wondering what kind of damage encouraged a girl to walk around in skintight jeans that hung low enough to expose thong and/or ass crack at every moment, not to mention a halter top that allowed for side-, top-, and under-boob to be on full display.

Daddy didn't love her. She had a boyfriend that abused her. An uncle or cousin that molested her.

All of them could be true. Or none of them. There were infinite ways a person could be damaged.

And, somehow, all of them paraded through this place. The terminal. The end of everything.

Another glance at the inert TV. Another thought of Coot with his guns a-blazin', another moment when Paul wondered if madness was the evolutionary imperative of humanity.

Another swig of whiskey.

"What would your bosses do if I told them you're drinking on the job?" said Bella.

Paul turned toward her, knowing from the sound of her voice what he would see: a cocky smile, hands resting on hips canted so far to the side she would have fallen out of her pants if said pants weren't so tight that it probably took a bottle of Vaseline and a mechanical vise to squeeze her out of them.

Paul toasted her, then drank a third time. "They'd ask me why I didn't invite them to join me," he said after swallowing.

He said it calmly, knowing it would elicit a rise from the girl. Same thing every time: they were only cocky when they felt in charge – and the feeling was easy to knock out of them. Nothing more than casual distaste would do it most of the time.

Bella followed the pattern. Her hips straightened, and the hands went from there to the bars of the small holding cell that took up most of Paul's "office." She shook them, looking disappointed when they didn't rattle like some olde tyme jail in a John Wayne western.

"Come on!" she shouted. "Let me out, man! I got places to be!"

Paul looked from her to Officer Beam, still in his hand. He considered a fourth swig.

No, too much.

He capped the whiskey and put it slowly back in the desk. Locked the desk.

He saw Bella, yanking on the bars again, in his peripheral vision. "Didn't you hear me! I got somewhere to be! I got someone to meet!"

Paul straightened, his back popping audibly as he did. "Then you shouldn't have been loitering in the locker room with no bus ticket and no money."

"At least give me my phone," she said. She pointed at Paul's desk, where the latest iPhone sat in its Hooker-Sparkles case.

Paul picked it up, turning it over in his hand. The thing had been buzzing every few minutes since he tossed the girl in the cell. Honestly, he probably would have just told her to get lost when he found her in the locker area earlier that night, but before he got a word out she started in on him, cursing everything from his parents to his potential progeny. Even so, she probably would have gotten a warning and a swift verbal kick in the ass on the way out – but she actually took a swing at him.

Paul had sidestepped the feeble attack, then spun her around and put her in cuffs before marching her into the cell. He called it in to dispatch and they said they'd have someone come around to pick her up and take her to the county jail for processing for assaulting an officer.

That had been four hours ago. Four hours of her nonsense, of TV nonsense, and of the nonsense of life in general, punctuated every few minutes by the buzzing of her phone.

He clicked the home button on the iPhone. It was locked, but an alert banner showed. He read it. "Seventeen messages?" he said. "Aren't we Miss Totes Popular? I bet I could find about a dozen parole violators and drug dealers on your contacts list, and another hundred in your Friends on Facebook."

She snorted. "Who uses Facebook? That's for old people."

He snorted right back, then wiggled the phone at her. "Don't suppose you'd share the code?"

"Don't suppose you'd bite me."

Paul shook his head. "Sorry, but I haven't had the right vaccinations for that."

Bella looked away from him, glancing at the wall clock that hung above the door to the terminal lobby. Her expression morphed from irritation to something approaching desperation. "Come *on*. I have to meet someone. This is cruel and unusual – *shit!*"

She stumbled back from the bars so fast she banged her knee on the metal slab that served as a "cot" for the drunks Paul tossed in from time to time. Bella cried out, but the pain didn't reach her eyes, which were full to brimming with terror.

Paul whipped around, following her gaze to the one-way window. To the night.

To the fog.

"What is it?" he asked, surprised at how high-pitched and strained he sounded.

Not surprised. Because you knew, *didn't you? That's not a normal fog. There's something out there.*

"What did you see?" he asked, this time forcing his voice to a whisper – better than the cracked, strained sound of terror clawing at his throat.

He gazed into the fog as he spoke. Staring into the glowing wall of gray outside the window. Its depths roiled, but the impossible vertical line of its boundary remained perfectly in place and inviolate.

Not possible.

Paul swiveled away from the fog, glancing at Bella, who was now pressed against the back wall of her cell. The lights flickered.

She looked at him. Then forced a smile to her face.

"Maybe it was nothing." She pushed away from the wall, cocking her hip to the side, her hands balled into fists at her waist. "You're a jumpy one, aren't you?"

"Ha, ha," said Paul sourly. "Very funny."

She *had* gotten him, and that stung. But worse than that was the fact that she had spotted him in the middle of an irrational moment of panic.

Losing it, Paul. You better get out of this place before you go Full Coot.

He turned his back on Bella, intending to head out to the terminal. Maybe he'd go outside and see the fog up close.

No way.

As he turned, he glimpsed the cocky look on Bella's face disappear, to be replaced by something he recognized.

"No, there really was something –" she began, pushing herself toward the bars again. Paul ignored her, walking to the door. "Hey!" she shouted. "Hey, at least leave a shot of what you were drinking before –"

He ignored her.

He walked out the door.

3. MS-13

The step from the office and holding area to the lobby was a short trip from gray to gray. The lights out here were the same, but somehow Paul always thought the feel shifted from one type of desperation to another. Like his office held the desperation of hope long-dead, and the main terminal nurtured the desperation of hope about-to-die.

He rested his hand on his gun as he entered the lobby, knowing that the gun was an empty show of force by a man who had little power, but never quite able to stop himself from doing it. It was another holdover from the days when being a cop had mattered. When he tried to make a difference.

He had never drawn his gun in this place. He didn't expect to have to. No going Coot for him if he could help it, and he'd taken steps to prevent that from happening. Maybe he'd go nuts, but he'd be damned if he would gun down a bunch of innocent people.

He looked out the big lobby window, and sure enough there was that damned fog. He couldn't see the sidewalk from here – the windows only went down to about waist-height, and below that was the same cinder block construction the rest of the place was made of. But he guessed that if he went outside the fog would be hanging on this side of the terminal just like it had outside his office.

But that meant that the fog wasn't just *hanging* outside the terminal. It was *surrounding* the place, but not actually touching the terminal building anywhere.

Impossible.

Impossible? Like fog that hangs in a perfect vertical line?

He had no answer to his own argument. So he avoided it. As good a strategy as any.

He let his gaze rove over the passengers waiting for the next connection. It was an unusually busy night, with seven people sitting on the benches. Most of them looked like the usual type who passed through here every day of the year.

One did not.

Paul walked toward that one, not caring to even try and look nonchalant about it. The guy would be expecting attention. How could you not, with a face like that?

Paul walked over to the man and stood with one hand still on his gun, staring. The business suit the man wore looked expensive. Gray, with a fine weave that had a subtly metallic glint, as though the threads were interspersed with spun silver. The tie looked expensive, too – silk, a solid black marred only by the silver tie bar that kept it tight against the man's immaculately-pressed, highly starched white shirt.

From the neck down, the guy looked like a lawyer or stockbroker, the kind you saw on TV who banged their secretaries in discreet (and not-so-discreet) affairs before going home to McMansions in big-city suburbs.

From the neck up: a whole different story. Hell, an entire different *library*.

He was Latino, probably from El Salvador, which Paul knew not only from the skin tone and hair and eye color, but from the story written across the man's face. Short and sweet, consisting only of a half-dozen teardrops tattooed under his left eye, and an intricately-scrolled "MS-13" on his right cheek.

His only baggage was a small, expensive shoulder bag on the floor beside him.

The man was reading a tattered paperback book that had obviously been read and re-read time after time. *Guerra y Paz,* it said on the cover, and though Paul didn't read Spanish, the translation was easy enough to figure once you saw the author's name, "Leo Tolstoy," written in words as big as the title.

The guy was reading a Spanish translation of *War and Peace.*

Body of a banker, hands and reading preferences of a college lit prof. Face of…

Paul had been standing in front of him a good ten seconds, and the man showed no sign of noticing him. He turned the page in his book.

Paul waited another five seconds. He recognized that the guy was manipulating him. Making him wait, like he held all the cards.

Paul had played into the guy's hand, too – he had waited long enough that if he spoke, it would be a loss of sorts. The other man would have made him speak first, winning a strange first round in an even stranger fight.

But if Paul just kept on waiting, then he was on the guy's timetable, too. The guy would continue ignoring him until the book ended… or until he did whatever he had come here to do.

Screwed either way.

So Paul spoke, because the guy's book still had hundreds of pages to go, and waiting for him to just *do* something could turn out to be extremely dangerous,

"You getting on the next bus?" he said. The other man's only answer was to turn the page. He was either a very fast reader, or he was doing it as a silent but elegant way of telling Paul to get lost. Paul shifted his gun belt. "You gonna be any trouble?" he asked.

No answer.

"Good," said Paul, knowing he was saying it only to save face; knowing it wasn't working. But what else could he do? Arrest the guy for failure to stop reading? He supposed he could have forced the issue… but then he'd end up tossing the guy in holding.

And this was a guy you definitely didn't want sticking around, even in a cell.

Paul turned away. As with Bella a few minutes before, he thought he saw the man's expression shift to reveal something else beneath. Only where Bella's eyes had gone from cocky to fearful, the face of the man with the MS-13 tattoo went from aloof to deadly. It was just a flash, but something in the eyes changed and for an instant he looked less man than shark.

Paul turned back, but the face was now impassive again, seemingly engrossed in the book the man still held.

Paul waited.

The gun still felt useless under his hand. More so, now that he knew there was a *Mara Salvatrucha* gang member in his terminal. Most members of *Mara Salvatrucha*, or MS-13 as it was also known, were Salvadoran, but the gang was international in scope. It had started in Los Angeles in the 1970s, but had spread all over the US, and pushed fingers into Mexico and Central America to the south and Canada to the north. Unlike some gangs, which were mostly bluster and bullying, MS-13 was renowned for its cruelty.

Paul remembered reading about an event in 2004, when MS-13 members had sprayed a bus with automatic weapons in Honduras, killing dozens and wounding more – including women and children – as a protest against the Honduran restoration of the death penalty.

The people on the bus screamed. They ducked. They hid behind the metal body of the bus. It didn't matter. MS-13 gunmen climbed aboard and put guns to the heads of passengers, blowing them away with no more emotion than Paul would have shown swatting a fly.

In 2008, the MS-13 were again in the news – this time for killing a man and his two sons because their car blocked him from making a left turn.

2017: two MS-13 members were arrested for kidnapping, then raping and torturing, a fourteen-year-old girl.

Those weren't the only things they had done. They weren't even the worst. He wasn't sure if that title would go to the MS-13 gang member who killed a two-year-old for screaming after he murdered the child's mother, or the ones who were in charge of ongoing child prostitution rings that trafficked girls as young as fourteen, luring them from schools and public shelters before kidnapping them and forcing them to live lives Paul could only think of as the embodiment of Hell on Earth.

Bumping into MS-13's work was likely to count among any cop's worst days. And here was a member of the gang.

Or maybe not. Maybe he was one of the rare ones who escaped. The suit argued for that – not to mention his choice of reading materials. Maybe he was one of those guys who escaped, but kept his tats in order to provide more power as he toured around talking to teens about the dangers of gang life.

Only there was none of the contentment and smiling he expected to see from people like that. Everything about the guy screamed "Danger!" as surely as if he'd been a rattlesnake shaking his tail.

Paul didn't want trouble here. The man hadn't done anything, and hadn't even shown any of the attitude most gang members did when called out by cops.

He was just reading.

The man turned another page.

"What's your name?" Paul asked.

Pause. Another page.

Paul thought about turning away. He thought about ignoring this. He thought about Coot.

He dug deep, finding a bit of good cop still survived. Not much, but…

"Sir, please identify yourself."

The man still didn't look up. "Jesús Flores. Do you want identification, *abuelo*?"

"What's that mean – *abuelo*?"

The 'banger smiled a tight-lipped smile. "It means, *sir*."

Paul doubted that. "You here on business or pleasure, *Jesus*?" he asked, intentionally mispronouncing the name.

The man's smile remained tight, but the ends curved higher. It reminded Paul of the Joker from the Batman movies. "Business."

Paul's insides suddenly shriveled, leaving a vast empty space that filled with fear. "What kind of business?"

"*Cálmate*," said Jesús. "I have no business here. Just passing through." His eyes narrowed slightly as he added, "Unless you want me to start my business early. I could do that, too. Depends on what you want."

Paul's fear thickened: an oil slick inside him that curdled his guts. "No," he said. "Just… don't do anything stupid."

The man turned back to his book. He said nothing further.

Twenty years ago, Paul would have made a bigger deal. He would have asked for ID, would have run the name through the system to check for warrants or BOLOs. He would have frisked the guy and, if he'd protested, tossed him in holding.

Ten years ago, Paul would have stood firm. He wouldn't have tossed the guy in a cell unless the guy really asked for it, but he wouldn't have backed away.

Now, though… now he did back away.

His hand still sat on his holstered gun. Waiting. Not sure if he was more worried about the man reading *Guerra y Paz* behind him, or the mist that still swirled outside.

Doesn't matter. Neither of them matter. The fog will clear, the guy will go. No problems – at least not here, and that's what matters.

Paul took a deep breath, held it, then let it out in a half-hearted attempt to purge himself of the fear he felt. He didn't like feeling that way.

Be a cop. Be a man, *for shit's sake.*

Paul walked away from the still-reading 'banger. He looked out the lobby windows. The fog hung outside, roiling and angry… but holding itself in check.

Controlled.

A crazy thought. But it was what Paul kept thinking as he started counting the minutes to the end of his shift; wondering if, when that time came, the fog would still be outside.

4. Phones

Shelly Sherman was fifty, and until recently that had made her feel old. She had gravitated from job to job over the course of her life, and though the jobs varied radically, they all held two things in common: they aged a person, and they made a person acutely aware of her age.

The current one wasn't the worst – not by a long shot – but definitely had its downsides. Which was why she smiled so much. "Nothing hides the ugly like a smile," as her mother was so quick to say when life beat her down. She said it as she beat Shelly, too – one of the main reasons Shelly had run away from home three months shy of her fifteenth birthday. She saw her mother all the time back then, even in her dreams. Smiling as she brought down the hard cane that had belonged to her father and which said father had used to show her the errors of her ways.

"Life is errors, life is mistakes, and all we can do is make the best of them." That was another favorite saying, and Shelly came to understand that the best way of making the best of a life of errors was beating after beating. "Smile," her mother would say then, and out would come the cane, and the less Shelly smiled the longer the beating would last.

She learned to smile a lot, and though Mother was long dead – she had rotted from the inside out, dying of liver failure and other cirrhosis complications when Shelly was in her twenties – Shelly still saw the woman's face from time to time. She was always smiling, both in Shelly's nightmares and in the waking dreams that plagued her every so often.

She smiled. She worked jobs that relied on a pretty face and a young body. She knew no other way to live, and so felt each year as not just a passage of time but a laying of weight upon her. The weight dragged her down, added wrinkles, and gave her the pains she covered with smile after smile after smile.

So yes, she felt old.

Until she found out about Michelle.

Michelle, so close and so far.

Michelle, who even now waited for her.

Shelly had felt old, tired, washed up and washed out… before Michelle. Now she felt different. She felt hope.

Hope was a strange thing. It was wonderful, and filled her with a cool, clean feeling. It also amplified fear, because what was hope but a fight between two possible outcomes: the wonderful and the terrible?

Mostly, though, the hope was a good thing. It made the days crawl by, full of wondering what Michelle would be like, what things she would like and what things she would hate, and most of all what she would think of Shelly.

She'll think you're old. Old enough to be a grandma.

Will she call me that?

Shelly still hadn't decided if she would like that or not. The idea of being a grandmother was one that had never crossed her mind. She worked as a beauty consultant for Mary Kay, and beauty consultants weren't supposed to be grandparents, were they?

She didn't know.

She only knew that Michelle was waiting. And, for the first time in her life, Shelly felt like that reality – the reality that waited so close to her now – might be enough to make the smiles real.

For now, though, the smiles were still pasted over layers of makeup, more layers of doubt, and – deepest of all – the fears that she might, in some important way, be just as broken and terrible as Mother had been.

I won't be that way.

But she didn't believe it. She saw her mother's eyes staring back at her in the mirror some mornings. She saw her mother's own cheekbones – a bit too severe and sharp to be truly beautiful – poking out from under the flesh of her face. She sometimes felt the urge to smile… and to hurt something.

She always tried to tamp down that feeling to resist, and not become her mother. She had made mistakes, yes, plenty of them. But she wasn't going to be like her. Not with Michelle. And that was something, wasn't it?

She watched the other passengers in the terminal, wondering idly where they were going, and if any of them was heading toward something as bright and wonderful as the thing that waited for Shelly. She doubted it. Didn't think such a thing could possibly exist.

Shelly had traveled a lot in her life, too. Not so much working for Mary Kay – there was a lot of travel in that job, but mostly of the close-by, stop-and-go-traffic variety, delivering batches of beauty products to her clients and the salespeople she had managed to recruit to work for her. Still, whether stuck in traffic on a five-mile trip from her apartment to her next makeup party, or waiting in a bus stop during one of the many longer trips she had taken in her life, she could count on the travelers around her being many and varied.

These here were no different. Some made her smile – not Mother-smiles, but real ones – like the two obvious lovebirds in the corner, who couldn't keep their eyes off each other. Some made her wrinkle her brow in confusion, like the young man playing some game device a few seats down.

A few just gave her the creeps, like the guy in the expensive suit and the tattoos.

The cop gave her the creeps, too. He strutted a lot, but he also kept sweating like he was constantly nervous. Not a good combo, in Shelly's experience: people who pretended to strength as a cover for nervousness were often the most dangerous, because you could never really tell what they might do. They might protect people in an emergency, but they might also worsen bad moments or even be the cause of them.

So when the cop walked out of his office and went over to talk to the scary guy in the suit, Shelly tensed. She could feel it happen, but was unable to control it. The only thing she could control was the smile that plastered itself over her face. The Mother-smile that came out strongest when she was worried.

A nervous cop and a guy who had said nothing that Shelly had heard, but seemed as though he would kill you as quickly and easily as he would look at you. He had been on the same bus that Shelly came in – the last few buses, actually – and had not so much as acknowledged a single person. But she knew he saw *everyone*. Probably knew them from the inside out, or knew at least enough about them to divide them into the various categories of prey.

He would not, Shelly knew, see anyone around him as a possibly stronger predator than himself. Such people – and she had known more than a few like him – never did. They just looked long enough to figure out how to hurt you should the need or desire arise, then dismissed you until you had something they wanted.

Then you gave that thing to them, or you suffered the consequences.

So the question was: would the cop be seen as enough of a threat that the suited man would take action? And if so, how bad would that action be?

Apparently it was a moot point. The man read his book, the cop moved away. He walked past one of the other passengers, a guy whom Shelly had chatted with a bit at the last stop and knew his name was Jeremy Cutter, that he was balding rather unpleasantly, that he had been constantly calling someone on his phone (someone who never picked up, from the look of things), and that he had shifty eyes that guaranteed she would keep a hand on her purse whenever he was near.

The cop, whose name was Kingsley according to the tag over his shirt pocket, barely noticed Jeremy, other than to do a quick double-take and ask, "Don't I know you from somewhere?"

Jeremy shook his head, eyes wide in innocent confusion. "I doubt it. I'm not from around here."

Kingsley thought for a moment, then nodded and said, "Okay. Have a good night."

"You, too," said Jeremy, the confusion still on his face.

He was good. Shelly knew people – that was part of every job she'd ever had. That meant she was also pretty good at spotting liars – apparently better than Kingsley was.

And though Jeremy had done a great fake-innocent look, he was lying as he did so. He did know the deputy… or expected Kingsley to know *him*.

Shelly wondered if she should say something about her suspicions. But she knew, too, how that would go: Kingsley would ask what her problem was. She would say something inept, like, "I just don't trust him." Kingsley would roll his eyes and put her in the twin categories of "Maybe Crazy" and "Keep An Eye On Her." She didn't like either of those categories, so she kept her mouth shut, watching as Kingsley sauntered over to the lovebirds. He let his eyes rove over both of them, stopping longer on the woman, and Shelly's Mother-smile grew at the look in his eyes.

Not that she could blame him for spending more time looking at the woman than the man. The man was okay-looking, but nothing special. He had Japanese features, which Shelly could spot because she had dated a Japanese-American for a while. He had gone nuts the one time she referred to him as

"Asian." In an effort to please him, she'd put real effort into learning to distinguish between Japanese, Chinese, and Korean features. That seemed to mollify him, though when she pointed out there were numerous other countries in the region and asked if she should work on memorizing *them,* he just shrugged as though those places were immaterial.

Shelly could never quite figure out if that qualified as some weird racism.

Racism or not, though, she could now state with authority that the man nearby was, indeed, of Japanese descent. And the observational skills she had honed over a lifetime of "people-related" jobs, as she put it, also told her that he was a white-collar guy; that he probably had a decent job; and that he was deeply, stupidly in love with his wife, the gorgeous woman beside him.

The woman who had drawn that man's attention – and the more-lecherous attention of the grizzled deputy who now appraised her openly – was an interesting mix of darkness and light. She was beautiful, with enough curves to present femininity in spades, but wrapped in a body that moved with the economy of an athlete. She wore vaguely sporty clothes as well – jeans and a long-sleeved T-shirt that were, like the woman, feminine but also fit-seeming. She looked like the kind of girl you would not be surprised to discover had been prom queen, valedictorian of her high school class, and had then gone on to distinguish herself in college, taking courses in social work or teacher education. A "people" person.

But there was also something furtive about her – something that didn't quite mix with the rest of the aura she presented. Shelly didn't believe in auras the way some of her clients did – she saw no vaguely orange or purple or puce-crimson with hints of blue at the edges that she had heard those women talk about, nodding as they murmured things like, "probably a Virgo," or "watch out for those oranges – too feisty," or "Well of *course* she knew her husband was cheating! Did you see that bright yellow around her? She's got more than a touch of the psychic!"

No, none of that for Shelly. But she *did* believe that different people gave off different kinds of energies. Most of the time the energy the beautiful woman exuded wasn't the same as the look she presented to the world. She *looked* outgoing, confident – but only on the surface. Shelly suspected that beneath that façade hid something coiled tight. Not ready to spring forward – she wasn't a predator like the man in the suit who focused on his book while still somehow managing to check out every person who came within a mile of him – but ready to jump *back*. To flee.

The beautiful woman looked strong on the surface, but Shelly wondered if there was someone like Mother in that other woman's past. If there were smiles and canes raining down aplenty.

The deputy, who had been watching for long enough to be noticed by both the man and the woman – though only the woman *really* noticed him, because her husband was utterly oblivious to anything not his wife – cleared his throat.

The woman glanced up at him.

Oh, no, don't do that, honey. That's what he was waiting for.

The woman didn't hear Shelly's thoughts – definitely no yellow aura there! – so she *did* look at the deputy, and continued to look as he pointed to the dangerous man in the suit and whispered conspiratorially, "Don't worry. That guy won't bother you. Not with me around."

The woman's companion finally noticed someone else existed. He blinked, looking around as though surprised that there was a world other than the one he apparently fell into when looking at his wife. "Sorry, what was that?" he said.

Kingsley ignored the man. He nodded at the woman. "That's a beautiful ring you got."

Shelly saw the way the woman reacted. The woman was a newlywed – that was the only thing she *could* be, wearing that ring and so completely captivated by her man – so she should have flashed the huge diamond on her finger –

(Good Lord, that thing is enormous. *What is someone who can afford a ring like that doing on a* bus?*)*

– and made a series of innocuously appreciative statements before turning back to her husband. Or, if creeped out, Shelly would have expected the woman to put her hands in her pockets or behind her back, or at least half turn so as to obscure her ring and herself from prying eyes.

Instead, though, the woman tugged nervously at the long sleeves of her shirt. "Thanks," she said noncommittally, her clear, even voice totally at odds with the nervous energy she exuded.

The deputy leaned in close, ostensibly to admire the ring further but also, Shelly couldn't help but notice, openly ogling the woman's figure. "Pretty thing like you probably worries that a rock like that isn't safe in a world like this. But as long as you're here," he said, gesturing around at the terminal with one hand, the other resting on the butt of his gun, "you're completely safe." He grinned a not-at-all-friendly grin at the husband. "Completely safe with *me*," he finished, making the words into a clear judgment of the lack of safety her office-working husband probably provided.

"Officer…" said the woman.

"Deputy, actually," said Kingsley. A correction, unnecessary given the circumstances, that would position him as the authority figure.

"Deputy," said the woman with a nod.

Oh, honey, no. No. *Just ignore him.*

But the woman surprised Shelly. She figured, given the way she tugged at her shirt and the subtle quaver in her voice, that the woman was about to be embarrassed in front of her husband. Instead, though, her spine straightened and when she spoke the next two words, they were steely. "We're fine." Then she added, "Thanks," in a way that clearly said, *"Now go screw yourself."*

Kingsley either didn't hear the tone or didn't care. He leaned in a bit closer and said, "Well, I'm here. Just so you know."

Again Shelly was surprised. The husband was himself no shrinking violet, and she would have expected the average male to get a bit of gorilla in him, to pound his chest as another male threatened what he saw in his domain. But the man just watched as his wife batted her eyes and said, demurely, "The big *stwong* man?"

Kingsley, absolutely without shame, leaned in closer still, ignoring the husband now as he waggled his eyes and said, "If that's your type."

And the woman finally turned away. Not in a manner that suggested she was afraid, or that she had anything to hide. It was a dismissive move, a queen turning her back on a roach. "It *is* my type," she said, and laid a possessive arm around her husband, who did his best to stifle laughter. "So I think I'll be fine, but *we* both thank you for your concern."

Kingsley froze. The leering grin on his face could have been carved in stone, but for all its rigidity Shelly could tell it was the smile of someone who had been hurt – and badly. The air of impotence she had sensed when she first saw him – powerlessness painted over with a thin veneer of bravado – now bubbled to the fore.

Shelly had seen lots of cops in her life. More than most, she knew. She had been up close and personal with many of them – some in good ways, others less so – and knew that the average law enforcement type, regardless of whether a he or a she, whether they went by "officer" or "deputy," would not let this kind of sleight pass. There would be some kind of reminder – a few favoring the subtle, others the overt – that you Do Not Screw With The Man.

Here, though, The Man was the one who flinched. He turned away, and the couple watched him go.

In the moment Kingsley turned, the woman seemed to diminish. She tugged at the sleeves of her shirt with a near-desperate air. Her husband gathered her into his arms. "It's okay," he whispered. Shelly didn't think Kingsley noticed, but she saw *others* in the place noticing.

She saw Jeremy noticing, and saw the balding, thin man smile knowingly before dialing a number on his phone yet *again*. That was a smile Shelly had seen before. Not for a long time, but it was the kind of smile you never forgot: the kind of smile of a barker noting an easy mark. A barker, or a thief.

She saw the man in the expensive business suit and tattooed face notice as well. His glance was quick – so fast she doubted anyone else would have seen it. But she knew what she saw in his face: the look of someone preparing for mayhem.

She looked away. She had no desire to be the focus of the dangerous man's mayhem, so she whipped around to face something else. And she saw the fog.

It had been weird on the way in – thick enough that a few times the bus driver on the previous leg of her journey had slowed to a crawl. It was agony, because this trip was the most important of her life. The trip where everything would change, and Shelly would no longer be what she had been. She had spent her life as an ugly caterpillar, gagging down the rotten leaves that fell to her. But the buses – this trip – would be her chrysalis. She would emerge a butterfly, ready to float upon happiness; to *be* happy.

So when the bus driver slowed on the last leg of the trip, calling out a quick, "Foggy night, folks!" over his shoulder by way of explanation, she had wanted to scream. The chrysalis was the place of transformation, sure… but it was also a cramped, rolling metal tube that smelled like the saturated B.O. of ten thousand travelers and sported a tiny "lavatory" that had a door thin enough Shelly would rather explode than use when anyone was within a hundred feet.

But they got through it, and Shelly figured that by the time her next – and last – bus came, the fog would be gone and that would be the end of that.

The fog, it seemed, had other plans. It had thickened, and seemed almost to glow with an inner light as though it were less natural occurrence and more something *constructed.* Something *directed.*

Shelly looked away from the fog almost as quickly as she had looked away from the venomous gaze of the tattooed man. She glanced at the large sign that showed departure and arrival times. The next bus still had a brightly-lit "ON TIME" beside it.

This is ridiculous. I'm waiting in a bus terminal at the end of my trip so that I can take a short hop to a stop only a few miles away. Why why why *couldn't there have been a faster bus? Or at least a rental car company in this place?*

But she knew, even as she thought it, that the anger and irritation she felt weren't really about the wait. She had a few hours before what she traveled to – before the end of her chrysalitic journey – would even be ready for her. She might as well wait here as anywhere else.

The irritation was simply veiled worry. Because what if the end of the trip *wasn't* the change she hoped? What if she wasn't… *different* when she reached her destination?

What if Michelle didn't like her?

She pushed the thought down, into the deepest, darkest places where she kept all the other fears and regrets that plagued her. There were a lot of fears, a lot of regrets down there, and the newest one bounced into its fellows, all of them nothing but jagged edges and sharp memory.

Shelly stood, turning away from both the hinky-seeming Jeremy Cutter and the outright dangerous-seeming tattooed man. The only direction left to her was the end of the aisle of seats in which she had been sitting. The aisle dead-ended at the outer wall of the lobby, and a young man sat in the chairs there, the farthest spot from anyone else in the terminal.

Shelly decided to go chat with him. Why not? Maybe he'd be nice. Maybe she'd be able to make a business contact, or a sale. Maybe there would be some way to profit from this moment.

That was Old Shelly thinking. Old Caterpillar, Mother-Smiling Shelly.

But that Shelly, for the moment, was still in charge. And would be until she had her arms around Michelle. Until she could look in that little girl's eyes and see the reflection of herself in them.

The thought warmed her enough that it almost felt normal when she sat down beside the young man at the end of the aisle. He was black, in his twenties. He was thin – not gaunt, but made up of the lack of flesh that plagued some people who worked under fluorescent lights or in front of glowing screens for their entire lives.

The thin young man was staring at a screen now, hunched over a gray box about the size of an old tape-cassette recorder. Shelly wasn't much up on video games, but she decided she should learn – what if Michelle liked them, and Shelly had to talk about them? – and now was as good a time as any.

She sat beside the young man. Waited. The young man didn't acknowledge her, though; didn't even seem to *notice* her.

Shelly looked at the box in his hand. She dug through her memory, trying to remember what such a thing was called. "Is that a... what's it called... a Gamebox?" she finally ventured.

The man didn't look up. He kept playing, his thumbs jabbing down on buttons with precision and speed. "GameBoy," he said.

Shelly waited a moment. The man said nothing further. She thought about going back to her other seat. Then remembered the tattooed man's expression. No, here was safer.

And there was Michelle's video game interest, of course, which Shelly had no reason to believe actually existed at all, but which had suddenly become not merely a possibility, but a likelihood – rapidly morphing to a certainty.

"Of course," she said. "What are you playing on the... GameBoy."

The man kept playing, speaking without looking away, his voice oddly monotone. "Tetris. Pseudorandom sequence of tetramino blocks that fall into a ten-block by eight-block field. The goal is to create horizontal lines, each of which disappears and thus allows for gradual clearing of the playing field."

Something beeped on his screen. Shelly glanced at it. Looked like a level had been cleared, or maybe the man had just paused his game. Either way, he was now looking not at her, but past her, with eyes that somehow managed to look both absent and intense.

Autism? Asperger's? Something else?

She didn't know. The thought of it made her uncomfortable. She thought of herself as a pretty open-minded, tolerant, caring gal. Mistakes of her past notwithstanding, she liked people and thought everyone deserved a fair shake.

But like most people, she also came smack against moments like this one. Moments where she realized her fellow humans didn't always make her feel comfortable. Being different was a sin for many. Differences meant uncertainty, and uncertainty meant the possibility of danger.

But she forced herself to lean in close, to say, "Interesting," even though she had understood not a single word of the man's infodump.

The man nodded. "Yes." Then without preamble he switched gears from game to system. He held the GameBoy a bit higher, like an auctioneer showing off the night's biggest piece. "This GameBoy is one of the first thousand sold in the U.S., and this Tetris cartridge is the original one it came with."

Now Shelly *was* interested – and not as a pretense at civility or politeness. She looked at the box, which was a dull gray with a monochrome screen. But she understood what words like "original" and "first thousand sold" usually meant. "Is it –" she began.

The man returned to his game, speaking over her in the same monotone as before. "My teacher gave it to me. My therapist says I like it because it gives me the illusion of control in a world that makes little sense."

The comment caught Shelly off-guard enough that she stuttered out the thing she had been about to say: "Is… I… I bet games like that are valuable."

The man shook his head. "Not always. Sometimes. To the right people." He kept playing a moment more, sighed, then punched a button. The game froze. "I am Adam S. Miles. My therapist says I should try to talk to people more." He held the game toward her. "Do you want to play?"

Shelly smiled wanly. The kid hadn't looked at her once. Not even when holding out the game, at which point he settled his gaze on empty space just above her right shoulder. "No, thank you," she said. Adam looked vaguely relieved as he pressed a button. The game started beeping and his thumbs started moving.

Shelly watched for a few seconds, then said, "Think we'll get out of here on time?" She looked at the arrivals/departures board again. It flickered, the display darkening for an instant before brightening once more. "I hope so," she said. Adam grunted noncommittally. "You going somewhere for work? I'm not. Pleasure. Real pleasure, not business for once. I travel for work sometimes, but never this far."

Shelly heard herself talking. The voice was too loud, the words too fast. She was nervous – the bald little snake Jeremy, the more terrifying viper of a tattooed man, the creepy cop –

(The fog. Don't forget about that.

What's wrong with it? Just fog.

You ever see fog like that?)

– and what waited for her at the end of the trip had all pooled, deeper and deeper until it spilled out in a flood of nervous chatter.

"You smell nice," said Adam.

Shelly smiled a bit more genuinely this time. "I'm an Independent Beauty Consultant for Mary Kay. It's more than just lipstick, you know, it's a great family of products that –" She finally managed to stop herself, clamping down on her lower lip hard enough it made tears rise up behind her eyes. "Sorry. I guess the fog's getting to me. I talk when I'm nervous."

Adam glanced up from his game. He looked out the lobby windows for an instant before returning to Tetris. "Strange," he said, and she didn't know if he was talking about the fog or about her.

For some reason, the idea that this kid – this strange, off-kilter kid – might be referring to *her* as "strange" was more comforting than the idea that he had noted the fog as unusual.

"You smell nice," Adam said again, "but you wear too much makeup."

Shelly nearly gasped. Then she laughed a bit. "When you get to a certain age, it's either too much or too little. I'd rather hide a bit."

"You can't hide," said Adam. "You are right here. With everyone else who is in here in the bus terminal."

Shelly hadn't realized that anyone else was listening. But Adam suddenly paused his game and held it out toward Deputy Kingsley, who had approached with a silence she would not have expected. In exactly the same tone as he had asked her, and with the exact same lack of eye contact, Adam said to the cop, "Would you like to play Tetris?"

The cop snorted. "Not in the least."

Adam seemed to slump, and Shelly couldn't tell if it was sadness at the dismissive way Kingsley had spoken to him or relief that he had tried to be more social and, failing, could now return to his own personal cocoon… from which, Shelly thought, he would be happy never to emerge. A cocoon of ones and zeros, of varying shades of green that combined to form ordered blocks that he could march whichever way he pleased.

Kingsley sat beside Shelly. She didn't like him being there. But she didn't want to just ignore him. She pulled out her phone – the best way to shut someone down before they started talking, she knew, was to demonstrate they were less important in the flesh than was someone who could be anywhere in the world. A text message was a great communicator, but it was also the *ultimate* shut-down trick.

She brought up the message string that had been all she thought of for days, scrolled to the end, and texted:

SHELLY: Is she there? Are you there?

She waited only an instant before the answer came:

PI: i am here her bus gets in at 5 am

A moment later, another text popped up.

PI: stop stressing it'll be fine

She thought about texting him back, saying something witty like, "easy for you to say."

But apparently Kingsley had tired of undressing her with his eyes, because he leaned in close and whispered, "I'm so tired of this shit."

Pretending she hadn't noticed his interest was one thing. Straight-up ignoring him was probably unwise. She'd never liked attention from people like him, but she also knew that trying to ignore them just tended to make them more interested, aggressive…

… curious.

She didn't like any of those options, so she put away the phone and said, "You must have a lot on your plate."

"Damn right."

She glanced at her phone again. If another message had come, maybe she could say, "Sorry, gotta take this," and phone Petey. He'd charge her for it – but he was probably charging anyway, waiting on her errand as he was.

As she looked, the phone's screen flickered. She squinted at it, surprised. She'd never seen that before. Glitches, sure – who hadn't had a call cut off at the most important moment, or an app fail to load? But nothing like this. For a moment the home screen just disappeared, replaced by a formless gray field. Then it was back again.

Shelly squinted. "What –"

"Work, dammit!" Shelly looked up, aware that Deputy Kingsley had done the same. They both watched Jeremy the Snake as he shook his own phone, which he'd apparently been trying to make a call on.

Shelly looked at him, wondering if *his* screen had flickered. Had gone gray.

She looked at the fog beyond the windows. So thick she couldn't see more than two feet into its depths. But – and she hadn't realized this until now – it wasn't right outside as she had first assumed. It was outside, but not *right* outside: it had halted a few feet from the windows.

Two thoughts popped into her mind. For the first time in days, not a one of them was about Michelle or this trip.

The first: *I wonder what happened to my phone?*

The second: *I wonder if the fog did it?*

The latter was insane, because she wasn't wondering if the fog meant some random weather pattern had interfered with her cell signal. No, she was asking if the fog – itself, consciously – had caused the phone to glitch.

Insane.

But it was what she kept thinking, as she watched the fog roll around, wafting this way and that, side to side.

But never any closer.

6. Isolated

Mary tried calling her daughter again. And again.

Each time she did, she became more convinced her daughter wasn't answering because something dreadful had happened to her.

Each time she did, the reception worsened.

The last time, it was nothing but hiccups of noise:

"... eans... either a.. arketer or... om. Either ... go..."

Beeeep.

Then the line died. Absolute silence, and though Mary left yet another message, she knew that she was speaking to a dead line.

7. Lockers

Paul wasn't interested in the woman who had finally introduced herself as Shelly Sherman. Not mentally, emotionally – certainly not physically. She was good-looking enough, he supposed, in an aging beauty queen sort of way. But Paul had found it hard to find much interest in the opposite sex the last few years.

Just one more step on your way to the real *retirement party. The one where there's no gold watch at the end, just a wood box and a bunch of dirt on top of it.*

And yet he kept talking to her. Kept yammering away like a horny teen trying desperately to get the object of his high school infatuation to notice him. Paul had done that himself in high school. She *had* noticed him, and look how that turned out: marriage at nineteen, divorce at twenty-five. No kids, thank God. Then a string of relationships that always ended the same: tears, anger. A few empty threats.

No, he was not interested in Shelly Sherman, Mary Kay Beauty Consultant and Nervous Talker. But he kept on speaking, and as he heard himself Paul wondered if he was really talking to her at all, or just using her as a mirror – talking to her so that he wouldn't talk to *himself*.

Talking to yourself was one of the things the nutjobs did. The drunks who were so far out of it they thought they had fallen back in it again – whatever "it" was, whatever harsh world "it" was a part of.

He wasn't crazy. He wasn't a drunk. But he needed to talk to someone. And Shelly had seemed like the best bet, after being shut down by the gorgeous gal with the Asian boyfriend or husband or partner or whatever they were calling it these days.

He was gesticulating wildly as he spoke, too. Gestures far too big for a conversation he shouldn't have been having in the first place. He should be walking around the lobby, then checking the locker area and bathrooms before checking in with Mary.

But he wasn't doing any of those things. And he knew why, too: because after those things, the *next* thing on the list would be a walk around the outside of the terminal. Making sure no one had come on the property who didn't have actual business there. The drunks who would frequent the area generally knew that they weren't allowed to come into the terminal without a ticket in hand, but that didn't stop them from occasionally trying to sleep off a bender in one of the cars that might be parked in the lot, or just sleeping *under* the car, if the vehicle was high enough off the ground to let them wiggle under.

Usually he didn't mind those patrols. They broke up the monotony a bit.

Tonight he had no desire to go outside. Not with the fog still hanging there, curling around and up and down but never reaching out to cross the final few feet to the terminal.

Paul didn't know what would cause such a strange atmospheric event, but then, he didn't really *want* to know. He wasn't paid to figure out such things.

So he talked, because talking to a non-entity like Shelly Sherman was better than talking to himself, or turning on Coot's shitty TV, or just pulling his gun and starting his own retirement party in style.

"… don't even get good passengers here. Just foreigners and hipsters and douchebags and…" He had been pointing at the different passengers waiting in the lobby as he spoke, and now his finger jabbed at the kid who was playing the GameBoy. "… and whatevers."

"They're not that bad," said Shelly.

Paul smirked. Typical kneejerk response. But faced with reality, he had seen many a "kind, compassionate, right-thinking" person suddenly reevaluate their core principles. When facing threats, it was amazing how many people lost their kindness.

Paul pointed at the MS-13 guy, who was still reading his book. "And him?" he said.

Sure enough, the tolerant, gee-why-can't-we-all-see-we're-in-this-together smile on Shelly's face cracked a bit as she looked at the thug. "I'm sure he's got his good points."

"Sure. His name's Jesus, so I'm sure he absolutely walks on water as he goes forth doing good deeds."

The 'banger looked up. He saw Paul looking and smiled the same smile Paul figured a diver would see in the final moment before being eaten by a great white.

Paul tried to hold the other man's eyes. Tried not to look away. Failed.

Looking at his hands, which were clenched tight in his lap, he murmured, "Buncha assholes. I wouldn't trust any of them to hold a bag of shit."

Sounding amused – though still a bit nervous – Shelly said, "Why would you want them to?"

Paul's eyes snapped to hers. He could see something battling there, and knew what it was: the forces of societally-inculcated "goodness" duking it out with reality.

"You think different?" he said. He gestured at the 'banger. "Then by all means, go have a chat with him. I'm sure you two will have tons in common."

Shelly's mouth firmed into a thin, bloodless line. "Fine," she said.

Paul reached for her as she stood, maybe trying to stop her from doing anything that would upset whatever balance existed now, but she skittered to the side like she was avoiding the touch of a leper. She walked toward Jesús, who was still staring at her. She faltered a bit, but Paul had to admit a grudging respect as she kept moving forward. Her hand jutted out, obviously hoping Jesús would reach out and shake it and they would all fall into a big happy bowl full of the milk of human kindness.

Instead, she tripped on her own feet and pitched forward.

Paul half-stood as she stumbled toward the well-dressed 'banger, her hand still outstretched but now in an odd parody of a person drowning. Before Paul's legs had fully unlocked, though, the tattooed man had folded down the page of his book, put it down, stood fully, and caught Shelly in his arms.

Good shit, he's fast.

Paul tried not to imagine what someone with that kind of reaction time would do in a fight with an over-the-hill Sheriff's Deputy.

"Thank you, I…" Shelly's voice, full of happiness at being saved, petered away as she got the full force of that blank-eyed stare. The 'banger still looked like a great white, and Paul was hard pressed not to shiver while standing ten feet away. He imagined it must be a hundred times worse when the shark actually had you in its teeth.

"I'm sorry," Shelly mumbled. She pulled away from Jesús, who dropped his hands but did not move away from her. "I'm so clumsy, I…" Again her voice faltered. She took a halting step backward, then turned and all but ran to the bathrooms on the other side of the lobby, disappearing into the women's room without a backward glance.

Paul finally finished standing. Jesús smirked, and Paul got the impression the other man had caught Shelly specifically to show Paul how fast he was; how outmatched Paul would be in any physical confrontation.

Again, twenty years before, Paul would have gotten up in his face. Ten years ago and he wouldn't have pressed as hard, but wouldn't have backed down either.

Now he didn't stand his ground. But at least he could choose to stop hiding from the basics of his job. He had avoided checking out the lockers and bathrooms, knowing that would draw him closer to the moment he would have to go out into the fog. But what was fog when you were trapped in a glass and concrete box with a great white?

He turned toward the lockers. They were in their own room of sorts, a twenty-by-twenty space with a single bank of lockers in the middle of the room, another line of the metal boxes attached to the back wall. The whole thing was separated from the lobby by a doorway with no door: just an empty rectangle that gave little illusion of privacy for anyone putting their bags in a locker. That was by design, Paul knew: since the Towers, public lockers were nearly all monitored, and the folks who owned them wanted people to *know* they were monitored.

Not that anything dangerous had ever been hidden here. Other than Coot.

Still, part of his duty was to walk through the locker room, and even if he wasn't quite the cop he had been, he was still enough of a man to walk around an empty place like that, wasn't he?

So he squared his shoulders, kept his hand on his useless gun, and walked into the locker area. It was a bit darker here than he remembered it. Glancing up, he saw that one of the fluorescent bars that lit the place was flickering. The other was dark, dead. It reminded him suddenly of the dry husk of a fly curled in a spider's web.

First the computer, then the phones. Whole place is going to hell.

He didn't anticipate finding anything dangerous in here, but movement caught his eye. He had thought all passengers were present and accounted for in the lobby or (in Shelly's case) hiding in the women's bathroom. So what was moving in here?

He lunged around the bank of lockers in the middle of the room. Saw what was there, and hollered, "Gotcha!"

8. Reunion

Mary heard the door click open. She felt the slight gust of air that always accompanied someone coming in through the door in the lobby. She felt the presence of someone in a room that until this point had been solitary as a coffin.

But she didn't react to it. Sometimes you know someone is talking, but you keep watching the TV. Sometimes you know a car is changing lanes dangerously close but you don't honk the horn. Sometimes…

… sometimes the cop who can rat you out comes in the room and you keep talking on the phone.

The fact was, Mary was getting scared. Taylor had ignored her calls before, but it was rare for her to ignore this *many*.

But worse than that was the dead, nothing sound on the other end of the phone whenever Mary called her daughter's line. Not like there was a problem with the cell service, but as though everything outside the bus terminal had simply *ceased*. Or had never existed in the first place.

Row, row, row, life is just a dream.

Something else Big J had taught her, slurring the words to the old song before ranting about how *some* people's lives might be dreams, but not *his*.

She hated that song. But it came to her in times of stress, worry, and fear. Times like now, when she spoke into a dead line and worried about her daughter. When she feared the nothing on the other side of the line so much that she *heard* Deputy Sheriff Paul Kingsley come in, and knew on some level that she had to put the phone away… but didn't. Just kept talking into the nothing, because if she stopped talking then she might well start to scream.

"Call me *back*, young lady. You get this and I don't –"

Reality finally penetrated. She hurriedly terminated the call and turned toward what she knew waited: Kingsley with his too-knowing grin, that smile she saw a hundred times a day, and that she always felt like was his way of hinting that he could make her life difficult if he chose.

Had he ever actually done such a thing? Not really – other than just by his presence – but the smile was so weird, like a vase that had been broken and superglued back together with a few pieces missing, so you could see the shape it *should* have been, but that phantom shape only served to highlight how wrong the remainder looked without its missing pieces.

He was smiling now, and as Mary turned, hiding her phone to the side, already speaking her excuses, that smile was all she saw for the first moment. "I swear, I wasn't just…" She blinked, as though she might see something different when she opened her eyes. She didn't. She glanced at the phone she was no longer hiding. Relief poured into her, then was shoved roughly aside in favor of maternal irritation. "What are *you* doing here?"

Her daughter matched her gaze, irritation for irritation. Only that wasn't all anymore, was it? Every kid – especially every *teenage* kid – stared at their parents with irritation. But the look Taylor was tossing at her mother had shifted from that normal teenage gaze to one of contempt.

It hurt.

Taylor turned away from Mary, and began swatting at Kingsley with the small purse in her hand. "Let me *go,* you shi –"

"Language, kid," said Kingsley. He frowned at Taylor as he said it, then turned back to Mary. The fractured smile was gone, replaced by a look of weariness so great it was almost heartbreaking.

Mary wondered – not for the first time – if the real reason Kingsley disturbed her wasn't because he was a creep, but because she saw so much of her own failure in him. Both had hidden from the world in this box of concrete and glass. Both existed in a place populated almost entirely by the Just Passing Through.

"Mary," said Kingsley, "how many times have I told you? You can't just –"

Mary began speaking, overlapping the officer's words as everything she felt was driven aside by the fear of what a negative report by him might do to her. "I know, I'm sorry, I –"

Kingsley, still talking himself, as though he didn't even notice her speaking, continued, "– come around here. It's against policy, and you know that."

"Please, don't report me, Deputy. I can't... I can't lose this job."

Kingsley still held Taylor's arm with one big hand. He ran the other across the lower half of his face, like rasping his palm over the stubble there would make the world go away. Or at least stop bothering him.

"How many times do I have tell you to call me Paul?" he said.

Mary, desperate, finally did just that. He'd told her to do that for years, but she never had. She felt weird doing it. Not just because of the over-respectful attitude she had felt she needed to convey to cops, both as a black woman and as someone who came from a background where police were just as likely to be the bad guys as the heroes. It was also, in good measure, simply the fact that she didn't want to be that close to the officer. Like calling him by his first name would let him stand closer, let him loom a bit more. Let him smile that fractured smile a bit wider, and she might see cracks in her own soul that mirrored his.

But now, she used that offer in the hopes it would bolster her position. "Paul, please don't... please don't report me. I need this job. Taylor just got into college and..." She stared at Taylor as she said it.

Her daughter was beautiful. She had thick, black hair that tumbled around her shoulders in curls so tight they looked like the springs from a clock, and bounced subtly up and down as she walked. Her eyes were deep brown, but striated through with threads of green and silver that created an exotic look. She was a beauty, straddling the line between "hot" and "cute," which gave her access to the best of both worlds.

And the worst.

Taylor stared back at her mother. At this moment, her eyes were less exotic and lovely than they were disgusted and world-weary. That was the biggest fashion today, Mary knew. The right cut of jeans, the right logo on a shirt... those things mattered, but the accessory that was a Must Have for young people today was the affectation of cynicism that would have been more appropriate to someone three times their age.

They weren't Millenials or Gen Y or Gen Z or whatever they called themselves. They were the Generation of Hopeless Derision.

Mary couldn't stare at that face, that look. She turned back to Kingsley. "Please," she said again.

Kingsley sighed and repeated his stubble-rubbing move. "Don't worry about it, Mary. I've never told yet, have I?"

Mary nodded. He hadn't, though she had a feeling he was running a tab on her, and eventually the bill would come due.

Kingsley turned to Taylor, and smiled, and Mary returned to the knowledge of how very beautiful her daughter was. Kingsley was old enough to be Mary's father, and so Taylor's grandfather. But there was nothing grandfatherly about his smile as he stared at the teen he held. It was a smile of longing.

"She can stay, I guess. Gives me a chance to get to know your... *beautiful*... family a bit better."

Mary's skin crawled. She did her best to ignore it. To put a smile on her face as she took Taylor's other arm, pulling her daughter close to her and *away* from Kingsley.

He let go. Still staring at Taylor.

Mary stepped between them. "Thanks, Paul. I owe you."

The last words fell from her lips before she could catch and shove them back unspoken. Kingsley looked at her, his expression suddenly unreadable. "Yeah you do," he said. The moment stretched on, and Mary had no idea how to end it.

Thankfully, Kingsley turned to the desk that held the CCTV feeds. He nodded at them. "You ever see fog like that?"

Mary turned toward the monitors, surprised at how completely the fog had taken over every external view. The security monitors showing the outside feeds held only blank gray. She would have thought they were all broken, but there was a diagnostic feed blinking at the corner, a green dot that meant everything was working fine. She supposed that could be malfunctioning, too, but *all* the outside cams being down and *all* their individual diagnostics also being wrong was too much of a coincidence – even if she couldn't see the fog with her own two eyes by looking out the ticket window and the lobby window beyond.

The fog hadn't come in here, of course. But outside it reigned supreme.

She shook her head. "No, never," she said. "It's weird."

Kingsley suddenly darted forward, his finger stabbing toward the monitor that showed the parking area behind the terminal. "There!" he shouted. "You see that?"

Mary glanced at the monitor he was pointing at. She shook her head. "See what?"

"A shadow or…" Kingsley frowned. "Or something."

"Maybe it's a drunk. Think you should check on it?" said Mary, trying not to let the hope that he would do just that show too obviously in her voice.

"Maybe," said Kingsley. He sounded a bit like he was in a trance, hypnotized by the blank gray of the screens. "Maybe." He looked away from the screen with visible effort.

Mary looked away, too, but as she turned she thought *she* saw something moving this time. Just a subtle eddy in the gray on the monitors. A slim line of darker gray in the strangely-glowing mist.

A drunk. Has to be. Maybe that gross guy with all the teeth missing.

Kingsley said something. Mary didn't catch it. "What?" she asked.

"The next bus still on time?" he repeated.

Mary looked at her desk computer. "So far as the computer knows."

Kingsley looked from the monitors to her computer. Back again. He rubbed his face, then bit his lip, then nodded. "Okay," he said. "Don't let this happen again, Mary." He looked at Taylor as he said it, then sighed and said, "I better get back to my desk."

He left. Every ounce of the worry and anger and disgust Mary had been feeling suddenly fell out of her as she said, "You mean back to your *booze*." She contained herself as best she could, then turned to Taylor, who still stared at her with contempt. *Disgust*. Mary shook her head, not sure whether she herself felt disgusted, or afraid, or just tired. "What are you *thinking*?" she demanded. "I've been written up twice for you skulking around. Do you want me to lose my –"

Taylor's face changed. She had apparently decided that Loving Daughter was more likely to avoid trouble than Cynical Teen Daughter. She contrived a blush and actually blinked those big brown eyes like some caricature of teen innocence. "Gee, Mom, I was just coming to visit you and –"

Mary cut off whatever came next with a quick slash of her hand. "No. Do not lie to me, child. You're good at it, but not *that* good."

The disgust returned, shattering the innocence Taylor had been affecting. "Then please, do tell me what to do. I'm all ears."

"How about not ditching school?" demanded Mary. When her daughter got the tell-tale look she knew meant a denial was coming, Mary waved her phone in Taylor's face. "Don't deny it. You want to know what to do? How about obeying me? You want to *know what to do*? How about not showing up here in the middle of the night and –"

"Oh my *god*!" Taylor managed to make the three words into a nuanced expression of boredom, irritation, and rage. "It's not like you care what I'm doing the rest of the time. What, I'm supposed to entertain myself for the twenty hours a day that you're gone and –"

"And for a girl who claims she hates it here," Mary belted out, "would you mind explaining why this is the third time that someone's found you sneaking around outside in the middle of the night?"

"I wasn't in outside. I was in the locker room."

"Oh, well, thank goodness for that!" Mary shouted, throwing her hands upward. "I'll make sure to include that fact in my prayers later. 'Yes, Lord, she was in the bus station, skulking around so well that no one even spotted her on the security monitors, for only-You-know-what, but at least she was in the *locker room*. Hallelujah! Praise Jesus!"

Taylor's eyes narrowed, and at the end of Mary's screed she whispered, "Does it even matter?" Then she squared her shoulders, then said in a louder voice, "The only thing you care about is my precious 4.0 at school. The only thing you want –"

"You don't know the *first thing about what I want!*" Mary shouted the words. She glanced toward the ticket window, worried that she might be drawing a crowd at this point. Thankfully, the two-inch-thick slab of plexiglass that saved her from potential attackers, and made half of all ticket requests into gibberish, also shielded the passengers from the sound of her outburst.

She swiveled back to Taylor, who looked taken aback at the outburst. Good. Mary rode that moment, hoping it would take her somewhere where she would find her daughter again, instead of the angry, withdrawn girl Taylor had become in recent months. "I know all about the world you're getting yourself into, girl, and it's not what you think. You think I *enjoy* leaving you alone at all hours of the day or night? No!" She realized her hands were clenched. She wondered – not for the first time – how much of her daddy might be hiding inside her. If she had a little bit of Big J inside. She thought she had killed off that part of her, but at times like this…

She unballed her fists, which had been clenched so tightly that the fingers were already cramping, before continuing. "I did whatever I had to, to get out of the gangs, out of the slums, when I found out I was pregnant with you. I've slaved and scrimped and saved every day since then to keep you far away from that world, then to keep you in a good school, then to come up with a deposit for a college good enough to keep you far away from the life I had to lead when I was your age. Lord only knows how I'm going to keep doing it, or how I'm even going to find the money to get you the rest of the way through college, but I *will* do it and you *will* go to college and you *will* get away from my dead-end world."

Taylor looked strange. Mary couldn't place the expression on her daughter's face. She had never seen it before, and had to play back the final moments to realize when it happened.

"*My* dead-end world." That was what she had just said. Not *a* dead-end world, not even *this* dead-end world.

My.

It was the first time, Mary realized, that she had flat-out told Taylor that she didn't want her daughter to be anything like her or end up anywhere near her. She had always dreamed of a better life, but never for herself. That die was cast, that fate was inevitable. But Taylor could have something better. Something more.

Mary reached out. She didn't deny what she had said. Instead, she clung tightly to her daughter and whispered, "You will grow up to be nothing like me. And that's a promise."

For a moment, Taylor held her back. For a moment, Mary felt like her daughter had returned. In saying she wanted her daughter to be far away, to be nothing like her, she had discovered her child closer than she had been in a long time.

"It'd be easier if you'd trust me a little," Taylor said quietly.

"It would be easier if you gave me reason to," Mary chuckled. She meant it as a joke, an easing of the suddenly-too-real emotion in the air.

It was the absolute wrong thing to say. Taylor stiffened. She pushed away from Mary, and threw up her hands in a mirror of the movement Mary herself had used only seconds ago. She stomped to the door to the lobby, still holding the purse she had entered with, her own fists balled so hard that the purse would probably have a permanent mark.

"Where do you think you're –" began Mary.

"To *pee*. Is that okay with you?"

Without waiting for an answer, Taylor threw open the door. She left.

Mary watched the door close behind her daughter.

Then went back to her desk.

Interlude

This is what happens in the final moments before the end truly begins:

Taylor Holiday, teenager extraordinaire and daughter mediocre, slams out of the ticket window while her mother watches her from the desk behind said window. Daughter's eyes: hard. Mother's: haunted.

Sheriff's Deputy Paul Kingsley watches Taylor, eyes following her as she walks in a straight line to the women's bathroom, the teen almost colliding with Shelly Sherman.

The Mary Kay consultant murmurs half of an "excuse me" before her eyes widen. Shelly Sherman points out the window, where the fog now – at last – presses hard against the glass. "Get a load of this," she says.

Everyone in the terminal looks, except Adam S. Miles, who just scored a Tetris and now grins as four complete lines of blocks disappear.

The rest of the passengers, though, gape. Most had not noticed how completely the outside world has disappeared. The entirety of the universe now seems to consist of the terminal, with nothing but gray, formless void beyond.

"Anyone ever see anything like –" begins Shelly.

"Sure," says Paul – too loudly to be believed. "Lotsa times."

He is lying. Everyone who cares to notice can tell.

The first passenger to look away from the fog is the unpleasantly-balding man, Jeremy Cutter. He pulls his bags, which are already clustered so tightly around him that standing without stumbling over them would be a challenge, a bit closer. He is afraid of people stealing them. People steal things all the time; he knows that well.

He looks at the sign on the wall.

Current Time: 1:38 A.M.

LA to SLC arrive 1:38 – ***NOW BOARDING***

BOISE to LOS ANG. arrive 3:20 A.M.

"NOW BOARDING" blinks on and off in a steady mockery of reality. Jeremy looks from the two words to the empty window that shows nothing at all beyond the terminal – least of all a bus arriving from Los Angeles via parts unknown – back to the sign.

NOW BOARDING.

Blink off.

NOW BOARDING.

Blink off.

Jeremy Cutter looks out the window again. Back at the sign. Back out the window.

"Where's the bus?" he demands. I have to get –"

"Unpucker," says Paul. "You'll get there."

"Look!" Shelly suddenly shouts. Everyone follows her pointing finger. Everyone sees the twin lights in the glowing fog: headlights.

Everyone sighs. Even Jesús Flores, whose life has been so full of blood that little scares him, lets out a slim breath. The world exists, after all. He of all the people in the terminal occasionally worries that such is not the case. He has taken enough lives that he absolutely knows how frail the gossamer-thin thread that tethers us to reality is. So thin it cannot be seen, and occasionally he wonders if it is real at all. And if life is not real, then what else might be false?

Is he an imagination? A dream in the mind of some unknown and unknowable god?

He does not know. So he focuses on the headlights as they grow steadily brighter, and tries to think of the job he has to do. More blood to come. Money after. A new suit – he likes nice suits, which a few people laughed at until he cut their balls off and showed them to the others he ran with.

So yeah, a new suit. Definitely. Then a bit of *blancanieve* – he rarely does cocaine, save after a successful job, but then he always takes a few days and lets himself ride the snowbank to a place where pleasant dreams hide. Maybe a woman or two. Then the next job.

The headlights grow brighter, but still do not pierce the gloom completely.

"Thank goodness," breathes Clarice Nishimura. She tugs at the sleeves of her shirt.

Her husband, Ken, takes her hand. Their fingers intertwine. He feels the huge diamond that sometimes seems to teeter on the band of metal that holds it to her finger. So big. He would never have been able to afford such a thing. But life turns out well sometimes, and it is certain that Clarice deserves a rock every bit as big as this one.

Ken stands, lifting Clarice's hand a bit. "Ready for the next bit of the trip, Mrs. Nishimura?"

She smiles. Ken bends to pick up his bags, and almost gets an elbow to the face as Jeremy shoves past him. "Watch it!" shouts Clarice, the nervousness she sometimes feels swallowed whole – as it always is – by the idea of something happening to Ken. He deserves *more* than the best. He is hers, and she is his, and that means that she has to protect him.

She takes a step toward the weaselly man who keeps pushing past, all his bags clattering and twisting as he pulls them behind. "Watch it!" she half-shouts again.

Ken tugs her hand. "No harm no foul, babe," he says. He uses his free hand to rub her shoulder. Kisses the back of her neck. "Let it go."

Clarice turns to Ken and kisses her newly minted husband.

In the ticket office, the security monitors flutter. Static obscures all of them, even the ones that were showing the inside of the terminal. The static appears to be the electronic analog of the fog outside. The interference grows in intensity. Electronic fog is replaced by an electronic blizzard. Then, with an audible snap, the monitors turn off as one.

Mary raps the side of one of them. It remains inert.

She looks out the ticket window, searching for Paul. He is staring out the lobby window. A moment later, Mary does the same.

In the satellite Sheriff's office, Bella Ricci stares at the monitors on Deputy Kingsley's desk. They flicker. Static obscures them. They flicker again, then turn off.

Movement draws her attention. She looks out the one-way glass window nearby. The fog billows, vomiting more vapor from inside itself, curling forward and outward. Tendrils caress the glass. Then the body of the fog – that is how she thinks of it, as a thing with a *body,* it was so thick – presses hard against the glass. The curls and eddies seem to disappear, like the fog has grown so much that there just isn't any more room to move.

Bella shrinks back against the wall. Then realizes that just the other side of that wall is more fog. She leans away from the cinder blocks, looking behind her as though the fog might reach through brick and mortar to catch her by the hair and yank her right through the wall.

In the lobby, Paul Kingsley hears Mary Holiday's voice. Tinny, broken to pieces the way it always is when she talks through the small speaker in the middle of the ticket window. "Paul? Can you check –"

Paul turns to her in time to see her break off. "What?" he asks. "Come on, Mary, just spit it out."

She doesn't respond. Just stares over his shoulder. Paul turns and sees only the fog and the two headlights. They are close enough now that they look like glowing orbs. Like eyes.

Paul gulps. Tries to convince himself that everything is fine. "What's so interesting, Mary?" he asks. His voice comes out rough. His mouth is suddenly dry. "It's just the bus."

The speaker in the ticket window clicks. Mary says, "Shouldn't it be slowing down?"

The bus lights grew. Faster, faster.

Ken Nishimura lets go of the suitcase he has been holding. It thumps to the floor. He grabs his wife and pushes her hard. "Get back!" he screams.

The women's room door opens. Taylor walks out. She doesn't notice the fog, even though she is standing right in front of the lobby window. She doesn't see the onrushing lights, even though she is closer to them than anyone.

"Taylor!" Mary shrieks. "Get away from there!"

People scream. They spin, looking for the best place to avoid the bus when – not if – it crashes through brick, mortar, and glass.

Ken holds Clarice's hand. He pulls her with him.

Clarice stumbles. Even in her panic – or especially with it – she pulls on her sleeves.

Paul trips over his own feet, moving away from the window.

Jeremy grabs onto his bags, heroically yanking as many of them away from danger as possible. He bumps into Taylor, who is also running. She falls, and the purse she has been holding drops from her hand and rolls loosely along the floor for several feet.

Jeremy does not stop. Does not offer to help. Just elbows Taylor to the side.

Mary, in the ticket office, sees her daughter shoved aside. "Taylor!" she screams. Then she abandons all thought of getting in trouble for leaving her desk in one moment, and abandons that desk in the next. She runs out the door to the lobby.

Shelly is running, too. Like Mary, she sees Taylor fall. She almost runs away, then wonders what Michelle – dear, sweet Michelle – will think if she finds out Shelly had abandoned the girl. She *will* never hear of such a thing, of course, how could she? But the thought turns Shelly nonetheless. She runs toward Taylor, reaching her at nearly the same moment as does Mary.

Jesús reacts calmly. He folds down the page of his book, puts it on the seat beside him, then stands and glides to the far corner of the terminal. That is where his eyes tell him he is least likely to be plowed down by the bus.

Adam does not move. He has scored another Tetris and is approaching his personal high score. He knows that people are upset – he has trouble interpreting expressions, but even he can tell that much – but he is mostly just glad no one is trying to talk to him any more.

Finally, though, he does look up. He sees the lights coming. He does not move. Just stares. Fear lashes his eyes, but it is clouded by calculation. After a moment, he looks back down at his game.

The bus can finally be seen through the fog. Not in details, but as a general outline. A gray leviathan swimming toward the aquarium windows of the terminal.

Its brakes squeal.

But the bus keeps hurtling forward.

PART TWO: The Other

1. Chaos

Mary saw her daughter fall. Saw the other woman – the one with the blond hair that was a bit too platinum to be natural – run for her. She saw the woman hook her hands under Taylor's shoulders and start yanking at the teen's suddenly dead weight.

Mostly though, she saw the bus. Displaced mist flowed over its front windows and grill, making it look less like a vehicle than like some monster of the deep, surging upward from places dark and cold and better left undisturbed. The mist recoiled from it, but there was still so much fog that the bus was more outline than substance; more intimation than detail.

But no matter how cloaked in fog it might be, there was no mistaking its speed or its mass. The lights blared at its front, dull gleams at first but quickly brightening to near-blinding levels. Mary saw Taylor hold up her hand, blocking the brightness that speared through the big windows at the front of the lobby.

The bus wasn't going to stop. Mary could tell that. And here was the moment that every story of near-death got wrong: she didn't see her life flash before her eyes. She saw *Taylor's* life. Saw her being born. The first steps as a toddler. The first day at kindergarten, and the day she came home from eighth grade because she found out her boyfriend was cheating on her with that "witch-with-a-B Kate Sterling."

Mary saw her daughter grow. Saw her become the teen she now was, so full of anger and disdain, but also so full of potential. She saw that potential bloom. Saw Taylor go to school. A good college. Saw her fall in love and marry. She saw grandchildren, and a few great-grandchildren. She saw her child grow, and bloom and bloom and never grow old.

All in the time it took Mary to run ten steps. All in the time it took her to leap over a line of chairs, almost tumbling to the floor as she did.

She saw the bus finally explode from half-light to sight, the last of the mist pulling away as though it sensed the violence about to occur, and had decided it could be no part of such awfulness.

Or maybe the mist wasn't departing. Maybe it was moving out of the way to give the bus more space. Maybe it had moved to the rear to push the bus forward. Maybe the fog was the reason the bus *was* moving forward.

All this: the time it took to take three more steps.

Taylor was still five feet away.

"Row, row, row your boat," Big J sang in her mind. *"Life is but a dream..."*

Mary kept running. Knowing the bus would plow through the front wall of glass and cinder block, and would continue forward to crush Taylor. Mary decided if that happened then she wanted to be a part of it.

Her life *had* flashed before her eyes, she realized: because her life was Taylor. And if Taylor's life ended, then Mary had no reason to continue.

The bus was going to steal it all away.

She reached for Taylor.

She heard the squeal of airbrakes pressed to the limit. Braced herself for the crash.

The brakes shrieked. Crescendoed. Mary winced, but could not help but turn to look at the violence that came for them.

The bus stopped. Two feet from the lobby windows. The mist puffed across it, its movements making Mary think of someone giggling at a great practical joke.

Not funny. Not funny at all.

The next moment, a new sound: the hiss of pneumatics as the doors on the bus opened. A form flung itself out, moving so fast and so strangely that he was hard to track for a moment.

"What the hell is that asshole –" began Kingsley.

The man – it was a man, Mary could see that now, though precious little other detail could be made out – stumbled across the pavement, tripping his way along as he hurled himself toward the lobby doors.

The bus doors hung open behind the man. No one else came out.

The man stumbled again, disappearing below the level of the windows before righting himself and pitching forward the last few feet to the sliding doors that opened onto the lobby.

The doors slid open.

The man ran in.

That was when Mary got her first look of him. He looked to be in his forties, with a lean, hard face that spoke of a life mostly spent in worry or perhaps anger. The kind of face you would see on a businessman who never quite turned a profit, or a blue-collar worker who looked at people with uncallused hands and raged at the unfairness of a God who sent him to a working-class family. The face of *any* person who had chosen to look at the hard parts of life as proof that the universe was out to get them.

But most of those people, Mary suspected, did not paint the angry lines of their faces with thick coats of blood.

It wasn't just his face, either. The man was covered in it, from top to bottom. Face dripped with it, his clothes were sopping with it. His hair stuck out in a thousand different directions in a clotted, gore-soaked mess. He looked like one of the extras from a war movie; the ones who got cut when the director realized that leaving *that* guy in would result in an X-rating.

Kingsley had been heading for the sliding doors, his own disappointment-ridden face hardened to righteous rage. He stopped when the bloody man tripped his way in. The man saw him at the same time. He looked from Kingsley to the door, and Mary thought she understood what he was thinking. He thought Kingsley wasn't heading for *him*, but for the exit.

The man screamed, *"NO!"* and body-checked Kingsley. Mary caught a glimpse of Kingsley's face, his expression contorted in a way that would have been funny had it been under any other circumstance. As it was, she felt no urge to laugh, simply grabbed Taylor, who still lay on the floor. She threw a protective arm across her child's chest and yanked her backward.

For the first time in a long time, Taylor didn't pull away or tense during her mother's embrace. She grabbed Mary's arm with both hands, crushing her mother close.

"NO!" shouted the bloody man again, screaming as he writhed his way on top of Kingsley. He began pummeling the deputy, shrieking as he did, "Don't go out there! Don't! You *can't... go... OUT!"*

Kingsley was screaming, hollering in pain as the blows rained down on him. The bloody man was so crazed that most of his attacks missed, or were so off-center that they were ineffectual. But a few of them landed. Kingsley's ear bloodied, and Mary saw one fist hit the deputy square enough on the eye that it was sure to leave a shiner.

"Help!" screamed Kingsley. "Someone get this guy offa me!"

Then he gagged as the bloody man started choking him.

"Don't go out!" the man screamed. "You can't!"

Mary looked around. No one was moving. Most of the people had expressions she knew were the mirror of her own: stunned, unsure, confused. What do you do when the world stops obeying normal world rules?

She held Taylor closer. Then felt herself move away. Taylor tried to pull her to her again, and that felt good, *so* good. Mary wanted to stay there, to bask in the moment where her little girl needed her, *wanted* her, again.

But Kingsley was turning red. She didn't want the deputy to die. She didn't like him, but that didn't mean she could stand by and watch him be murdered. Normally he would be the one to handle such a thing, but since he was the one in danger, that left Meriweather "Mary" Holiday. She was the closest thing to authority, and something inside her whispered that that mattered.

So she pushed Taylor away. She ran to the ticket office, hurriedly punching in the code that unlocked the door. It clicked open and she crossed to the locked box on the back wall. Yanked it open.

She heard Kingsley through the open door, heard him gagging. Heard the other man saying in a wheezy, half-laughing, half-choking voice, "Don't… go… out… there…"

Mary pulled open the box so hard that half its contents flew out and fell to the floor. The thing she needed, though, stayed in the box, clipped securely to the side with a bright red plastic clip marked EMERGENCY USE ONLY.

Mary broke the clip open. Grabbed what it held. It seemed simple enough to operate – she *hoped* it was simple enough, since there wasn't exactly time to take a class on the subject.

She ran back into the lobby. The bloody man still straddled Kingsley, but as Mary ran out she saw the young man – the one who was so googly-eyed over his pretty wife – fling himself onto the attacker's back, trying to help.

The bloody man whipped a fast elbow behind him. It found the new husband's nose, flattening it with a crack that sent the other man tumbling back and away, his face now masked with blood that eerily paralleled the countenance of the madman in their midst. Like insanity was a bloody, virulent, and above all *contagious* thing.

The man's wife caught him. His weight drove both of them backward, sending them tumbling into a line of hard plastic seats, then both of them continued over the backs and to a no doubt bruised pile on the hard floor behind.

Mary was still moving toward Kingsley and the crazy man who kept screaming, "Don't go out! Don't go out!"

Apparently he had decided that the best way to keep that from happening was to kill the deputy.

And then what? The rest of us?

Taylor?

She couldn't let that happen. She closed the distance between her and Kingsley. She only had one shot, and couldn't waste it.

Just a few steps closer.

Beside her, the man who had been playing a GameBoy since he walked off the bus that dropped him here sighed and put the device carefully on the chair beside him. He strode to the bags of the ugly, balding guy with the ferret features, then grabbed the laptop bag that perched atop that man's luggage.

"Hey!" shouted the man. "That's mine!"

The gamer kid ignored him. Two quick strides brought him beside the mad, bloody man and Kingsley. The gamer hefted the case, as though gauging its weight. Then he swung it right at the crazy man's head.

The madman snarled, sensing or seeing the case hurtling toward him. He twisted to the side, and instead of striking his head the case bounced off his shoulder. Something cracked inside the case.

"Hey!" screamed the man who had just seen his case sacrificed.

Jeremy. That was his name. Jeremy Cutter. That's what the ticket said.

Mary didn't wonder why her mind was vomiting up that tidbit right now. Just one more moment of madness – so that meant it fit right in, didn't it?

The case hit the madman hard enough to knock him to the side, and Mary heard Kingsley heave in a huge breath. His respite was short-lived, though, as the crazy, bloody man jumped right back on top of him again. And worse now, because he had somehow gotten Kingsley's gun loose of its holster. The madman waved it back and forth, screaming, "Get back! Get back or I swear I'll –"

As soon as the gun waved its dangerous arc away from Taylor, Mary shot her own gun. A sharp, angry *snnnap* as the twin darts at the end of the Taser launched out, connected to the trigger and battery mechanisms by trailing wires.

The darts made an ugly crackling noise, something halfway between a hum and small fireworks going off. According to the training – which mostly consisted of instructions that boiled down to, "But I wouldn't use it if I were you, 'cause you'll probably get sued and the bus line isn't in the habit of defending stuff like that" – the shock the Taser emitted should have disabled and paralyzed the bloody man.

Apparently he hadn't gotten the training, or read the manual. He stiffened, and the gun flew out of his hand. But he didn't fall. He remained atop Kingsley. His jaw locked for a moment, but then his back arched in a way that reminded Mary of a wolf howling at the moon and the bloody man screamed, louder than he ever had: *"ALL IN FAVOR! ALL IN FAVOR IS ME AND IF YOU LEAVE YOU DIE IF YOU LEAVE YOU DIE NOW LET ME –"*

Something faster and stronger than either a laptop case or a Taser hit the bloody man in the face. The bloody man stiffened as the man with the tattoos on his face kicked him so fast it was a blur. The madman toppled to the side, Kingsley gasping under him as the hands that had been choking the life out of him suddenly loosed.

The tattooed man looked at the man he'd just kicked, obviously checking to see if more violence would be necessary. The madman just lay there, motionless.

The tattooed man shifted his gaze to Kingsley, who was wheezing, "Jesus," over and over again.

"No. Jes*ús*," said the tattooed man. He shook his head, the most superbly disgusted expression Mary had ever seen gracing his features, and then muttered, "You're welcome."

Jesús turned as movement caught his eye, stiffening slightly as though ready to attack someone else. Mary felt like she was watching a tiger in the zoo: something contained, but far from tame.

Only unlike such tigers, Mary suspected that he held the key to his own cage. He would release himself if and when he felt like it, and the results would be bloody.

In the next instant, Jesús relaxed, seeing that the motion that had arrested his attention was just the man who had swung the laptop case. His name, Mary thought, was Adam. She had a good mind for names, and often remembered specific passengers whose names came across her screen.

Adam pulled the insane and now thankfully unconscious man away from Kingsley, then rolled the man onto his stomach and crossed his arms behind his back. Mary thought she saw a flicker of admiration on Jesús' face at that. Jesús yanked a pair of handcuffs off Kingsley's belt. Kingsley just lay there, still groaning.

Jesús shook his head, then cuffed the madman, who had started to groan as well. The bloody form started twitching, and Jesús kicked him in the side, then looked at Kingsley. "You got a holding cell, *sí*?" he said.

"You can't!" shouted another passenger, the newlywed –

(*Clare? Clara? No, it's Clarice, that's it.*)

– who had come in with her husband, Ken. She had been holding a cloth to her husband's face, staunching the flow of blood there, but when she glanced at him he nodded and gestured that he was fine and that she could go do whatever it was she was going to do.

To Mary's surprise, Clarice ran to the side of the now-moaning madman. She began running expert fingers over his sides, his limbs. "You can't move him, he could be hurt," she said.

Kingsley finally managed to sit up, huffing and puffing like a beached whale. "*He* could be hurt?" he managed. His voice was rough, abraded-sounding.

"What about the rest of us?" demanded Jeremy. The man was rubbing at his hairline as he said it, as though he might coax the angrily-dying follicles back to production. His already-whiny voice went a full octave higher. "That nut comes in here, tries to kill us all, and you're worried about *him*? How about you check the rest of us out before seeing to him?"

Clarice glared at Jeremy for a moment, finally spitting the words, "You're not the one covered in blood."

Shelly moved toward Clarice, sliding a scarf from around her neck and holding it out. Clarice took it without looking, nodding an absent thanks as she began mopping the blood away from the madman who was still moaning. "We don't know what's wrong with him," she said.

"What the hell are you, a doctor?" demanded Jeremy.

Clarice glared at him. "Nurse. Which means I know that if we move him it could hurt him worse or even kill him."

"So?"

Jesús said the word quietly, so low that it should have been lost in the heat of the moment, but everyone looked at one another as though he had just screamed the single word. He didn't wait for a response, though, simply moving back to where he had been sitting when the night dissolved into madness.

He picked up the novel he had been reading and held it tightly in hands, the only obvious concession to the terror of the past few moments the fact that he was no longer reading the book. Just holding it so tightly that the thick tome was bent nearly double.

Nearby, Taylor sniffed. Mary realized she was still holding the spent Taser, and now she dropped it and rushed to her daughter. She knelt down, gratified to feel Taylor hug her tightly. "You okay?" she asked.

Taylor nodded wordlessly. She opened her mouth to say something, coughed, then tried again. "Where's my purse?" she said.

Mary looked at her to see if the question was a real one, or one born of shock and fear. She couldn't tell. Taylor had a distant look on her face, but no more so than she almost always did these days. Mary couldn't decide if that was a good thing or a bad one.

She looked at Clarice. "Can you take a look at my daughter?"

"In a moment," said Clarice. She glanced up, though, and said, "She break anything when she fell? Hit her head?"

"I don't think so," said Mary.

"I'm fine," said Taylor, her voice full of acid irritation.

She sounds fine, all right – or as fine as she ever is, if pissed off and closed off and self-righteous count as "fine."

Mary said none of that. She stood, deciding that if Taylor didn't want her help, maybe someone else did. She looked around the room, trying to see if anyone else had been hurt.

Jesús was still sitting alone, holding the book, watching everything. The tiger deciding if it would be better to feed, or to stay in the cage for now.

Kingsley had scooched back a few feet, and now sat with his back against one of the rows of chairs. He unbuttoned the top two buttons of his uniform and felt his throat. Mary could see it had already started glowing an angry red. Other than that, he seemed okay.

She looked at the woman who had handed her scarf to Clarice.

Shauna? No. Shelly. That was it.

Shelly was scrabbling around in a purse that looked expensive, if not particularly classy. She found what she was looking for, drawing out a prescription bottle. She popped the top, then tilted the bottle and Mary saw a pair of pills tumble into the woman's mouth.

Still holding the open pill bottle, the woman fished around in her purse again, this time coming up with a mini-bottle of Smirnoff. She cracked it open, then tossed it back in one gulp, following the pills down with a vodka chaser.

She grimaced, then started screwing the top back on the bottle. Spotting Mary, she shrugged and said, "Nerves. Sometimes just the Xanax won't cut it."

"Guys?"

Mary heard her daughter speak, but her attention was diverted to Kingsley, who had rolled back to his knees, then stood. He started toward Clarice, pointing a big finger at the man she was still examining. "Get away from that guy. I'm putting him in the back until –"

"You can't!" shouted Clarice. "I'm telling you, you move him and you could –"

"Guys?" said Taylor again. Mary felt like she was watching a dozen TV screens at once. Too many.

"– could kill him," Clarice continued. "He could be sick, or have nerve damage, or –"

"GUYS!" Taylor screamed. Mary finally looked at her daughter, then her attention was stolen by Shelly, who screamed and dropped the pills she still held. The bottle bounced across the floor, the pills exploding out of it.

"That's not the right bus," said Jeremy. "That's not the right bus, is it? Not the right bus at all."

He spoke in a breathless, terrified tone that sent the words tripping over themselves. Mary looked at what Taylor had seen, what the woman had seen, what Jeremy had seen.

And when she saw it, too, she had to stifle a scream.

2. Nerves

Shelly knew a few things with certainty at this moment, the moment she screamed. The first was that she didn't want to be here; that she should have gone on and just waited for Michelle at the meeting spot instead of worrying about looking needy.

The second was that Xanax and vodka weren't going to be enough. Not in a place where the fog had rolled in so thick it made her unsure if she still *existed*. Not in a place where a madman had run in covered in blood and started attacking people.

Definitely not in a place where the bus that finally came wasn't the one that had *Final Destination – Los Angeles* written above it, but one that said instead *Lewiston Transit*.

"Not the right bus, it's not the right bus, where's the right bus?" mumbled Jeremy. Shelly barely noticed his words, but something in the back of her brain made her tighten her grip on her purse. She knew dishonest people – many of them, and some of them intimately – and everything coming from this guy *screamed* dishonesty.

But as the words sunk in, Shelly realized he was right: the bus that had appeared out of the mist *wasn't* the right bus. Instead of the long-haul bus line's logo she had expected to see, the vehicle outside looked like a short-line commuter bus.

And Shelly didn't know how the guy driving it had managed to stop the vehicle before he crashed right through the terminal. How could he, when he must have been driving blind? When every window – *every single window* – was caked in brown and black and red.

Colors that Shelly had seen.

Colors that she knew.

Blood. Gore. Bits of other things that could be brains or clumps of hair or simply so much blood that it had begun to congeal upon itself.

The windows of the bus were the nightmare eyes of a person suffering massive brain hemorrhaging. The bus' eyes bled, and freely.

"Dear God in Heaven," whispered the kind-looking ticket lady whose name tag said *Mary*.

Bet Mary wishes she worked for a different bus line right about now.

"Where's the right bus?" Jeremy asked again.

No one answered, but the cute new husband stood suddenly and began lurching toward the sliding glass doors that led outside. The deputy saw him and lunged between the groom and the door.

"What are you doing?" shouted Deputy Kingsley.

The husband gestured at the bus outside. "There could be people in there who need help. We –"

"Whoa!" Kingsley waved his hands back and forth like he was trying to scythe down the words as they emerged from the younger man's mouth. He jerked a thumb behind him, where the bus still sat. "Didn't you hear what…" and then the thumb jerked toward the still-unconscious madman, "… he said? Didn't you see *him*? Something's not right –"

"Understatement," muttered the guy with the tattoos.

"– and I don't want it in here with us," continued Kingsley. "Not until we've got some backup."

"There could be people hurt –" the young man tried again.

A different voice spoke up. The teen girl who was so obviously Mary's daughter – and who just as obviously wished she wasn't. "But we don't know for sure," she said. She had already pushed her mother away, which struck Shelly as rude given how fast Mary had come to her aid. Now she glanced at her mom as though daring her to disagree. When Mary said nothing, she jerked a chin toward the bus. "I don't know what's happening out there, but I do know I don't want it in here."

Adam, who had not looked at anyone during the exchange, said, "I think the deputy and the girl are right."

"Gee, thanks," said the girl. "And the name is Taylor."

"Taylor," said Adam, continuing in the herky-jerky tones that Shelly was coming to realize were his natural communication. "I am Adam S. Miles." He turned his gaze back to the new groom who was trying unsuccessfully to force himself past the deputy. "I am just passing through. I wish to be safe, and I do not believe it would be wise to leave. The man said we should not. He said, 'If you leave you die.'"

As though he had heard others discussing him, the madman moaned loudly and began to shift. Not awake, but coming back from whatever dark place he had been kicked into.

"He was nuts," said the groom.

"Maybe, but..." Deputy Kingsley's voice was surprisingly soft, gentle. "What's your name, kid?"

The guy looked surprised to be called "kid," but he nodded as he said, "Ken. Ken Nishimura."

"Okay, Ken," said the deputy. "I'm Deputy Kingsley. And I have *never* seen anything like what just happened. Going out is not a good idea."

Ken's face eloquently communicated what he thought of Kingsley's advice. "He was *crazy*," said Ken. He pointed outside, at the gore-streaked bus. "The guy probably did all that, and what if there's someone hurt inside the bus? Or do you believe if I leave I'll magically die or something?"

Adam said, "No. Magic does not exist. But it stands to reason that we should wait for assistance. Statistically, violence against one's person is less likely when in the company of trained assistance." He looked from Ken to the deputy – or from a space over Ken's shoulder to one just above Paul's forehead. "Are you going to call for backup, Deputy Kingsley?"

"Yeah," said Kingsley, obviously abashed. "Yeah, I –" Embarrassment shifted suddenly to angry bluster, which Shelly guessed was his SOP for any uncomfortable situation. "Don't tell me my job," he snapped. He unclipped the radio from his belt and held it to his lips. At the same time, he pointed at Ken, a gesture that said, *Don't you try to leave.*

Shelly watched Ken's face. She saw fear there, and more as he glanced at where his wife was still working on cleaning up the crazy guy. She saw him decide not to leave, and was surprised how glad it made her.

Why so happy, Shelly? What are you worried about? What could be out there?

The answer, when it came to her, was short, uncomfortable, and true: *Anything*.

"Dispatch?" Kingsley said into the radio. He let go of the button on the side, and a burst of static answered him. He keyed the button again, and said, "Dispatch, this is seven-six, come in. Deputy Kingsley at the Lawton Terminal Station, come in."

He let go. Nothing. Not even the burst of static this time. Just dead air.

Ken turned away from the deputy. "Clarice, you okay?" he asked.

Clarice answered. "Yeah. Great," as she cleaned the unconscious man.

"Shouldn't you move away from him a bit?" asked Ken.

Clarice smiled nervously and tugged at the hem of one of her sleeves. "As soon as I'm done checking him out."

Kingsley, meanwhile, was trying various buttons and knobs and dials on his radio. Shelly didn't know what any of them did, but she could tell they weren't doing anything helpful. Kingsley said, "Dispatch," into the radio a few more times, then grimaced and put it back on his belt. He took a breath, visibly trying to keep himself calm, then pulled out his cell phone. He put it to his ear.

As he did, a noise burst from it, so loud that Kingsley yelped and nearly dropped it. So loud that Shelly – and everyone else in the room – could easily hear it.

The noise sounded strange. Terrible. Frightening. It wasn't organic, exactly – Shelly was reminded of the old dial-up tones she had heard when connecting to the Internet when she was younger. Sort of like that, yeah, but also…

She searched for a word to describe the thing she heard. The clicks and grating shrieks. Finally she came up with "wet." That was it. It sounded wet, violent. If a machine could be drowned, she thought that this was what it would sound like.

The shriek sounded, louder and louder. Kingsley held the phone far from him, his expression one of a pet owner who has suddenly found himself holding a wild animal by the scruff.

The noise grew louder, and Shelly realized it was no longer coming only from Kingsley's phone. Jeremy was holding his own phone at arm's length, staring at it with horror as the sound echoed there. Then it started coming from all around the room, and Shelly heard it in her own purse.

All the phones. All of them are making the sound.

What is it?

She didn't know. But she knew that, whatever it was, it couldn't be good.

She wondered, fleetingly, where Michelle was right now. She wondered, fleetingly, if Michelle was in the fog as well.

She hoped not.

She feared so.

The phones silenced. All at once, the shrieking, drowning noise that had come from them just *ended*. The silence was somehow louder-seeming than the noise had been, and as everyone in the lobby looked at their phones then at each other, the phones all squealed again. The tone was shorter this time – thankfully – but when it cut off this time, the lights in the terminal all went out.

The only illumination, suddenly, were the brightly-blaring headlights of the bus that had started this nightmare.

No. The fog *did.*

Shelly didn't know why she would have thought that. Fog was fog, wasn't it? But as much as she tried to convince herself of that fact, something inside her *screamed* that it was true. This had started with the fog.

A few clicks arrested her attention. "What's that?" she murmured. No one answered.

She followed the sound and realized that the terminal lights were still off, but the emergency lights over each doorway had flickered on. They didn't help the atmosphere any, each of the smaller lights' beams swallowed up in the much brighter lights from the bus.

Shelly looked around and realized how much everyone looked like grim skeletons in that harsh light.

Bad lighting. Not at all flattering.

She felt, madly, like offering everyone a free beauty consultation. *"Worried about how you'll look in the terrible light of a gore-soaked bus, terrified in the middle of the night as your cell phones try to crush you under a wall of noise? Well I'm Shelly Sherman, Independent Beauty Consultant for Mary Kay, and have I got a few deals for* you!"

She shouted in surprise as the phones all sounded again. It wasn't the same wet, angry, painful noise from before, though. This time, tones rang out –chimes, a short beep or two.

Shelly's own rang out with a chipper arpeggio: the tone that alerted her a text had come in.

She looked at her phone, seeing others do the same. On her phone's screen was a short, simple message.

The Other: only 1 will leave
all in favor

Jeremy spoke before Shelly could, asking the question she herself had heard in her mind. "Who the hell is 'The Other'?"

Everyone looked from their phones to each other. "You got that message, too?" asked Shelly.

She was speaking to Jeremy, but Adam and Ken both answered instead: "Yes," they both said, and Clarice nodded at the same time. Mary was looking at her own phone, and though she neither nodded nor spoke, Shelly saw the affirmative in her bright, terrified eyes.

Then Mary's eyes changed. Still scared, but now surprised as well. She danced backward, barely avoiding Deputy Kingsley as he barreled past her, streaking with surprising speed to the locked door at the back of the lobby, the one that said, "Deputy Sheriff" on the door. He pressed a series of buttons on the side of the door, then yanked it open and ran inside.

"What the hell?" asked Ken, his voice shaking.

The tattooed man snorted. He was staring at the door in disgust, but his own phone shook in his grip, and Shelly could see that he was holding it so tightly the knuckles were bright white, bloodless burls.

That made her even more afraid. She had no doubt the tattooed man was dangerous. So what could make a man like him start to shake?

The fog.

No. The *fog* hadn't done anything. Okay, maybe the lights were out due to some weather thing causing the fog as well. But why wouldn't she think *"the crazy guy covered in blood who drove in on a bus also covered in blood caused all this"*? Why think *the fog did it*?

She had no answer to that. She stared out the windows. The fog curled around the lights of the bus, as though waiting to claim the light to itself. To eat it. To leave the world in darkness.

To be all that remained.

3. Going Places

Bella Ricci knew she was Going Places. That was, like, destiny. Nothing more, nothing less.

Sure, she'd been born in a crappy little town in Idaho. Sure, she hadn't *technically* graduated from high school. Sure, she didn't have much money, or any contacts outside of the area – except one.

But that one was important. He was going to take her places.

Unless she rotted away in this cell.

That was seeming more and more a possibility with every passing moment. It was her fault, she supposed – she hadn't been acting very innocent, waiting in the locker room of this tiny little place.

No, that's not true. Lockers are supposed to be used, right? So it wasn't me *that was doing anything wrong. It was that asshole cop.*

That sounded right in her head. She was Going Places, and that was great. But she'd also realized that it pissed off everyone who *wasn't* Going Places. People stuck in dead-end jobs and dead-end relationships and dead-end lives *hated* the folks who, like Bella, were destined for great things. They looked, and envied, and acted like crying babies.

That's what happened with the cop. He saw a girl who was Going Places, and knew that he'd never enjoy that privilege. So he tried to stop *her* from enjoying what fate kept in store.

She'd thought for sure he would let her off. Most guys did. She just had to cock out her hips, shove her boobs a few inches closer, and every bit of oxygen drained from their brains in favor of the boners they tried to hide.

Everyone wanted her. That was why she was Going Places. Hard *not* to do that, when you looked like an A-list movie star just waiting for her first deal to find her.

But the guy apparently didn't like movies. Because he all but manhandled her into the back room, then tossed her in the holding cell. She thought she *still* might be able to get out, but the dude was so deep in his own shit he couldn't even see the shining star in his presence.

And then… nothing. A few hours of watching him watch TV, followed by a few minutes of talking to him, followed by loneliness.

Bella liked many things. She liked movies. She liked texting. She liked doing her makeup and hair. She liked taking pictures of herself and monitoring the likes and the comments of "sexy AF" that inevitably poured in when she posted them on the 'Gram.

She did *not* like being alone or feeling lonely.

She especially didn't like it in here, with not a sound to distract her from the intrusive silence of the place. Even the noise of the tiny TV playing shitty local weather had beat the silence that fell when the cop left.

Crap. Crap, shit, crap.

She couldn't even tell what time it was. That scared her. What if her contact came and went?

Of course, that was impossible. That was *ridiculous*. He loved her, he said so often and repeatedly. So worst case scenario: he'd show up, find her not there, and just put off leaving until she did show up. He'd wait for her, just like fate was waiting for her in L.A.

But it was getting harder and harder to convince herself of that fact. Every passing moment of lonely silence, her own doubts started growing. Got louder.

They had just about started screaming at her when the lights went out. She actually *did* scream then, a tight yelp that made her glance around as though worried someone else might have heard such an ugly sound come from her beautiful lips.

No one was there. No one but her, the desk – geez, her phone was *right there*, and what would she give to have her hands on it now? – the silent TV, the grainy security monitors nearby…

And the fog.

She hadn't looked out there since she saw the *thing*. Had tried to pretend she hadn't seen anything at all. Just fog, because fog couldn't hurt her. Fog didn't do anything at all, other than make some cool lighting effects that highlighted her sexiness.

So fog… not a bad thing, right?

Right?

She kept saying that over and over; kept telling herself it was fine, that the fog was nothing, that L.A. was waiting with fame and fortune. She'd bang who she had to bang, get what she wanted, then laugh at all the people who used to tell her she'd be a failure.

It was harder to say such things when she stood in the dark. The darkness hid her beauty, and Bella knew that a big part – maybe all – of her success stemmed from her amazing face, killer bod, and knowledge of both.

In the dark, they didn't matter so much.

In the dark, it was just her and the fog.

The phone went off at one point, and that was what got her looking around again. The sound it made was awful, this grating, gravelly thing that made her think of a scene from some movie with computers that take over the world. If the Terminator texted, that's what it would sound like.

She looked at the phone when it stopped making that noise. It was dark, silent. A moment later it chimed, the sound of

Justin Bieber moaning, "Oh, baby," as a text arrived. The screen lit up, and she could make out the dark scrawl of a new text. But she couldn't see what it said. Couldn't see anything at all, other than white with a few squiggly black lines.

She reached through the bars of the holding cell, her fingers splayed as though doing so might allow her to squeeze between the bars.

Stupid? Sure. But every moment without that phone was a moment when she felt a bit less like Bella Ricci, Star On The Rise, and a bit more like Bella Ricci, High School Dropout With No Marketable Skills.

She dropped her hand as the phone's screen darkened again. Another missed message. She cursed under her breath.

She looked around. Deciding whether it would be worth it to start screaming. If the cop came, would her screams help or hurt the situation? If he was irritated, that would be bad. If it was some weird turn-on for him – and she wouldn't be surprised at that; one thing life had taught her was that men were *totes* screwed up when it came to turn-ons – then she could use that.

And what if he doesn't come at all?

That was the thing that locked her lips. That kept her quiet. What if he *didn't* come? What if she was alone… and would stay so, forever?

She looked around again. Same stupid office. Same nothing. The lights were off, but now she thought about it that was probably an improvement – at least she didn't have to suffer the sight of the industrial interior design all around her.

Keep telling yourself that.

It wasn't totally dark, at least. A pair of emergency lights glowed above the door to the lobby. It was a yellowed, nasty light, but lights meant power, power meant people driving that power, and people… they would all fall down before her someday.

Bella realized suddenly that not all the light was coming from the emergency lights. A softer, more even glow came in through the window that allowed a view outside.

She had avoided looking there.

She couldn't any longer.

She stared into the fog, trying to pierce its depths by will alone. She was a force of nature, wasn't she? So surely she of all people would –

Something moved in the fog. A dark shape that flitted close enough she could almost make out details. A long, thin form that looked somehow insectile. Arms and legs that snapped like whips, back and forth, back and forth.

The figure was the height of a person, she guessed. But something about its form was… *wrong*. Maybe that was a trick of the light, a function of the fog that revealed so little and hid so much.

Just someone walking around.

Then the thing stopped. Still barely more than a black smudge in the glowing gray mist, but Bella suddenly felt like it was aware of her. Like it was *looking* at her.

One of the barely-seen arms moved, touching its head. A trio of green lights glinted to life there.

Eyes.

Bella felt everything she knew falling away. She was no longer Going Places. She was just here, now, in a place cut off from reality by a gray wall of vapor. She was nothing at all but a thing in a cage, watched by something otherworldly, terrible.

She fell back, pushing herself into the wall, closing her eyes the way she had when hiding under her covers as a child.

It can't see me I can't see it. It can't see me I can't see it.

The words came as a mantra, a prayer.

Something clicked nearby, and Bella knew – *knew* – that it was the thing. It had come inside. It was in the deputy's office, and now stood watching her with those three green eyes. A monster or an alien, come down here and now deciding whether to take Bella from her cage, whether to load her in the mother ship or beam her up or whatever things like that *did*.

Bella liked movies. She knew these things rarely ended well.

Now it sounded like the thing was clattering across the floor, moving awkwardly. It was easy for her to imagine the thing: two legs, two arms. Humanoid, but clumsy on a planet whose gravity and environment were so different from those of its world.

She heard the clatter of plastic on plastic, followed by a series of rapid clicks. Bella frowned, because she knew that sound and had to ask herself what kind of alien would take the desk phone off the hook and then click the switch over and over to get a dial tone?

She opened her eyes, and had to consciously restrain herself from crying. It wasn't the alien or monster or whatever had been out there in the fog. It was just the deputy, and though he was a prick and disgustingly immune to her charms – which made him even more of a prick in her book – in that moment she would have kissed him.

Kingsley turned to stare at her. He looked different than he had when he left. He had already looked grim, sure, but now his mouth hung open the way mouths do when all a person's happy thoughts have taken a personal day, and his eyes were wide and frenzied. He looked like he was on a bad trip. Worse.

He was, she realized, terrified.

He kept clicking the switch on the phone. Tried dialing some buttons on the keypad. Apparently he didn't like what he heard because his mouth finally firmed enough for him to scream, "Dammit!"

Bella looked to the side. Out the window. Wondering what she would see.

The fog curled around the glass, touching it with eddying caresses that seemed both loving and somehow obscene.

Just fog. JUST FOG!

No matter how many times she thought it, or how loudly she screamed the thoughts in her mind, Bella could not make herself believe it.

She looked back at the deputy, who was staring at the phone with a mixture of horror and despair. "Excuse me?" she said. Her voice came out as a croak.

The deputy looked at her. Bella waited for him to say something. That was usually what happened when she signaled she was ready for a man's attention.

He said nothing.

She didn't either, not for a long time. Then, finally, she managed, "I don't know what's going on, but I could really *really* use that drink now."

4. Crutch

Adam S. Miles is different. He knows that, because though different he is certainly not *stupid*. People thought that for a time, but it is hard to call someone stupid who ruins the math curve.

So no, not stupid. Just not *normal*.

That suits Adam S. Miles just fine. He does not like normals. He is on a different scale, which rude people call "retarded" and less rude people whisper about being "on the spectrum."

Neither is accurate. He is simply who he is. He is a math genius. He likes computers more than he likes people. He is worried about his GameBoy more than he is about the other passengers.

That does not mean he does not notice them. That is a thing a lot of neurotypicals – what his mother always called "NTs" think: that he does not know what is going on around him. That is not the way it works, though. He is *more* aware of everything, he thinks, than they are. That is what it means to be neurodiverse, at least so far as he knows it: he sees *everything*. That is a good thing, because nothing sneaks up on him. But it is bad when, as now, there is so much happening that he cannot figure out what is the most important thing.

He sees it all. It all hits him equally. It hurts.

Adam S. Miles knows everyone's names, which is not unusual. He has a good memory for names and faces, though the expressions those faces wear is often a mystery. He has been called "retarded" for that, too, but is it retarded to not understand a twitch of the lips? A slight curl of the mouth or pinch of the cheek that could mean either anger or joy or disgust or ecstacy or any of a million other feelings?

No. Adam S. Miles thinks it is "retarded" that so many people do not say what they mean, then expect others to somehow divine what they wish.

Ken Nishimura, sitting beside his wife, is shaking his phone. Dialing numbers. He grimaces, and though the expression is mysterious as all expressions, Adam S. Miles figures it means he did not get through to anyone. Nearby, the man with the ugly hairline is shaking his phone and wearing the same expression.

Ken Nishimura's wife, Clarice Nishimura, finishes cleaning the bloody man who exploded into their midst. She sighs and sits back. "None of the blood is his," she says, with an expression and tone that Adam S. Miles *thinks* is relief, but might also be anger or irritation. So many mysteries. "So far as I can tell," she continues, "he's not wounded at all."

The woman who interrupted his gaming earlier, Shelly Sherman, says, "Then whose blood is it?"

Everyone in the room turns to look at the bloody bus outside. Adam S. Miles looks as well – a rare moment where he does exactly the same thing as the NTs around him. He wonders if that is a good thing or a bad one. He does not know.

Just like he does not know what the bus means. What the bloody man on the floor – who moans a bit louder every minute – means.

What *any* of this means.

For a moment, he wonders if he would be better off playing Tetris. He likes playing Tetris. He is an excellent player, but even if he were terrible at it, he would still play. Tetris makes sense. The pieces each have a shape, and that shape can rotate around four points. A maximum of four different configurations when they touch the other blocks that have come before. He likes that.

He decides not to play Tetris, though. He is afraid, and thinks he should pay attention to what is going on all around.

The man on the floor moans. Clarice Nishimura, kneeling beside him, leans close to him. She looks like she is feeling for a pulse, and doing so brings her close enough to the man that for some reason Adam S. Miles' own skin crawls. He does not understand this. He doesn't like to be touched, but Clarice Nishimura isn't touching that man, or Adam S. Miles. So why be worried or uncomfortable?

He does not know. Interesting. Interesting and scary.

Clarice Nishimura shifts and starts helping the man on the floor to sit up as he blinks and looks around.

"Hey, don't," says Jeremy Cutter. He has eyes that Adam S. Miles does not like. He does not do well with expressions, true, but he *does* have feelings of his own. He does not feel good around Jeremy Cutter. Something about his expression makes Adam S. Miles want to chain his GameBoy to him. "He might be dangerous," says Jeremy Cutter.

Ken Nishimura moves to help his wife, throwing a look that may be disgust or misery or excitement at Jeremy Cutter. "And he might not. He might be a victim in all this, and he might also be able to tell us what's going on."

Jeremy Cutter throws his hands in the air like he's in a Western and someone just told him to stick-'em-up. "Are you kidding me?" he shouts. "Guy tries to kill a deputy and you want to have a tea party with him –"

He advances as he speaks, and Ken Nishimura stands and puts himself firmly between Jeremy Cutter and Clarice Nishimura. "We need to stay calm," he says.

"I agree," says Adam S. Miles. He is speaking to himself as much as anything. No one seems to hear him. No one even looks his direction.

"No, *you* need to stay calm," shouts Jeremy Cutter. "*I* need to get on a bus and blow this place. *I* need to – *erk*."

The noise Jeremy Cutter makes is funny, and ordinarily Adam S. Miles would have laughed. He doesn't, though, because the reason Jeremy Cutter makes the noise is that Jesús Flores has grabbed him by the back of the neck and is squeezing hard.

Adam S. Miles does not understand facial expressions. But some *faces* he understands. He knows that anyone with tattoos like Jesús Flores' is to be avoided. So he does not laugh at the noise Jeremy Cutter makes. No one does.

"Be quiet," said Jesús Flores. "So I can think."

Jeremy Cutter's mouth opens, but Jesús Flores must have squeezed him again, because he makes the funny noise but says nothing.

Adam S. Miles wants to play Tetris.

He resists the urge.

He had a teacher, Mr. Eugene Canter, who once told him that video games were a crutch. Then he gave him the first GameBoy Adam S. Miles ever owned. Not the one he has now; the one he has now is a collector's item. But the one Mr. Eugene Canter gave him had Tetris and Super Mario Land and a few other cartridges. "It's a crutch, but sometimes we *need* a crutch," he had said. And taught Adam S. Miles the difference between needing a crutch and just wanting one.

That is why Adam S. Miles watches the people around him. Tetris could comfort, but he has the feeling that if he doesn't pay attention – close, close attention – that he won't be around long enough to play the game again.

Outside, the fog glows. Adam S. Miles doesn't think it is glowing because of the lights of the bus. He is pretty sure that the fog glows because that's just what it *does*.

Adam S. Miles doesn't understand expressions. He doesn't understand why people *want* to be "normal."

But most of all, he doesn't understand what is happening around him. He sees it all, but none of it makes sense.

That frightens him. It frightens him badly.

5. What now?

Normally Paul would rather die than show the kind of weakness to a prisoner that he now exhibited. The key rattled in the door of the holding cell as he opened it, and he was sure Bella noticed his shaking hands. But she didn't say anything. Didn't speak when he led her to the desk and poured them each a cup of booze.

Small grace: at least he didn't have a glass tumbler for each of them, and certainly no ice. Just a pair of paper cups that didn't jingle or clink when he brought his to his lips.

Bella's own cup wasn't too steady, either. She tried to play it off like it was because she was holding her cell phone in her other hand, but he could see the difference. A girl like her could probably tweeze her brows with one hand and text with the other, both while riding a rollercoaster. Now, though, she nearly dropped her phone twice just keying in her unlock code.

Bella's phone clicked, and the screen lit up. She pressed several places on the screen. Frowned. Her thumbs moved at light speed – probably texting. The phone made the outgoing text sound, which to Paul always sounded like a cross between ripping paper and someone blowing their nose.

A moment later the phone went *boop,* and based off Bella's face he could tell the sound didn't mean, *"Everything's groovy, baby!"*

"It's not working," she said.

"Told you."

The screen flickered. Bella's face underwent a similar series of light-to-dark and back again. "What is it?" asked Paul.

She showed him. The same message as had appeared on his own phone.

The Other: only 1 will leave all in favor

"What's that mean?" Bella asked.

Twenty minutes ago, Deputy Paul Kingsley would have ignored her.

Ten minutes ago, he would have mocked her – partly out of fear.

Now, he raised his cup in a silent toast. He didn't know if Bella understood what he was saying. Probably not; the girl didn't seem too bright, and what smarts she had seemed to be centered around using her body to get what she wanted.

But whether she understood it or not, Paul did: he was raising his glass to her, because something inside him knew that his path was now bound with hers. The people in the terminal were here, alone.

"We're all in this together." That was what his gesture meant. She was here, he was here. The rest of the passengers, along with Mary and Taylor, were nearby.

All in this together.

He drank. He looked out the window. The fog spilled into itself, roiled, and flowed to one side then to the other. Dark shapes moved deep in the mist... or maybe he only imagined that.

He drank again. Poured a bit more. He didn't offer to split the last bit with Bella because, together or not, there were some things that were still an "every man for himself" kind of thing.

"What now?" asked Bella.

Paul didn't answer. Just stared at the fog, savoring the last hot drops of whiskey on his tongue.

What now indeed?

He looked at Coot's old television, which stared back at him with its gray eye. It reminded Paul, suddenly, of staring into his mother's eyes, clouded with cataracts, in the moments before she died. She had smiled, but the smile never made it to her eyes. She was staring at nothing. Not Heaven, not Hell. Just darkness.

He looked at the fog. Wondered if that was just God, getting cataracts. Getting old and blind and no longer noticing when old men went nuts and gunned down passengers in a bus terminal, or when slightly *less* old men simply disappeared in the fog.

6. Itch

Taylor followed her mother into the ticket office. Mom had to key in the code on the door, which surprised her, but Mom had explained that the doors were on the same circuit – and the same power source – as the emergency lights. "Same with the front doors," she said.

"Well that's a relief," said Taylor.

Mom glanced sharply at her, and Taylor could tell she was gearing up for a fight. Taylor didn't rise to the challenge. She was tired, she was sore from tripping when that bus came barreling in and she fell. She was scared, too, though she would die before admitting it – especially to Mom.

Mom was moving around near her desk. She lifted the landline phone off its cradle and tried it.

"*Should* we leave?" asked Taylor.

"Oh, I'm sure someone's already on their way," said Mom. She avoided looking at Taylor when she said it, and Taylor could tell from her mother's posture – tense, stiff, with her shoulders up around her ears the way they got when she was really freaked or really pissed – that Mom didn't believe that for a second.

"We should try, shouldn't we? I mean, what's so bad out there? What do we know, really?"

Mom put down the phone and stared at her. "I don't know," she said finally.

"So it could be nothing."

Mom nodded. "Could be. Probably *is*. And if it weren't for the crazy man covered in blood, I'd be all for leaving."

"But..."

"But there *was* a crazy man, he *was* covered in blood."

"Still, someone's going to have to make a run for it eventually."

Taylor could see that Mom knew that. Could see, too, that she wasn't about to do it.

Typical.

That was Mom for you. Play it safe, hurry up and wait. Get out of the bad parts of the neighborhood, but do it without really knowing what to do once you left.

She wanted so much for Taylor, which Taylor used to find comforting and satisfying. Now, though, she just felt crushed.

Or maybe that wasn't the weight of expectation she was feeling. It was the itch. The *need*.

"Where's my purse?" she asked. She looked around, and tried at the same time to remember when she'd had it last. Things had gotten fuzzy the last few weeks, which she knew should worry her. She'd maintained her GPA in spite of… *things*. But that wouldn't last. Things were changing, and even Mom knew enough to notice some of them.

What happens when she finds out? When she realizes what her angelic little girl is up to when she ditches school or doesn't show up until way too late on way too many nights?

Part of Taylor suspected that Mom already knew, but didn't want to admit it.

Part of her suspected that Mom knew, and maybe wanted to join in. She wouldn't, of course, not Miss "I Got Out Of The Hood And Never Looked Back." But she'd *want* to.

Taylor looked for her purse. She looked on the floor, then on and under Mom's desk. She thought about looking in the file cabinets that sat against the back wall. Her skin felt hot and prickly.

Yeah, it was the itch. Definitely the itch.

The fog was outside.

But it was coming *in,* too. Into her brain, clouding everything. She needed clarity. Needed to find her purse; needed what was *in* her purse.

"Honey?" said Mom.

Taylor ignored her. That was what the itch did, sometimes. Made everything… not *disappear,* exactly, but *fade.* The things and people and places and activities remained, but they were ghostly. They were without substance. Only the itch remained. Only the itch mattered.

That was happening now. The itch had her. It burned, and she felt the need put its hooks into her flesh and pull her along. She didn't notice when she started mumbling, "Purse, purse, where's my purse?" over and over with the steady tones of a child repeating a nursery rhyme.

7. Scars

Clarice tried not to think about what was happening around her. She focused on cleaning off the man who had come into their midst. She focused on checking him for obvious signs of trauma – finding none. She focused on Ken.

Ken, most of all.

He was always there. Not hovering the way some men in her past had done. Just *present*. Ken was her sun and moon and stars. He was the thing that shone on her, and loaned her his light when she was in need.

Ken was the first man with whom she felt whole.

Clarice knew she was pretty. Maybe even beautiful. Lots of men had told her so, and though she hadn't believed them all, enough people echoed the sentiment she had to admit it was likely true.

Not that she *saw* "pretty" in the mirror. No, in her reflection she saw skin that was a bit too pale, eyes that were a bit too dull. She saw a body that had too much of severity and too little of curves.

When her shirt was off, she couldn't see anything of what the men – and more than a few women, for that matter – had told her they noticed. She didn't see the athletic body, or the muscles that rippled beneath thin layers of skin and fat. She saw herself, but only in a disconnected way. She watched a science experiment when she watched herself. She watched a study in dissolution.

She saw all of herself, but only really *noticed* the flaws. The mistakes. The scars that criss-crossed her forearms from wrists to elbows. Long, thin, white lines that marked the years she had run razors over her skin. Never deeply enough to kill her, but even superficial cuts scarred over time. She had avoided it for a long time, not wanting her parents to notice.

The cuts became deeper. The scars brighter. Livid pink things that faded to white lines over time, but never quite disappeared. She cut across her skin, then when skin became rarer and rarer, territory crowded out by the scarring, she cut across the old cuts and raised them a bit higher on her flesh. They were a city of sorts, a thing populated by all the old pains and insecurities and fears. The higher the scars rose, the more of those things she carried with her.

Eventually, she knew, the city would topple. It would demand sacrifices she could not make. It would take her into itself, and she would be found dead on some floor, surrounded by blood and wondering when it was that the scars ceased to ride her flesh and became instead the whole of her existence.

Then Ken came along. He didn't sweep her off her feet; more like he found a way to help her finally stand. The cutting stopped soon after she met him, though it was weeks before she connected those two dots. She just knew that she felt better around this quiet, unassuming guy.

He didn't have "big plans," like so many people she had known. He didn't have giant ambitions, or anything writ large at all. He wanted a decent-paying job, which he had, and a wife and family, which he was still looking for.

He asked her to marry him a month after that.

It took her almost a year to say yes. He didn't complain. He seemed content to have what she could give, and that contentment opened up a bit more of her each day.

He was there for her, and always would be.

She said yes, and he smiled. Not a huge reaction. No cartwheels, no over-the-top enthusiasms. He was quiet in his joy, as he had been quiet in his care and his courtship.

They married. They started a real, true, honest life together.

And now they were here, which she could bear only because it was *they* who were here, and not simply *she*.

"How's Red?" asked Jesús. Clarice tried hard to repress a shudder and didn't quite succeed – the guy was scary.

"Who?" she asked absently, hoping that the guy would take that as a cue to leave.

"Red." Jesús nodded at Clarice's patient. "Gotta call him something, and Red fits as well as anything." He grinned a grin that she supposed was meant to show mirth but only managed to communicate anger and hunger.

"No idea," she said. She cast a sidelong glance at Jesús. She saw Ken tense, knowing that she was about to say something stupid. She did that a lot, and couldn't help it. It was just one more thing she hated about herself. "He's not talking, either – *someone* kicked him in the face."

Jesús didn't seem at all upset at her observation. "Good kick, too," he said, and the hungry/angry grin stretched a bit wider. "Watch him, though. He's not as out of it as he seems."

Clarice eyed Red –

(Good Lord, I'm already thinking of that as his name, what's wrong with me?)

– and said, "Why do you say that?"

"It's the smart thing to do. It's what *I'd* do," said Jesús, then moved away.

Clarice looked back at Ken. She needed his calm, and as she looked at him that calm came into her. Even with a bloody nose and what looked like the opening stages of a truly magnificent black eye, he was an island of calm in a stormy universe.

"Can you get me some water, hon?"

Ken nodded, but before he could go in search of what she asked, Shelly stooped and picked up a half-full bottle of water from the floor. "Here," she said, holding it out with shaking hands.

Shelly smiled the crackling, torn smile of someone on the verge of panic. Clarice had seen that smile a lot on the patients in the ER. The smile of a woman who just saw her child drink something from under the sink. The smile of a parent whose first baby is coughing too much, and drinking or eating too little. The smile of a man who brings in his brother, bleeding from a gunshot wound after discovering the hard way that deer hunting and beer aren't the smartest combo.

She had seen the smile on many a face – including her own, on the nights when Ken worked late or the days where she found herself unoccupied, between shifts at the hospital.

Clarice smiled back at Shelly, hoping to calm the woman and, maybe, herself as well. She held out her hand. "Thanks," she said, taking the water that the older woman offered.

She had intended to splash a bit of it on Red's face, to see if she could raise him out of the unconscious state he'd been pounded into. But when she turned back to her patient, he was staring at her with eyes open and bloodshot.

Clarice gave a little gasp and sat down on her heels, surprised. She had expected him to wake up, but for some reason the fact that his eyes had opened while she looked away seemed intentional. Malicious.

"It's what I'd do," Jesús had said.

Clarice tried to push that thought away. "Drink this," she said. She put a hand behind Red's neck, half raising him to drink, half steadying him.

Red opened his mouth but didn't really drink. The water sloshed over his lips, pooled in his open mouth, then spilled out over his chin and neck. His bloodshot eyes darted left, right, left. They never rested. Even when they settled on something for a moment, they jittered as though ready to run right out of his head.

"What happened to you?" Clarice said quietly, unsure whether she was acting as a nurse trained to ask that question, or simply as a person wanting to know what mad turn the world had taken.

"They said I'd get to leave," said Red.

"Who did?" asked Clarice. "Who said that?"

His eyes finally came to rest, staring deep into her own. She nearly recoiled at the madness there. "They said I could. I won. I was the only one left."

Red suddenly careened forward, bending nearly in half before springing to his feet. Clarice crab-walked backward, feeling almost at the same moment Ken's hands on her back, pulling her away, pulling her to her feet, then stepping in front of her.

"Why am I here?" demanded Red. His wrists were still cuffed behind him, and they rose away from his back as he spun, turning so hard and fast his wrists were driven away by centrifugal force. *"WHY DID YOU BRING ME HERE?"*

Again his gaze came to rest on Clarice, and he lurched toward her. His fingers appeared around his side, wiggling as though hoping to get her neck into their grasp.

Ken was still trying to get in front of her. She pulled at his shirt, yanking him back. She wasn't going to let him die to save her. That would be the worst trade in the history of the world.

Something moved past both of them, a blur she only barely managed to realize was Jesús before he finished gliding across the room and kicked Red's leg.

A brittle, sharp *snap* sounded. Clarice saw Red's knee bend backward. For a moment he wobbled like a rocking chair.

Then the joint finished its destruction, and Red screamed and pitched to the side.

Leaning over the still-screaming man, Jesús pointed a finger at him and spat, "Stay. *Down.*"

Red rolled back and forth. Clarice had cleaned him with Shelly's scarf as best she could, but a lot of dirt and blood and maybe other, darker, more frightening things remained as a residue on his skin. Now, tears of agony cut tracks through the gore, leaving grooves of white that shone as bright as scars on a wrist.

"Why?" he cried between mewling screams. "Why, why?"

Clarice didn't know what he was asking. She had no answers for him. She didn't know the *why* of anything. Never had.

She tugged at her sleeve.

8. Bullies

The sound of cracking bone is not one that Adam S. Miles likes. It reminds him of Terrence Jonas Inglebrook. Terrence Jonas Inglebrook was in Adam S. Miles' third-grade class. He stood at nearly six feet tall, partly because he was thirteen years old, partly because he was, Adam S. Miles estimated, at least seventy-percent caveman. He had clearly been designed on a physical level to attack saber tooth tigers. Mentally, he would have lost a game of trivial pursuits to any peer from the Pleistocene era, *including* said tigers.

Terrence Jonas Inglebrook was an idiot, a brute, and he hated Adam S. Miles. The sound of Adam S. Miles' arm breaking as revenge for refusing to let Terrence Jonas Inglebrook cut in the lunch line still recurs in his dreams from time to time.

So the crack when Jesús Flores broke "Red's" knee was one that nearly made Adam S. Miles jump out of his skin.

The night had started out nice and quiet. A bus trip was always relaxing for Adam S. Miles, because a bus meant he could buy two seats, sit in one and put his bag on another. He would not be spoken to. He would not be bothered.

He could play Tetris all the way from wherever he was coming from to wherever he was going. That was good. He could sit quietly. That was better. He could pretend he was *alone,* while still sitting among enough people to stave off the loneliness that sometimes gripped him.

He had felt the night skewing when Shelly Sherman – ridiculous name – started talking to him. Then, soon after, *everyone* was talking. Everyone was screaming.

Bones were breaking.

Adam S. Miles glanced at Red, who rolled around as well as anyone with wrists cuffed behind their back could do.

He looked quickly away, though, because watching that made Adam S. Miles think of what he did to Terrence Jonas Inglebrook a week after the lunk broke Adam S. Miles' arm.

Adam S. Miles found him in the boys' bathroom. The huge boy was pooping, *loudly*. Normally this was the kind of thing that would make Adam S. Miles leave. Certain sounds were hard on him. There were always too many sounds, for one thing, unless he was plugged into his GameBoy. And the ones coming from Terrence Jonas Inglebrook were of a sort that typically sent him running.

But in an extreme emergency, such as this one, Adam S. Miles could be brave. He could even be crafty.

So he waited until Terrence Jonas Inglebrook was done pooping. One boy came into the bathroom – a second-grader – while Terrence pooped. Adam S. Miles simply said, "Caveman," and the kid left with a white face, grabbing at his crotch but unwilling to share space with the school's version of the boogeyman, even to pee.

Adam S. Miles waited. Terrence Jonas Inglebrook finished, as evidenced by the sound of toilet paper being unspooled by a club of a hand. The jangle of a belt as pants were pulled up and cinched around a thirty-five-inch waist.

The toilet did not flush – Adam S. Miles remembers being unsurprised, given that Terrence Jonas Inglebrook lacked the brain power to work such complicated mechanisms – but everything that came before gave him time to get into place by the moment the stall door clicked and swung open.

Adam S. Miles swung the pipe he had brought to school. He was small, and the pipe itself had to be small enough that he could fit it into his bag without it being noticed. That meant he had to go for something easy, close, and debilitating. He opted for Terrence's crotch.

He missed.

The swing took the big cave-child in the shin – either because Adam S. Miles' arm was still in a cast, because he had not practiced enough with the pipe to maintain accuracy, or because adrenaline had spiked his aim downward. Either way, it hit with a surprising *crack*, and then Terrence Jonas Inglebrook was falling backward, screaming as he clapped his fingers to his shin and then tumbled back to land in the toilet.

Adam S. Miles saw blood coating the Cro-Magnon's fingers. He saw white bone sticking out above them.

He did not like the crack of breaking bone. But he liked the sound when Terrence Jonas Inglebrook splashed into a toilet full of his own unflushed mess.

Adam S. Miles did not want to see such a thing, though, to be sure. That would make him vomit. So he ran from the bathroom, remembering to slow to a walk as he entered the hall so as not to draw attention. No one saw him leave. Terrence Jonas Inglebrook was carried away on a stretcher, and so far as Adam S. Miles knew he never told anyone who had broken his leg so severely that he didn't come back to school until the next year.

To this day, Adam S. Miles still does not know whether that was because Terrence Jonas Inglebrook did not know who had done the damage, or because he was unwilling to admit it was "that dummy retardo-retard," as Terrence Jonas Inglebrook called Adam S. Miles, who had done it to him.

Adam S. Miles does not care either way. The next year he left for a different, superior school. Terrence Jonas Inglebrook was out of his life forever, and so no longer his concern.

Only now, for an instant in the terminal, he does not see Red on the ground. He sees the big boy, clutching at his leg and screaming.

That is why Adam S. Miles looks away. He knows he should not. He knows he should be paying attention to everything that happens around him.

But he cannot look at that. Not at a leg bent so similarly to the way Terrence Jonas Inglebrook's was. Not at a knee cracked so thoroughly apart that Red will likely walk with a limp if not a cane for the rest of his life.

Adam S. Miles' eye comes to rest on his phone. The message still hangs there:

The Other: only 1 will leave
all in favor

"Who is The Other?" Adam S. Miles asks himself. He often does that, and knows about life well enough to know that a) no one will hear more than a low mumble, and b) that seeing someone like him making noises like that will make them look away. That is fine. He rarely likes being looked at. Eye contact makes him nervous.

"Who is The Other?"

Nearby, Terrence Jonas Inglebrook –

(Not Terrence Jonas Inglebrook, it is the man everyone calls Red, *and I did nothing to him, the man named Jesús Flores did it to him…)*

– continues rolling around, saying, "Why… why?" in a voice that grows smaller with each repetition.

Adam S. Miles stares at the words on his phone. "What is The Other?" he mumbles again.

He clicks the home button on his phone. It is the latest Samsung and he likes it very much. It is simple, with a design that is every bit as intuitive as that of an iPhone, but allows him a level of customization that no Apple product can match. Apple hates its customers, Adam S. Miles is convinced.

Now, though, the Samsung's design fails him. The click does not shift the phone away from the text message screen, as it always has in the past.

Adam S. Miles tries again. No result. The Other's message continues to hang on a white field. There is no return phone number, nothing at all in the field that usually declares the phone number and, if Adam S. Miles has programmed the corresponding name into his contacts list, the name of the person calling. That is unusual. There is *always* something there, every time a text message comes through.

Adam S. Miles touches the field. Nothing happens. He expected that.

He presses the home button again. Once. Twice. Then he clicks the place that *should* make the phone show a minimized view of the apps he has open – a time zone calculator; his email; and a game called The Room which he likes very much, if not quite so much as Tetris.

The message remains where it is.

Adam S. Miles tries pressing the sleep button on the side of the phone. The message remains.

He *holds* the sleep button. This should power the Samsung down. It has always done so in the past.

It does *not* do so now. The message remains.

Adam S. Miles does not ask this time, does not say, "Who is The Other?" because he is suddenly afraid what the answer might be. The phone is not frozen. It has been *told* to remain in this field. The Other has told it to do so.

Nearby, Red switches from, "Why… why?" to a new set of words. "They told me," he whimpers. Then, in a sudden shriek, *"They TOLD ME!"*

Clarice Nishimura, who has been watching all this, shifts her weight as though to return to Red's side. Adam S. Miles likes Clarice Nishimura. She seems nice.

Now the nice woman takes a step toward Red. Her husband, Ken Nishimura, whom Adam S. Miles also likes if not quite so much as he likes Clarice Nishimura, puts his hand on her shoulder and says, "Clarice," in a tone that could mean, "Don't go," or could mean, "I'm proud of you for doing this and taking such wonderful care of a man who is obviously a few blocks short of a Tetris."

From the reaction of Clarice Nishimura, Adam S. Miles extrapolates it is the second option. She throws his hand away, actually grabbing it and *tossing* it off her like someone might do if they found a bug on them.

Clarice Nishimura moves back to Red, trying to calm him while avoiding his flailing limbs. It is too much movement for Adam S. Miles to watch without feeling slightly ill. He looks back at his phone.

The message is still there.

He turns the phone over and cracks off the back. He pulls out the battery. He flips the phone back over. The screen is dark. He lets out a breath, realizing at the same time that he fully expected the screen to continue bright, The Other's message to continue staring at him.

Adam S. Miles counts to ten. Then he puts the battery back in the phone.

He looks at Clarice Nishimura. He cannot help it. She is glaring at Jesús Flores. She points at Red and says, "You didn't have to do that."

Jesús Flores is not like Adam S. Miles: he does not mind staring people in the eyes. He does that now to Clarice Nishimura and says. "Are you enjoying your trip with your husband?"

Even someone as ignorant of the subtleties of human facial expression and conversational tactics knows that this is an odd change of topic. It makes Clarice Nishimura wince – Adam

S. Miles cannot tell if it is pain or surprise, but she tugs on her sleeve.

Clarice Nishimura looks away from Jesús Flores. "Anyone have something I can use for a splint?" she says.

A muffled voice says, "I think I do." Adam S. Miles sees the outline of Mary the ticket lady, standing in the darkness behind the ticket window. For a moment it looks like a ghost is speaking. Then the form – chubby, short, and pleasant in the light but lurking, skulking, and creepy in the dark – moves away. Presumably to get something for a splint.

Adam S. Miles sees light from the corner of his eye. He looks at his phone.

The screen is white. If it acts per normal, the Samsung logo will appear in five to ten seconds. It does not do so this time.

Instead, a message blinks to life on the white screen. It no longer looks like a text message: all the typical fields are gone. It is just a white screen with black letters.

The Other: only 1 will leave
all in favor

Adam S. Miles does not fully understand what the message means. He knows it is important, though, and decides to put his considerable brain to work on the problem. He likes problems. Brain teasers are of interest. He finds few of them funny, but enjoys figuring out alternatives until the right, obvious one becomes clear in his mind.

This message is a brain teaser. He does not know what it means, yet, but definitely knows that it scares him.

"All in favor," he mumbles. Knowing no one will understand the words. Knowing anyone who hears them will look away from the neurodiverse, because that is what NTs do.

That is fine.

Adam S. Miles does not want to be looked at.

He is thinking. Maybe harder than he ever has before.

Terrence Jonas Inglebrook scared him, until Adam S. Miles figured out a way to deal with him. He wonders if *this* person, this bully taunting them all on their phones, can be dealt with so easily, or so permanently. He hopes so. He suspects it unlikely.

"All in favor," he mumbles. "All in favor."

9. Going out

A small window set beside the door to the lobby allowed Paul to see bits and flashes of what was happening out there. Not a lot, but enough to hint that things were still going to hell. The window, like the one that opened to the fog-stricken world outside, was smoky, one-way glass. They couldn't see him. He knew that beyond a doubt.

But every time someone flailed their way past his field of vision, he felt like they were looking through the window, seeing him, seeing his *soul.*

And what a wreck of a place that *is.*

That wreckage plagued him daily, but this was the first time in a long time that he felt actively ashamed of it. He knew that some of it wasn't his fault – but it certainly *was* his fault that he was in here, hiding away while the rest of the people in the place were left on their own to deal with what was happening.

And what *was* happening?

He didn't know.

But he knew he should be out there, in the lobby. Should maybe be outside the terminal building itself, trying to see what was what and actually acting like a cop.

He heard gunshots. Not in the lobby, thank God, but in his mind. The sounds that had started the slide that ended here, in this place.

Since he and Bella finished the last of the whiskey, he had been trying in vain to call out on the landline. Nothing. Not even the courtesy of a dial tone. But he had kept doggedly hammering at the keys, hoping something would be different if he did it long enough.

And watching, all the while, through smoky glass that let him see a blurry view of the world he should be in. The things he should be doing.

He made a decision without really realizing what he was doing. He pushed the phone toward Bella. The gal took it automatically, her gaze distant and bleary. "Keep trying the phone," he said. Nodding toward the glass that separated him from his duty as a cop and his self-respect as a man, he added, "I'm going to see if anyone out there has any ideas."

Bella shook her head and put the phone in its cradle. "I ain't staying here alone," she said. Her words were clipped, not the slightest sign of slurring. But that dull look in her eyes didn't change, and Paul wondered if maybe she'd had one too many swigs of liquid courage.

Didn't matter. He picked the phone back up and pushed it toward her. She backed away, shaking her head. "I said I ain't staying here alone!" she half-shouted.

Paul waited until she backed almost to the window. Waited as she realized where she stood. She cast a quick, scared glance over her shoulder then took a few steps back toward Paul and the phone he held, though she tried to sidestep a bit as she did.

"You are," he said when she stopped moving. "Either you'll stay here alone trying to call for help, or you'll stay here alone locked in a cell." He wiggled the phone in the air. "Your choice."

Bella huffed, obviously angry to be put in a position where she had little power, just as obviously unsure what to do about it.

"Fine," she finally said. She stepped forward and snatched the phone from Paul's grip, holding it the way she might hold alien technology. "How do I use it?" she asked.

Paul rolled his eyes and said, "Oh, for the love of –"

"What?" she barked. "I'm not good with old people phones."

Paul refrained from grunting "old people phones." It was an effort.

Good lord, I've become the Coot of a new generation.

That thought led inexorably to thoughts of how Original Coot lost his shit, became Crazy Coot, shifted to Murdery Coot, and ended up as Dead Coot.

Not me. I'm better than that.

(Are you?)

Rather than answer the whispered question his mind had presented, he pointed at the numbers on the phone. "Press this button. Dial 9-1-1 – which is pretty easy. You just hit this button with the number nine on it, then –"

"Yeah, yeah, I get that part. Where's the text button?"

Paul tried not to sigh as he continued, "Hang up, then call the number here," he said, pointing at a piece of paper with the direct line to the sheriff's station that someone taped to the top of the phone. "If no one answers that one, then hang up and call 9-1-1. Rinse, lather, repeat. Just like your beauty regimen, okay?"

"Like that's all it takes to look like this," Bella muttered. But when Paul turned toward the door she was already dialing. He watched her for a second, noting how fast her fingers ran over the numbers. "Old people phone" or not, Bella's fingers knew how to fly. She was probably hashtagging messages between each call, Paul figured. Something like #horrorshow or #oldpeoplephones.

But she was making the calls. Or trying to.

He turned back to the door. Keyed in his passcode on the lock. The door clicked. He stepped out to see Mary entering the lobby from the ticket office at nearly the same time. She spared Paul a look that could only be described as thoroughly disgusted, then hurried over to Clarice and handed her the big white first aid kit that usually hung on the wall in the ticket office.

Clarice opened it, then removed a roll of bandaging and some medical tape. "This'll do," she said. "Thanks."

Mary nodded a quick "you're welcome," then glared at Paul again.

"Where's Taylor?" he managed.

As much as he hadn't liked the look of disgust Mary tossed his way before, he *hated* the look of revulsion she gave him now. "Looking for her purse," she said.

That was a weird answer. "Now?" he asked, his brows knitting themselves together over the bridge of his nose. "Why does she –"

The rest of the question was lost in screams as Clarice tried to wrap the leg of the guy who had started the night's descent into lunacy. Everyone in the room but Clarice and Jesús put their hands over their ears. "Can't someone shut him up?" yelled the weaselly guy with the bad hair.

The gamer, Adam, went over to the bloody, screaming lunatic. He squatted down in front of him and said, "You should hold still. I am going to call you Red because you are covered in blood. But Clarice Nishimura is trying to help you," which struck Paul as beyond weird but apparently it was the right thing to say because the bloody, screaming guy became instead a bloody, whimpering guy.

Clarice kept working on her patient's leg as her husband held up his phone and asked, "Anyone else's phone working?"

By way of answer, Baldy McWeaselface shook his cell phone in the air and said, "What the hell does this even *mean*? Who's The Other? What does he want? Where –"

Paul didn't like the way the guy's voice was amping up, fraying at the edges as it rose in pitch. He stepped toward him, surprised that he was taking this level of initiative. The other man cringed but kept speaking. "What is this? What is going on and why's it happening and *where's my damn bus?"*

"Easy," said Paul. "What's your name?"

"Why? Who's asking?" the guy asked. The tone kept cracking, but he blurted the questions so fast Paul got the feeling it was a pat answer that he gave every time someone asked his name.

Twenty years ago, back when he was still a good cop, Paul would have gotten suspicious at this answer.

Twenty hours ago, back when he was a shitty cop in a shitty world, he would have shrugged and ignored it.

Now he wasn't sure which version of himself was showing up to the party. But he didn't want the guy to lose it, so he answered calmly, "Deputy Paul Kingsley. My friends call me Paul, and I just want to know what to call you." He tried for a disarming grin and, surprisingly, felt like he probably succeeded. Some of the tension went out of Weasel-face's stance. "I could call you 'Hey, you,' but that usually gets too much of a response."

"Har, har," said the weasel. His shoulders slumped a bit more as he said, "Jeremy. Cutter."

Again, Paul felt a twinge of Old, Good Cop Paul. He doubted very much that Jeremy Cutter was this guy's real name. But right now wasn't the time to press the issue. Too much was going on, and doing a spot-check on a guy's ID was low on Paul's To Do list

"Okay, Jeremy. Just take it easy." He looked around. "No one else's phones work?"

"Just this odd message," said the gamer kid.

"Okay. The landlines don't work, either." Paul looked at the sliding glass doors that led outside. He didn't want to go out there, but there wasn't much else he *could* do, was there?

He had just about decided to head that way, and then to keep walking, right outside and act like a real cop for once, when he saw Mary. The look on her face told him in an instant exactly what she expected him to do: a big fat *nothing*.

The look drained the momentary zeal right out of him. She knew him. She'd observed him for years, and she knew what he was: a piece of shit who did nothing, helped nothing, and *was* nothing.

Paul shook his head. He weaved a bit, leaning a few inches toward the exit as the last bits of his determination fell away, but then moved not at all.

Mary snorted, the disgust on her face deepening, then turned to the bloody guy in the middle of the room. "Sir?" she said quietly. "Can you help us? Please? What's out there?"

Paul was disturbed that she spoke to a bloody madman cuffed on the floor with more care and respect than she had ever shown him. He wondered, not for the first time, if he should tell her what he thought of her – what he *really* thought.

"You think he's going to help us?" Jeremy said. "He's the wrongest thing about this whole situation." He turned his fevered eyes on Paul. "What about your squad car? You have guns in it? A shotgun? Riot gear? Just a *radio* that works?"

Paul, so close to going out just a moment ago, now felt his nuts draw up tight as Jeremy presented the idea. "First," he said, "you been watching too many movies. Second, my car is a good hundred yards away. And I don't feel like going that far in this kind of weather." He pointed at the sliding glass doors that were all that separated them from the fog. "If you get my meaning," he said.

Jeremy moved forward, coming close to the big windows and pointing at the commuter bus that had nearly exploded through the wall. "But there's a radio in that thing, isn't there?"

The bloody man's screams had become whimpers as Clarice helped him. Then they became hitching breaths. Now he spoke, his voice surprisingly lucid sounding, if pleading. "Don't go out there. You'll die if you take a single step out there." He giggled, the madness creeping back into the sound. "All in favor!" he shouted.

Jeremy wheeled on the man. "For the love of God, *shut up!"*

His fist balled in the air, raised as though he would hammer it down on the madman's head. Shelly stepped forward, the Mary Kay gal's face betraying more than a little surprise at her own move. She stood between Jeremy and the madman, her hands raised placatingly. "Let's all just stay calm, okay? I'm sure we can figure out –"

"You shut up, too!" Jeremy shrieked. "All of you shut up! I can't stay here, I can't –"

Something clicked, and the emergency lights turned off. Now the only light came from the commuter bus outside the windows, its headlights scything the air and turning everything and everyone into a mix of washed-out whites and fathomless blacks.

Everything in the place was one or the other. All shades of gray disappeared, and there was only light or shadow.

The ticket office door opened and Taylor ran out, flinging herself into her mother's arms. Paul was still enough of a cop to notice how the relationship between them had changed in recent months, and it gladdened him to see Taylor holding to her mom like she meant it. The circumstances sucked, but maybe something good would come of this.

"I got you, baby," said Mary. "We're okay."

Again, Paul felt a stab of duty. It hurt a little less than it had the last time. Maybe he was actually going to *do* something before all this played out. He turned to stare at the bus outside. Black and red and gray gore still coated the windows. Some were completely coated in the stuff, others just smeared from side to side.

What could have done that?

Whatever it was, Jeremy was right that the bus should have a radio, and it was certainly a damn sight closer than Paul's own squad car. Maybe...

"Can't see a thing in the bus," he said. He wasn't talking to anyone in particular, just voicing the words as a part of a thought train that he hoped would get his ass into gear. He was assessing the situation, and that was the first thing any good cop did: assess the situation, determine a course of action, and then *act*.

Ken, apparently misreading Paul's question as fear, walked to stand beside him. "I think we should check it out, though."

"Yeah," said Jeremy. "Maybe there's a radio or a cell phone in someone's pocket."

Paul didn't answer. He was too busy wondering what could make the kind of gorefest he saw splashed all over the inside of the bus. His mind coughed up the image of bodies, tangled across seats, sprawled on the black rubber that provided grip in the aisle of the bus. The image made Paul gulp and, again, the burgeoning feeling that he might manage to do something – and walk a bit back toward the self-respect he had so often lost sight of in his moral rearview mirror – dissipated.

Choking back vomit that wanted to rise in his throat, he said, "You two want to try going out? Be my guest."

Ken looked at Red, who had also turned in place to stare at the bus. "What's out there? Is there anything in the bus that might helps us?" he asked.

Red stared directly at the headlights, and Paul wondered if the guy was trying to blind himself, to burn the away the memory of whatever he had seen out there. "No people," he whispered. "Not people."

"Then what?" said Paul.

Red didn't answer.

Shelly stepped forward as well, rubbing her hands on her arms like she was trying to warm herself. "What if we wait for the next bus?"

Surprisingly, it was Jeremy who answered, "I can't wait for that. I gotta go *now*."

"Give it a rest," Paul sighed.

Jeremy swung toward him, jabbing the fist that was still clenched around his cell phone at Paul. "No, *you* give it a rest! I have to get out of here!" He looked at the phone he held. "Has everyone tried their phones again?"

"No one is getting –" Ken began.

"I said tried them *again*!" shouted Jeremy. "Maybe someone –"

"I have tried it again," said Adam. He showed the screen of his phone. "I cannot bypass this screen. Even if I remove the battery, as soon as I put it back this message displays." He frowned at the screen. "Cryptic."

A small laugh met that comment. Paul turned to see Jesús watching from the same seat he had been using the first time Paul saw him. Paul had forgotten about him, he sat so silently. He looked like a statue, even now, laughing.

"Cryptic indeed," he said.

Jeremy screamed. It was half fearful, but also half frustrated, and the noise actually made Paul cringe enough that Jeremy easily sidestepped him and walked toward the door.

Paul realized they had no reason to stay here, other than fog and the word of a madman that something bad awaited. He realized that every rational part of his mind should be crying out for him to investigate what would no doubt turn out to be something deeply banal.

But the rational part of his mind just said, *"Anyone who leaves this place will* die!"

"Wait!" someone screamed. Paul didn't know who said it. Maybe it was him.

Yeah, it probably was. Because Jeremy *was* going outside.

And that meant whatever was outside might be about to come *in*.

10. Why bother?

"Going Places. I'm Going Places."

Bella mumbled the words at first, continuing them over and over, sometimes slurring as they tumbled over themselves in their hurry.

She sounded just like her mother had during her last days.

Those were bad days. The days when there was nothing but the sound of oxygen hissing through tubes, the *beep-beep-beep* of a heart monitor, and the burbling sound of her mother's non-stop praying. The prayer filled the apartment, the words pervaded everything.

Bella could never quite hear words within the murmured sound. But she saw her mother holding her prayer beads, counting them down with fingers made scrawny by cancer and chemo, and knew that her mother was praying.

When Bella asked her mother why she bothered repeating nonsense that changed nothing. Her mother heard less and less of reality each day, as she fell closer and closer to the final abyss, and by the time Bella asked the question she neither expected nor received an answer. That was okay. Mother dying was just another step toward Going Places. Not much inheritance to speak of, but every penny saved was a penny earned. Or at least a penny toward the new iPhone cover Bella had found on Amazon.

It became a ritual, Bella hearing that sound as she posted videos on Vine or Instagram, her mother's continual entreaties to Heaven getting in all the cracks of her mind as she read the most recent box office reports and dreamed what it would be like when she did her own Marvel movie. Bella would stop what she was doing, go into Mother's room, stare down at the haggard old bitch, and say, "Why bother? No one's listening."

Now those words came back to her. She murmured, "Going Places, I'm Going Places," over and over like the prayer of a dying woman, and tried not to pause because every time she did she heard her own voice saying, "Why bother? No one's listening."

She hung up the phone. Let go of the plunger. No dial tone. She dialed anyway. 9-1-1.

"Going Places…"

No tone. No nothing.

(*"Why bother? No one's listening."*)

"Going Places."

Plunger down again. Dial the number Officer Dipshit had shown her.

"I'm Going Places."

No tone.

(*"Why bother?"*)

Hangup. Dial.

"Going Places."

No tone.

No nothing.

Nothing.

NOTHING.

(*"Why bother?"*)

Slowly, without realizing it, Bella's chant changed. She no longer gave voice to the core belief of her soul. She no longer spoke of Going Places. Instead, two new words took hold. She said them…

"Why bother?"

… over…

"Why bother?"

… and over…

"WHY BOTHER?"

She didn't realize she was saying it. She didn't hear herself speaking. She was Going Places, right?

She kept making the calls. And kept on hearing the same thing in response, which was nothing at all.

She stared out the window. The fog became a part of her movement, each whirl of vapor seeming to inform her actions. She felt like the actress she knew she would someday be, with a strange, cloudy coach just offscreen, giving her whispered hints and tips that no one but she could hear.

"Why bother?" she asked, not hearing the words she spoke. The fog twisted and spun, and drew her deeper into its mass.

She dialed. Listened. Hung up. Dialed. Listened. Hung up.

She stopped dialing. Stopped listening. She stood still, the dead phone cradled against her ear and the line of her jaw, watching the fog spin and twist.

Something moved in the fog. A twisting, turning line of dark gray that became larger, wider. Coming toward the window.

She ran without thinking, pounding on the glass. "Hey!" she screamed. "Hey, you!"

The gray line stopped moving. It came closer. "Hey!" she screamed again. Her confidence returned in a rush. She was Going Places. This was help, come for her! Nothing could stop the freight train of destiny, and that train was taking her out of this place right damn now.

The thing stopped moving. It looked to be about the size of a man. More important, it looked to be about the same *shape* as a man.

Fog, weird stuff *in* the fog, weird cops who didn't respond properly when she shook her boobs at them... all these things were outside Bella's comfort zone. But she knew in her heart that the guy outside –

(Has to be a guy, right? What else could it be?)

– would respond properly to her. He would come to the window, would see her –

(How? Window's one-way so how will he see you at all?)

– and everything would go back to being the way it should be: with Bella Ricci on top of things, and climbing higher every moment.

She slapped the window so hard it rattled in its casing. "Hey!" she shouted. "Get over here you –"

Her mouth hung open but no more words came.

Not a guy.

The thing that stared at her did so through a trio of green eyes. That was all they could be: glowing green orbs fixed along its head where the normal, *un*glowing eyes of a guy would have been.

No, not a guy at all.

The green eyes flared.

Bella's mouth, already open wide, cranked open another half inch. She inhaled, her body already knowing it was about to scream whether her mind had decided on a course of action or not.

The green eyes blazed.

The thing approached the glass.

11. Ghost

Mary hated every moment of this strange, terrifying night. But she would have relived every one of those moments a dozen times over just for the feel of Taylor in her arms. Not the way she was when she wanted something – that was a quick, cold grasping that always ended in an outstretched palm or with hands on hips – but the way she held Mary when she ran out of the ticket office. The lights had gone out, and there was a frightening mist outside, and a man covered in blood kept saying crazier and crazier things…

But her daughter *held* her. And that felt so good.

It was over too quickly. The good things in life always were. Big J always woke up, grabbing for his Kools with one hand and reaching for Mary with his other. Beautiful children grew up to be surly, distant teenagers. Hugs ended with screams.

Jeremy was headed toward the front doors, obviously intending to go outside. Mary had to ask herself why that was a bad idea – and had to answer herself that she didn't know, but she *absolutely* knew it *was* a bad idea. The way the fog hung out there was so strange, so *wrong*, that she wouldn't have wanted to go out there even without Red's dire warnings of doom and disaster, or the strange message from The Other, whoever or whatever The Other was.

Yet Jeremy wanted to leave.

So shouldn't we just let him? Just let him go and maybe he'll find a radio or phone like he said or – even better – just discover that there's nothing out there but fog, nothing to be scared of at all?

Taylor let go of her when Jeremy started in earnest toward the exit. "No!" she called out.

The glass exit doors slid open as Jeremy approached. Mary blinked and took a step back. The doors shouldn't have opened. The power was out; even the emergency lights were out, so how could the doors slide open?

She stepped forward now, fingers reaching for Jeremy, intending to say all this. She remained mute, though, fear chasing away words and thought alike. She suddenly saw nothing but the fog. It *puffed* a bit when the doors slid open, but it didn't enter the terminal. It hung there as a frothy, squirming mass, a straight line that did not pass over the threshold of the terminal lobby.

How is that possible? How is any *of this happening?*

She heard a gasp – she thought it was Clarice. "Look at it," said Ken. "It's…" But his words failed, too. He gaped like everyone else.

Jeremy paused. He turned to face the rest of the group. Mary figured he was going to step away from the open door with its pillowed mass of fog just beyond. But the moment he turned, she knew that wouldn't happen. Even before he said, "I'm getting out of here."

"No!" shouted Adam. He darted forward. "Wait!"

Jeremy gave a strange, almost *sickly* smile. And stepped out.

He walked into the fog. The backsplash of the bus headlights kept him from fading into nothing. He didn't look *real,* though – just a misty, vague outline with silvered edges marking where the light had fallen on him.

He turned. Mary *could* see his face. Well enough to see his wide eyes, his thin gash of a mouth. He waved at them all. The motion was jerky and taut, like someone else was controlling the motion, and Jeremy was only along for the ride.

He stepped toward the bus. He grew brighter and firmer as he approached it. The headlights cut him out of the fog, and

Mary felt herself relax. He was out there. He was *real,* the bus was *real,* and surely he would find something that could help them.

Behind her, a door clattered open. Mary wheeled, surprised to see the door to the deputy's office slam open. She wondered how that could have happened – the door had a code that you had to enter to get in.

But not if the door decides to open the way the exit doors did. It doesn't need a code anymore than the sliding doors need power.

The rules are all gone.

Bella, the girl Kingsley had found in the locker area hours ago, came stumbling out of the dark hole beyond the door. "There's something out there!" she screamed.

Kingsley had swung around to see what was making the noise, but now he turned back to watch Jeremy make his way toward the bus. "We know. He just left."

"No," said Bella. "Not someone. Some*thing*."

12. How... does... it... feel...

Jeremy Cutter was the latest name he was using. He had used no fewer than a dozen over the course of his life. They were many and varied, but they had several things in common, one of which was that they described a man who was anything but brave.

He was at least as surprised as everyone else that he was the one who decided to actually do something and *leave*. At first, he was content to stay where he was, waiting for the next bus or just for the fog to lift. But every second that ticked by made the world seem smaller; made it seem more as though he waited not in a bus terminal but in a morgue. He had to get out.

Maybe it was the look of the cop – the deputy suspected something about Jeremy, for sure he did. Maybe it was the creepy vibe of the 'banger in the nice suit. Maybe it was just because Jeremy didn't like feeling trapped. And oh, boy, did he feel trapped in the terminal.

Still, it wasn't like him to be the explorer. He prided himself on walking the road less traveled, but that wasn't the same as walking the road less traveled when it was a foggy, creepy road that wended along the empty edge of a cliff below which only darkness could be seen.

He had come to this nowhere place with big plans. He had something to look forward to for the first time in a long time. Not just the usual con or grift, either. This time he looked forward to beautiful eyes, long hair that he could already feel between his fingers, and a set of world-class tits.

Bella was supposed to be waiting when he got there. But when he arrived she was nowhere to be seen, and with every moment that passed, Jeremy realized more deeply how stupid he had been to come here. Sure, he had anticipated an easy road to some epic-level sex – a girl with blouse bunnies like that *always* knew how to use them in bed, along with everything else she had going on – but that shouldn't have clouded his judgment so much. Even with the added promise of the money she said she was bringing to the table, and which Jeremy had countless ways of stripping away from her (*after* getting well and truly laid, of course), he shouldn't have done any of this.

Coming to this nothing place, this nowhere stop between nowhere stops? It wasn't like him, and that divergence from the norm had bitten him in the ass.

So he had left the terminal, bolted out of the doors to get away from the tiny room with far too many people who were giving him side-eye. He regretted the move almost instantly, finding himself in the thick fog that had seemed to mock him when he was inside the terminal, but which now seemed to be…

He struggled to find the word.

It's stalking me. Hunting *me.*

Even through the cloying mist, he could see the bus well enough, and could also see the bus terminal and the wraith-like forms of the people watching inside. But everything else was as cloudy as his judgment had been when he decided to come here in the first place.

He suddenly realized why he *had* come: he was lonely. Bumping into Bella online had been purposeful – she was just one of many women he had on fishing lines of various lengths and with various hooks. He knew how to set those hooks, how to get the girls he chatted with and messaged to open up to their new "soul mate." He knew how to get them in bed, and get their money. He knew how to leave without them knowing it was coming.

With Bella, though, he realized that he hadn't been the one to set the hook this time. Or maybe he had done so, but she had done some hook-setting of her own. He had moved plans around to come here tonight, to meet her where she said she (and a hunk of cash from some "business" she was closing out) would be waiting.

None of it – at least not the *emotional* stuff – had been planned, but it was something he had had to follow through on. Because as much as he told himself that he liked what he did, that he *loved* moving from place to place with the only consistent throughline being separating suckers from their dough… he hadn't had a friend in years. Hadn't been able to talk to someone as himself, rather than as an alias with a hidden agenda, for longer than he could remember.

Bella might have started out as just another potential mark – and still was, in some ways. There was the cover story he maintained, for instance. To her, he was Jeremy Cutter, producer of movies and maker of stars. She didn't even know what he looked like – he'd sent her a photo, but it was one from some years before, when he'd had more muscle and when his hairline didn't look like a follicular rendering of Scandinavian fjords. She'd be surprised when she saw him, but he had long ago learned that the appearance was less important to these kind of women than the sense that someone had come to take care of them, to fix their lives and make them into princesses.

Ha. As if.

But something happened. Somewhere during their communications, he started being honest. The cover story remained, but everything he told her about his life before becoming "Jeremy Cutter of Cutting Floor Films" was true.

It felt good. Being himself – or whatever remained of himself after years of being everyone *but* himself.

So he came here looking for her. And, of course, he found only disappointment. The night did a sideways shuffle out of reality, and Jeremy couldn't stand sitting there in the fog waiting for someone to come and bail them out of whatever was happening, because whoever *did* come wouldn't be Bella, and whatever bail-out happened wouldn't involve either tremendous sex or a bit of spending money. It *especially* wouldn't involve a beautiful young woman showing up to live and die for the chance of Jeremy Cutter's smile.

He couldn't stay. So he went. That had been, was now, and always would be his *modus operandi*.

He moved toward the bus, trying not to look at the crimson windows. He focused on the headlights at first, then when he'd gotten close enough he focused on the bus' front doors. They hung open, as they had since Red dashed out of the vehicle.

The rubber edging on the doors made them look oddly like the sideways lips of some grim monster, hunkering in the mist.

"Open wide," Jeremy muttered. He jumped, surprised at the sound of his own voice in the nothing-noise of the fog. He laughed, trying to use the laughter to convince himself that everything was fine, like this was no big deal and this kind of thing happened every day.

He failed, but he convinced himself otherwise. He was good at that – at convincing himself of unrealities.

Just like Bella. Never a reality. Never gonna happen.

He was only ten feet from the bus. He could see inside, to the driver's seat and the gearshift. Beyond it hung the usual silvery pipes that served as skeleton to every single commuter bus in the world. The place where people would toss briefcases or packages, the bars people would hold onto as they swayed their way down roads that existed only as things that would bring them from one place to another. "Just here for a sec, just passing through" – that was what those bars and poles always said to Jeremy. It was a comfort.

"Just passing through," he said, and giggled, hysteria beginning to paint the edges of the sound.

He peered into the bus. He didn't think there was any blood visible up front, other than the windows, but the driver's seat was the usual dark green leather-substitute material designed for masking stains, and the bus' interior lights were off, so there *could* have been blood and worse on the seat and everywhere else.

But, again, Jeremy chose to believe otherwise. The inside of the bus was fine. Had to be. Just like the stuff on the windows *couldn't* be blood or gore or brains or skin or hair or –

He stood at the doorway of the bus. He couldn't see beyond the driver's area: the rest of the bus was hidden behind a plastic sheet that would only be about waist height for anyone in the bus, but for him out on the street it was well above the level of his head.

He would have to go in to see what was inside.

He almost didn't. He almost turned back to the terminal.

But Bella wouldn't be there. She wouldn't be there, and the cop would be. That meant there was no one waiting for him in there other than a sheriff's deputy whom Jeremy was certain was going to cause trouble for him at some point.

So he didn't go back to the terminal. He reached out, grabbing the pole that slanted up the side of the entry stairs. The metal felt warmer than he expected. Gummy, too. Sticky.

He didn't look at the spot he held. He just pulled himself forward. His front foot was on the first step, though his back foot remained on the concrete outside. Jeremy took a deep breath, then lifted that foot away.

He was fully inside.

This was the part of any horror movie where the doors would slam shut, trapping the hero inside with whatever monster waited.

It didn't happen here.

This wasn't a movie.

Jeremy took another step. He could see over the plastic wall into the rest of the bus. Before he could take in any details, though, the doors *did* slam shut.

Jeremy spun, his body so keyed up to this moment that he actually got his fingers wedged between the doors before they closed. He screamed as the doors clamped painfully around the flesh. He battered on the doors, but they wouldn't open.

He screamed again, half-turning and looking for the lever or button or whatever the hell it was that he could press or pull or push to get the doors open.

He saw a lever that looked like it was probably what he wanted. He reached for it. Couldn't quite get to it.

He turned and yanked on the wrist of the hand clamped in the doors. "Come on, come *on*!" he shouted. "I'll go back inside, I promise. I'll wait, I'll just stay there."

He didn't know who he was talking to. He didn't know who would hear the promises he was making.

But maybe *someone* heard, because all of a sudden his hand popped loose. The fingers slid out from between the rubber lips of the doors with an audible pop. Air hit fingers that had been bruised and abraded, and Jeremy would have screamed to feel such pain under normal circumstances but this time he just laughed as he fell back. He was free!

He kept laughing as he tumbled backward, cradling his fingers against his chest as he hit the steps with his hips and ass and back. His head hit something, too – the lever he'd been trying to grab – and he felt everything swim around him for a moment.

When the universe solidified, Jeremy turned his head to look down the center aisle of the bus. Now, this close, there was no way to fool himself about what coated the windows. Definitely blood. He could tell because of the redness that coated every other surface, as well. The smell hit him at that moment, too, a coppery odor that seemed to crackle in his nostrils. A shock to his system.

Not as much as for the folks who lost all the blood.

His brain was kicking in now, and Jeremy realized that, though blood *was* everywhere, something else was noticeably absent. Namely, the bodies the blood had come from.

The bus had been painted in dark reds, blacks, and grays. Painted by an insane artist with a hard-on for the dark things that hunkered just beyond the edges of sanity.

But no bodies.

Jeremy turned to his stomach, levering himself upward as he put his feet under him. He stood in the aisle, just past a turnstile that separated the driver from the unwashed masses.

He climbed over the turnstile. Maybe he could find a phone, and then maybe he'd actually come out of this whole thing looking like a hero. Bella would show up somehow, begging him to let her give him the attention she had withheld. He'd laugh and find some other hottie to play hide-the-sausage with.

Yeah. That's what I'll do.

He walked all of two steps into the main part of the bus before it really sank in – where he was, what he was doing. The smell of the blood turned thick and festering in his nostrils, and in the next instant Jeremy threw up all over the row of seats to his right. The burger and fries he'd grabbed at the last bus stop came up hard and fast, and he was left blinking tears away, staring at the chunks he'd spewed across the seat.

Turned out to be the best thing that had happened that night, though, because when he turned his head away from the sight and stench, he saw the cell phone.

It was just a cell phone. Nothing big, nothing unusual. But it was what he'd *hoped* to find, and seeing it like this, bent over his own explosion, seemed to be a sign. Things were looking up. Everything had gone to puke, but now everything was going to be a-okay.

He stumbled over to the cell phone, which lay atop a seat a few feet away. Still shaky from the sudden violence of his vomiting, he had to flail around before actually managing to get the phone into his hand. A few more shaky twitches before he managed to hit the button that would activate the screen.

As he touched the button, Jeremy realized that he was still likely screwed: people all had their phones programmed with passwords, or with facial recognition. This phone would no doubt have the same features, so even if there was a signal he doubted –

"Yes!" he screamed, shocked and pleased at the fact that hitting the button resulted not in a lock screen, but in the home screen of this person's phone. A smiling woman holding a child looked up at him from the phone's screen, peeking from behind the rounded squares of the apps she preferred.

Where are they? Where's this woman and where's her kid?

Don't think about that, J-Diddy. Just make the call and get outta here.

Jeremy ignored those, focusing on the space at the top of the field that showed the mobile carrier… and a full four bars!

He whooped for joy, turning toward the closest window and wiping off the gore with one sleeve while he dialed 9-1-1 with his free hand. He didn't know why, but it seemed very important that the others in the terminal see this. A moment of heroism, where Jeremy Cutter saved the day.

That's right, me. I *did it.*

He barely noticed the feel of the sludge as he smeared it across the window, the warmth of it as the blood and other, less identifiable, things seeped into his sleeve and pressed against his skin.

The sound of a phone ringing on the other end of the line filled Jeremy's ear. He grinned so hard it hurt. His arm, still wiping grungy textures off the window, finally won the battle and he could see through to the terminal.

A sea of faces in there.

And one in particular. Bella. She was looking at him – *right* at him. She didn't recognize him, he could tell. Again, he had expected that. It was something he was used to dealing with, and he would deal with it now.

But she had come.

This is all going to be fine. Everything's going to –

The phone clicked as someone picked up. Jeremy opened his mouth to speak, to tell the operator what to do, where to go. He was going to be a hero.

The person on the other end of the line spoke. It sounded weird, and it took Jeremy several seconds of listening to realize why: each word sounded different. A different voice, speaking a single word each, then disappearing as the next voice spoke.

"How..." said the first voice, the gruff tones of an old man.

"... does..." continued a child's voice, high and light.

"... it..." said the third, a sultry, smoky woman's voice.

"... feel..." continued a fourth, this one androgynous; the kind of voice you could hear coming from anyone old or young, male or female.

The voices continued, and Jeremy's smile shattered. It became a rictus, then a stretched circle of horror as the voices spoke, each being born for a single word, then dying in his ear as the next voice took over for their short life:

"How... does... it... feel...?" The voice said, and to Jeremy it sounded in that moment like Death whispering in his ear. "To... know...," continued the voices that Jeremy suddenly understood belonged to The Other, "... that... you're... the... first... to... *die*?"

Something rasped nearby. Jeremy spun, still holding the phone to his ear. He saw what had been hidden in the back of the bus.

His eyes widened. The perfect circle of his mouth stretched a bit wider as well.

Then the perfect circle was perfect no more. It became a ragged, quivering slash in his face as Jeremy screamed.

13. Pop goes the weasel

It all happened so fast. Faster than anything Paul had ever seen before, faster even than the moment the girl held the shotgun and tried to pull the trigger. Maybe. One moment, everything was fine. Then the world had fallen to darkness and fog. A moment or an eternity later, Jeremy left the terminal.

Something clicked, a door opening, and he heard Bella scream, "There's something out there!"

Kingsley had swung around to see what was making the noise, but now he turned back to watch Jeremy make his way toward the bus. "We know. He just left."

"No," said Bella. "Not someone. Some*thing*."

"No, some*one*," said Paul, and gestured out the lobby windows as Jeremy entered the bus.

Bella's entire posture changed. She gave an odd mix of sob and giggle, then frowned. "Where'd he –"

"There he is," said Adam, pointing at a window where Jeremy was wiping off the coats of blood and holding up a phone.

"Who's that?" asked Bella. Paul could tell she didn't really care who it was.

"His name is –"

"Shut up," said Paul.

Jeremy's eyes were gleeful as he pointed at the phone he held to his ear. Then the eyes shifted to something like surprise, then to horror. A slight turn of his head as he looked at something that no one in the terminal could see. Something in the bus, hidden from sight by the swaths of blood that coated all the windows.

Then Jeremy's head was gone.

It happened in an instant, but at the same time, Paul saw it draw out in his mind. Jeremy's eyes, so wide. The mouth, shifting from smugness to screaming.

No sound that Paul heard with his ears, but for some reason his brain conjured up the sharp, bright noise of a balloon popping. Jeremy's head popped just like that balloon: one minute fine, then some thought filled his head to overflowing and his forehead shifted sideways and the back of his head exploded in the same instant.

Pop. And Jeremy Cutter's headless body slid out of sight. An instant later the window he had smeared some of the gore off of was painted again, geysering spurts. Blood splashing over the glass that could only have come from the stump at the end of Jeremy's neck.

People screamed. Paul barely heard it. Mostly, he just heard that bright, sharp noise. *Pop*. And then words:

"He should not have left," said Adam.

He turned to see the GameBoy kid, Adam, staring at his phone. Paul could see the phone, but he didn't have to look at it to know that the young man was staring at the message sent by The Other.

The Other: only 1 will leave
all in favor

"He should not have left," Adam said again.

Paul experienced another one of the strange, bouncing instants where time dilated, collapsed, then expanded again. He was standing in front of the sliding glass doors to the terminal one moment, staring at the blood arcing over the inside of a bus window. The next moment he had somehow conjured himself in front of Adam S. Miles and his fist buried itself deep in the kid's stomach as Paul screamed, "What's going on? What do you know?" He pointed at the phone Adam still held. "What does *that mean*?"

He raised his fist, ready to send it into Adam's stomach again, but something cold and hard pressed against his ear. Paul froze. He flicked his gaze sideways and saw Jesús standing beside him, the 'banger pressing the muzzle of Paul's own gun against the side of his head.

"I wonder what your bosses will say about you failing to recover your firearm. Or even remembering that you lost it in the first place."

Paul, surprisingly, found that he really didn't want to die. It wasn't about the gun Jesús held, either. just the entirety of what had happened. *Pop.*

"You really want to shoot a deputy?" he said quietly.

Jesús shrugged. The gun didn't shift so much as a millimeter. "Not so much. But I would not be too bothered by it, either."

The moment stretched into an eternity. Then the gun pulled away from Paul's head. Paul exhaled a pent-up breath, then saw Jesús aim the gun at Adam.

"What do you know? You figured something out, so what was it?" said Jesús, and his voice was even darker and more fraught with danger than it had been a moment before.

Adam, gasping, held the phone out for everyone to see. "Only one can leave," he said.

Jesús advanced on Adam, growling, "Talk plain, *idiota*!"

Adam wheeled back, his hands going up to both shield his face and simultaneously point at the screen he held in front of him. "Only one is allowed to leave, and no one else," he shouted.

Shelly stepped forward, her need to understand any of this obviously outweighing her desire to stay out of Jesús' view.

"But if one of us could leave, then why did… that… just happen?"

She nodded toward the window, through which the bus could be seen. Paul noted with odd detachment that new blood was no longer sluicing over the inside of the window recently showcasing one Jeremy Cutter.

No more blood. Heart's finally stopped.

Adam gasped a bit, both arms dropping as he realized Jesús wasn't going to shoot him. They went to his stomach, where Paul had punched him, and he groaned. Paul flushed, his cheeks burning with shame. He hadn't meant to do that; hadn't meant to slug the kid.

He held out a hand, intending to say as much, but Adam shied away from him. He turned toward Shelly and said, "Because, 'All in favor.'"

Paul, hand still outstretched, frowned, "What does that mean?"

The answer, surprisingly, came from Taylor. Sounding more like the little girl she had once been than the woman she was fast becoming, she said, "A vote. It's what they say in a formal vote."

Mary turned a horrified gaze on her daughter. "So we have to *choose* who leaves?"

The words hung there, and Taylor seemed to shrink into herself. She nodded, though, adding, "And it says, '*all* in favor.'"

Paul frowned. "So? What –"

"So that means it has to be unanimous," she said.

Beside her, Adam nodded. "All in favor," he said. "All."

Shelly had been rubbing at her arms like a woman trying to dry off after a dip in an icy pool. She shivered now, too, her face draining of color as she said, "And what happens to the rest of us?"

Paul looked out the lobby windows. At the bus, at its red-streaked windows – one of them sporting a newer, fresher coat than the others.

"No," said Ken. "I don't believe it. Can't you hear yourselves? This is *insane.*" He shook his head so hard Paul wouldn't have been surprised to hear his neck –

(Pop. Like a head exploding.)

– crack under the strain.

Adam finally let go of his stomach, grimacing. Paul reached out to him again, intending to say something. To apologize, or to explain… or *something.* But his breath caught in his throat as he tried to speak.

"Why not believe it?" asked Adam. "It makes sense, given what little we know."

Ken laughed, an utterly humorless sound. "If what you guys are saying is true, then we're all dead." He looked around, grimacing as gestured at everyone in the lobby. "There's no way you could get a group of strangers to vote unanimously on which one of them doesn't get murdered."

For some reason, Paul's eye was drawn to Shelly. If he had to pick one of them as the omega, the member of this impromptu herd most likely to be cast out as an offering to the predators outside, it would be her. But in the instant he saw her, she looked less weak than cunning. Someone who knew she wasn't cut out for survival, but who was figuring out a way past that obstacle. "There is a way to make the vote unanimous for one person," she said. She looked at Red as she added, "If that person is the only one still alive."

Red had been watching all the drama unfold, strangely silent, his expression caught in a null zone between madness and unconsciousness. When Shelly said that, he snapped into awareness enough to wink.

Paul looked away from the two of them. He caught Adam staring at him, his expression unreadable. As soon as Paul's gaze found him, Adam shifted to avoid eye contact, and Paul saw the guy look first toward Ken, then in the general area of Clarice.

Ken and Clarice stared back at Adam for a second, then they looked at Mary, at Taylor, at Bella. At Red. Back at Paul.

They were all sizing one another up, he realized. Looking for weakness, for the person who might hurt them, or the one they might be able to sacrifice to whatever dark gods hid beyond the glass, in the darkness and the fog.

"What kind of people would –" Mary began.

"Not people," said Red, his voice high and sharp. Everyone looked at him. He smiled slyly, the smile of a kid who knew that a practical joke was coming, knew that it was the kind of joke that wasn't really funny so much as hurtful, and that knowledge made the coming "joke" just that much more delicious. "And soon *you* won't be people anymore, either."

Everyone did their best to ignore that. Everyone failed.

Jesús was the first to mimic a normal expression. He had looked dismayed, but that dismay fled before his more normal mask of bored mayhem-to-be as he tucked Paul's gun into his waistband.

Paul pointed at the weapon. "That's mine," he said.

Jesús responded exactly as Paul had expected: he ignored him. He turned instead to Bella, who had screamed when Jeremy's head exploded but now sat curled in on herself, looking small and pitiful on one of the terminal's hard plastic seats. "What did you see?" said Jesús, his voice surprisingly gentle.

Bella's eyes snapped to his, tears winding silvered tracks down her cheeks as she said, "He… he died. That guy's head –"

The kindness of a moment before disappeared as Jesús snapped, "Not him," jerking a thumb toward the windows outside as he did. He pointed toward the deputy's office. "In there. You came out and said you saw something. What?"

Bella shrank away from him, the sullen tone of her voice made a lie by her obvious terror. "I don't know. Some kinda monster or alien or something."

Paul shook his head. He hadn't realized how much he wanted her to say something helpful until she came up with that pile of stupidity. "I knew you were high when I first laid eyes on you."

"I'm not high!" Bella screamed, and erupted out of the chair. Paul had seen this before, lots of times: people taking fear and transitioning it to rage. It was a kind of emotional alchemy that he had always found shocking, watching someone shivering and quaking in one moment and then turning to a screaming, shrieking ball of potential violence in the next. It shocked him now, as Bella was suddenly in his face, shaking her finger at him and screaming, "I saw something, you ignorant asshole, and unless your inbred relatives had glowing green eyes to go along with their tiny dicks, *it wasn't human*!"

Silence fell around her last words. Jesús was the first to break free from the effect of Bella's words. "So no one can leave until we choose who gets to go," he said.

Ken shook his head slowly. "We don't know that. We don't know anything at all. And even if what you say is true, we don't know what happens with the rest of them – the rest of *us* after we vote."

"Dead," someone whispered. Paul looked at Shelly: the voice had been the quavering voice of a middle-aged woman in the grips of fear. But Shelly was looking at *him* as though *he* was the one who had just spoken.

"Did you say that?" she said.

"Dead," someone else said. Paul looked around again, wondering who had said it this time – it sounded like a little kid, and for a moment he wondered if there was a child in this mess, and what would he do then?

"Dead," came a third voice. A man's voice, deep and rumbling.

"Dead," said a woman.

"It's coming from the speakers," said Clarice, pointing at the spots in the wall.

"And from the phones," said Adam, holding out his own as another voice – female, this time, someone in her thirties if Paul had to guess – said, "Dead."

The voices continued, each one speaking a single word, then cycling through to another voice which said a single word, then another and another and another.

"Dead…"

"… dead…"

"… dead…"

"… *DEAD.*"

The last was spoken by what sounded like a toddler, someone barely old enough to make the sound and certainly *not* old enough to understand what the word actually meant.

"Who is that?" whispered Shelly.

"The Other," said Adam. He stared at his phone, almost dropping it when voices began speaking again.

"Dead… dead… dead…"

Something flashed, and Paul turned with the rest of the passengers. It was the electronic sign that had until recently announced the arrivals and departures. Now, though, instead of that information, a series of words appeared, blinking into existence as they were spoken by the voices that sounded everywhere at once.

"You'll... all... be... dead... So... choose... choose... *CHOOSE!*"

The voices cut off, but the word "CHOOSE" blinked on and off three times before disappearing from the sign. The sign blinked out as well, whatever power had illuminated it now just as obviously gone again.

Paul looked at the dark sign. At the bus outside, with its red windows like stained glass in a church of the most profane gods. He looked at Jesús just as the 'banger looked at him. The tattooed man grinned tightly and rested a hand on the butt of Paul's gun, still jutting out of his belt.

Paul had come to this place, this dead-end nothing at the end of the world, for a very specific reason. He had wanted to avoid the ugliness, the despair –

(the shotgun and the girl and the memory of her that came to him so often)

– and now he was in the worst of it. Not just what was happening, but the reality that he was staring at a group of people who would be only too happy to see him die if it meant they would live.

Jesús' hand curled around the butt of Paul's gun. Paul didn't know if the 'banger was going to try and use it on him or not. He wasn't worried about the gun itself, so much as the intent he saw everywhere around him.

He chanced a glance in Mary's direction. Wondering if he would find her looking at him that way.

She was.

That was enough, and too much by far. Paul turned and ran for the safety of his office. He had spent years hating the space, and now it was all he could think of.

"Paul!" Mary shouted as he ran. "Get back here! You gotta help, you're supposed to be a –"

Paul's fingers fumble-flew across the keypad that allowed access to his haven. The keys were dead, though. Whatever had cut the power in this place had rendered them inert.

That was fine. He yanked open the door, now unsecured by any lock, and threw himself into the darkness beyond.

He slammed the door behind him. The electronic lock was not engaged, but there was an old-fashioned deadbolt that he slid into place just as the first fists began hammering on the door.

"Kingsley!" Mary screamed. "Get your white ass –"

"Sorry, Mary! But I ain't waiting around to lose a vote or for someone to just kill me!"

Mary shouted something else, but Paul didn't hear what it was. All he heard was the silent *pop* of Jeremy's head exploding, and all he felt was the loud sound of his own heart turning to stone.

"Don't wanna get voted off the island," he said to himself. He sank down, too-ample ass wedged into the space where the door met the floor, and put his head in his crossed arms and cried.

Interlude

One is dead.

That leaves ten. Eleven if you count the one who had come in from the previous Cycle.

The fog hangs outside, wafting gently back and forth without ever actually dissipating. If it had had eyes, it would have watched the people separate into ones and twos; micro-cliques that serve as reminders of how very alone each of the survivors has already become.

Isolation can be every bit as deadly as any gun or knife.

The fog drifts, but does not go anywhere. It presses at the windows, turning each sheet of glass into a writhing gray eye that will never blink, never look away.

It will stay this way until the end.

Whenever that comes.

And whoever it comes to.

PART THREE: Caucusing

1. Cycles

Ken saw Clarice catch him staring at her. She smiled her beautiful smile, and he smiled back. She mouthed something at him, and he didn't know what it was but he smiled and mouthed, "I love you" as though that was all that was needed.

That was what all the songs said, what all the movies claimed: that love was enough. Love won out over all.

Clarice adjusted her wedding ring. It caught the bus' headlights and sparkled. The brightness of the ring dulled any happiness her smile brought. That wasn't her fault – she didn't know what the ring was, or what it meant, and she never would if he had his way.

But *he* knew. He knew what that sparkle meant, and the compromises required to bring its brightness to her hand.

Ken didn't believe he'd had a choice in the matter, not really. A woman like Clarice could have anyone. She didn't have to choose him, but she had. Now it was up to him to show her the world she deserved. The ring wasn't the biggest indicator of that world, but it was certainly an important one.

Ken had always thought he'd have to settle for a plain gold band for his bride – whoever she was. When Clarice came along he knew that would never be enough. *Nothing* would be truly worthy of her, but a simple gold band on her finger would be a blasphemy.

That's when it all came together. When the job came that allowed him to get the ring for her. When the money came into play, the money that would let him gift her with the life she so richly deserved.

Had it been the right choice? Of course. It was the only way Ken could give his wife the life he wanted to give her – the life she *needed to have* – and so it was the only option. He did what he had to.

But now… they were in this awful place. He tried to convince himself it wasn't true. But though he could lie to his wife – and had lied to her every day for months – lying to *himself* was getting a bit harder.

I didn't do anything. This isn't my fault.

Every time Clarice's ring caught the light and glinted, the edges of the lies eroded a bit more. He wondered if he might actually tell her someday.

And then she really would *leave. No two ways about it.*

He pushed the thought away, focusing instead on what was happening now. That was all that mattered.

He looked at the wall, and frowned. "It's still going."

"What?" asked Deputy Kingsley.

Ken pointed at the simple, round, analog clock hanging on the wall near the bathrooms. It continued ticking down the clock as though the rest of the world hadn't effectively ceased to exist.

"Battery powered," said the deputy.

"So they can't run everything in here," breathed Ken.

"Or they simply want to make sure we are aware of the time," said Adam.

Ken glared at him, which was by and large wasted since Adam avoided his gaze. "That's not helpful."

Adam shrugged. "I was not trying to be helpful. But hiding from our reality is not going to help us."

Shelly tittered. "Sometimes hiding from reality is all you *can* do, honey."

Ken looked at the clock again. According to it, the time was 2:49 a.m. That meant a little over an hour had passed since the nightmare had begun.

He turned back to Clarice. Her ring caught the light again. Broke it into pieces smaller than old, dead dreams, and sent the shimmering bits right into Ken's eyes.

He looked away. He had to. If Clarice saw him looking at her, if she looked into his eyes, she'd know. She'd intuit the reality of their world, and would never speak to him again.

His gaze settled on the ticket woman and her daughter. Mary and Taylor. They sat close together, Mary's arm around her daughter's shoulder. Taylor shivered, though it wasn't particularly cold in the room. The teen looked not just afraid, but physically ill. Like the fear of the night hadn't just caused a rise in emotion, but actual physical deterioration.

That was the right word, too – the more he thought it, the more Ken realized "deteriorating" was the right descriptor for the teen. In the hour since this had all began, her cheeks had sallowed, her eyes had begun to shine with fever lights. She looked like she was being hollowed out, and the flesh that remained stretched taut over some invisible torture device.

Taylor saw him looking. Her eyes shone like lying wedding diamonds. Ken looked away from her.

Everyone else sat as far from their neighbors as possible. Ken sat close to Clarice, Mary sat beside her daughter... but everyone else was spread out, their heads on perpetual swivels as they all looked from side to side in a vain attempt to keep everyone in sight at all times.

That wasn't exactly true, though: two of the people weren't watching everyone. One was Red, as everyone was now calling the crazy guy who had driven the bus from Hell into their world. Red still wore the handcuffs that had been placed on him by Adam S. Miles, and no one – not even kind-hearted Clarice – seemed inclined to take them off.

Red didn't appear to mind, or even notice. He had pushed himself into a sitting position some time ago, and now sat staring out the lobby windows at the bus he had ridden into their midst. Once in a while his lips moved as though he was saying something, but no sound ever emerged.

The other person who wasn't totally devoted to the "sit and look around to make sure no one is creeping up on you" school of action was Adam. The gamer had removed a small pack of tools from one of his bags sometime before, and he had been using them to slowly, methodically dissect his cell phone. The components of the phone were now placed in an orderly grid pattern on a white handkerchief he had laid out across one of the benches, and Adam would occasionally pick up a piece and look at it in the light of the headlights streaming in through the windows, then put it down and move on to musing over the mysteries of the next bit of electronic detritus.

Ken couldn't fathom what the guy was looking for. He suspected Adam didn't know, either, but he didn't want to ask. It was a small comfort, thinking maybe Adam had some idea of what was happening and was investigating it as they sat there. Ken didn't ask what Adam was doing, though, because he didn't want to face the likelihood that the guy would just shrug and say, "No idea."

"Is anyone cold?" said Shelly. She'd been sitting near where she had been when all this started. Her bags were piled neatly beside her, and now she opened the top one and pulled out a bright red jacket that she shrugged into. She looked at Bella, the girl who apparently had been in the holding cell an hour ago and who now alternated between glowering at nothing and cursing at everything. "You know," said Shelly, "you'd be much prettier if you used summer colors instead of the cool blends you're wearing." She opened another bag and pulled out a small makeup kit. "I could loan you some –"

Bella gawked, which Ken heartily approved of since his own face was making the exact same expression. "Are you kidding me?" demanded the girl.

Shelly, sheepish, closed the bag and tucked it into an inner pocket of her jacket. "Sorry," she said. "I'm just going crazy waiting."

Bella snorted. "So you decide to drag everyone else into your poor life choices?"

Shelly's smile froze into a rigor mortis version of itself. "Selling cosmetics is nothing to be ashamed –"

"No," said Bella, snorting again. "Clearly. I mean, look at you: you're obviously winning at Life. What are you, sixty? Divorced, I bet. Going from one place to another and hoping –"

The smile that had frozen across Shelly's face melted into something momentarily ugly and oddly frightening. Ken would have bet money that in a fight between her and the hard-faced young woman, Bella would win in a heartbeat. Now, watching Shelly's face crumble into an expression of rage that fled as quickly as it had appeared, he wondered if he had that assessment backward.

"I used to be just like you," said Shelly. Her voice was low, almost threatening.

Bella snorted yet again and said, "Now you're getting mean," she said.

Shelly kept talking, speaking in the same low, dangerous tones that rolled right over Bella's louder voice as though it didn't even exist. "Young, beautiful, thought I knew it all. I was going to Hollywood, to be a star – I even knew a producer he said he'd get me into the biz." She paused, then smiled again. Unlike her previous smiles, though, there was no warmth or kindness in this grin. "I bet you know someone like that, too, don't you, sweetie? Bet you're just saving that last little bit of cash off whatever hustle you got going until you can shake the dust off this little nowhere town and make it big."

"You don't know anything –" Bella began.

"Yeah, I do," said Shelly. Her smile returned, bright and cheery as though this were nothing but a cold call trying to get some stranger to sign up for the Mary Kay Starter Package. "Let me tell you how that story ends: the 'big-time producer' turns out to be a fraud. Mine was a lonely liar of a makeup artist who knew almost no one and made less money than the average grocery store clerk." With every word, her smile widened and brightened. Ken blanched, and he wasn't even the one she was aiming the grin at; he couldn't imagine how Bella felt. "Maybe you won't even get that much," Shelly continued, "so I'd be careful who you make fun of, because my guess is that I'm you as a best-case scenario."

Shelly withdrew the makeup case she had tucked away. She opened it, flipped expertly through the contents, then withdrew a lipstick. She ran it over her lips, transforming them with a casual swipe to something whose brightness would be more appropriate to a night on the dance floor than… whatever this was.

She put the cap back on the lipstick tube, pushed it back into the makeup bag, and stared at Bella the whole time. "At least I learned how to do makeup," she said. "And that's something, because sooner or later *everyone* gets wrinkles. Sooner or later *everyone* needs to hide something."

She stood as she said this last, sauntering over to a Bella who was trying to both appear tough and rebellious and openly cringe away at the same time. Shelly held out the small makeup bag. "So would you like a sample pack?" she said, her smile now nothing more than the shmoozy grin of a professional saleswoman. "It's a great way to freshen up, not to mention a fantastic opportunity to learn about the great Mary Kay product line in case you ever discover that you're in need of a little extra cash."

Bella shook her head. Ken watched it all with the fascination of a kid in a reptile house at the zoo during feeding time. So did everyone else, he could tell; even kindhearted Clarice couldn't look away.

Bella mumbled something. Ken couldn't make out what she had said, and doubted Bella would know herself. It was just noise to cover the fear that she felt – that *all* of them felt.

Sometimes noise – any noise – was the closest you could come to hope. The dead did not speak, so the ability to make sound was sometimes the easiest way to prove you were still alive.

Taylor looked up at her mom and said, "Do you think it'll really happen?"

Mary rocked her daughter back and forth as she said, "Do I think what will happen?"

"Do you think we'll all die if we don't… *choose* someone?"

Mary's gaze went rigid. She kept rocking her daughter back and forth, her arm draped over the teen's shoulders in a motherly mockery of safety. "Don't you worry, sweetie. Someone will come. Promise."

Ken saw her eyes. He saw the lie there. Saw what everyone, including him, was feeling: there was no one coming. Maybe there was no one, *period*. The fog outside cloaked the world in gray nothing, as though they had returned to a pre-Genesis moment.

Ken's parents had been churchgoers, part of the aggressive "Americanization" that his great-grandparents had undergone while in a concentration camp for Japanese during World War II. His great-grandparents had found Christianity during their internment, and though Ken never really found out whether their conversion was sincere or just a matter of convenience/personal safety, the rest of their line had certainly followed suit. Ken had grown up in a world of Sunday School and mid-week church activities, Bible studies among them.

He remembered the verse, *"The world was without form and void, and darkness was over the face of the deep."* A preparatory scripture, readying the universe – and the reader – for the moment when God would shift the universe from *nothing* to *something*.

Only here, in this formless nothing, this place where the terminal had become the end-all, be-all of existence, Ken doubted that God could possibly exist.

Bella whispered sullenly, "There *was* something out there. And I don't think it was human."

Ken answered automatically with a response that would have made his parents proud, assuming they knew nothing else of how their son had turned out: "I don't believe in monsters or aliens. Or ghosts for that matter." He flashed a smile at Clarice. "I only believe in the occasional angel."

She didn't seem to notice the strain in his voice. She just smiled back, and the gratitude he saw in her eyes was just one more knife in his heart.

Adam was still working on his phone, and without looking up he said, "Until someone puts forth a better hypothesis, it would be unwise to discount hers." He *did* look up then, and smiled an awkward, ungainly smile at Bella.

She rolled her eyes and shook her head. "Great. So the only person on my side is the moron."

Another knee-jerk moment as Ken half-stood and said, "Hey, there's no need to –"

"Everyone, *cállense!"* shouted Jesús. Then, clarifying as though it were necessary, as though everyone hadn't understood from his eyes and the way he rested his hand on the cop's gun, "Shut up."

Everyone did. Except Red, who had begun to mumble. Ken focused on what he said, hoping against hope for some clue as to what was happening. The man had come from the fog, hadn't he? So he had to know what – if anything at all – was out there.

But the mumbling had all the coherence and continuity of a stream broken up by jagged piles of wood and rock. Whatever was out there had fundamentally broken this man. What could do that? What could destroy not just a man's body, but his sanity?

Clarice moved closer to Red. She crouched beside him – though Ken at least pulled her back far enough to keep her out easy reach of the madman – and said, "Can you tell us what happened?" Red didn't stop his susurrations. "What was out there?" Clarice asked.

The questions had already been asked, and Ken expected no better response this time. He was wrong. Red stopped murmuring, if only for a moment. He glanced at Clarice, then a sly smile spread across his face for an instant before his gaze went blank again and he renewed his nonsense burbling.

Clarice glanced at Ken. He felt the weight of her attention as a tangible thing. Always before it had felt like a blanket, covering and comforting him. Now, though, it suddenly felt more like a sheet of lead, weighing down on him and smothering him.

Only that was wrong, wasn't it? It wasn't her attention that did that. It was his guilt. It was that damn ring.

Ken turned away from her, looking at Red "Maybe he has a wallet," he said.

Clarice knocked the palm of her hand against her head. "Stupid. Nursing 101 in the ER, and here I am forgetting –"

"Don't be too hard on yourself. I think we're all going a bit crazy in here."

Wrong thing to say. Ken knew it as he said it, and saw Clarice pulling at her sleeves as the smile that had graced her features now turned to a self-conscious smothering of the pain she carried. Ken reached for her. He touched her hands. "None of us are thinking straight. It would be weird if we *were*," he said, hoping she heard the words he was really speaking: *"There's nothing wrong with you."*

She paused, then nodded. She turned back to Red, but something in the man had changed. He stopped mumbling and gazed on Ken with eyes that glinted with mad, animal cunning. He looked the way a predator would look, feigning weakness to lure in the *truly* weak.

He looked at Red's leg. Clarice had wrapped it well, but there was no mistaking the wrongness of the knee's bend, or the fact that it would be a long time, if ever, before Red stood on his own again. Between that and his cuffed hands, there wasn't much the man could do to anyone. So Ken leaned a bit closer – just close enough to put himself between Red and Clarice – and said, "Do you have a wallet?"

Red said nothing. Just stared. Clarice moved, and Ken knew that she was going to go for the man's back pocket. She'd lean in close and he'd grab her and tear her throat out and she would die and then Ken would be alone and –

Ken stopped the train of thought, derailing it with his own movement as he darted out a hand to grab for the other man's back pocket. Red began to laugh hysterically. The laughter came hard and fast, jagged as the sharp edges of a broken-out window.

The laughter ended abruptly, singing into a register so high Ken thought he would go deaf as Jesús glided forward –

(So fast the guy's so damn fast.*)*

– and stepped on Red's broken leg. He ground down on Red's knee, slowly, purposefully, waiting as Ken reeled back into Clarice's waiting arms. Jesús kept the pressure on, glaring about the room as though daring anyone to try and stop him.

No one did.

Jesús looked back at Red, then let up on the knee, just enough that Red gasped with the sudden *lack* of pain. "*Silencio, amigo*, okay?" whispered Jesús into the moment of silence. Red nodded, moaning, his eyes bright with pain but more fully present than they had been. "Now," said Jesús, "do you have a wallet?"

He enunciated each word separately, bullets from a silenced pistol, muffled but still deadly.

Red shook his head. "Lost," he whimpered. "Everything lost."

Jesús nodded, his face holding the expression of a dog trainer who had just coaxed a trick from a recalcitrant poodle. "What is out there?" he asked, and Ken saw him lean forward as though about to grind down on Red's leg once more.

"Them. The Other," said Red. His eyes started to fade into the vague nothingness so like the fog outside. He gasped sharply as Jesús put more pressure on his knee. "Four Cycles I've been alive. They said I could go but it was a lie." He paused, inhaled deeply, and Ken felt himself blanch in anticipation of the scream that must come.

No scream. Just three words, spoken in haunted tones: "They herded me."

Red inhaled again. Again Ken braced for a scream. Again, the scream did not come. Instead, Red lowed out a convincing imitation of a cow mooing.

"*Moooooo…. Moooooooooooooo.*" He stopped, then giggled, though Ken could see Jesús once more putting pressure on Red's knee. "They herded me. *Moooooooooooooooooooooooooo.*" The last lowing ended in a writhing, undulating sound that Ken felt as a vibration more than audible sound. He imagined the glass of the windows breaking, the fog rushing in.

For a moment, even Jesús looked panicked. He no longer ground down, he stomped his foot, and a *crack* punched through the air. Ken winced and looked at the lobby windows, waiting for the explosion, the moment when form and void would win out, would overtake the measly moment when the Word made all into reality and once more the world dissolved into nothing.

The glass remained whole.

Red continued laughing, biting out words between gales of hysteria. "I thought it was over, but it's just another Cycle. It never ends." He laughed harder and harder, and Jesús finally fell back, the man's mirth forcing a retreat the way Ken suspected nothing else could have.

The laugh ended so suddenly Ken would not have been surprised to see Red's head rolling across the floor. Only a guillotine could have cut off the sound that completely. But when he looked, Red was still there, his head still attached. He was kicking his legs, even the broken one thrashing from hip to knee, while below that point the rest of his leg flopped back and forth like a pendulum.

The guy had smashed Ken's nose. Maybe broken it, and the spot where he hit hurt like a sonofabitch. Ken didn't like the guy, and feared him, but in this moment Red looked so crazed that he transformed from frightening to pitiful. Fear had made him first into a rabid thing, and now into an object of abject misery.

Red stopped thrashing as abruptly as he had stopped laughing. He looked at everyone in the terminal.

Mary. Taylor.

Shelly.

Bella.

Adam.

Jesús.

His gaze moved to Clarice. Then settled on Ken.

Red smiled, and the dangerous madness was back in his eyes as he said, "It. *Never*. Ends."

2. Cut strings, whole strings

Paul had thought nothing could possibly save the group. Certainly nothing could save *him*. He had seen too much, done too much. Then, at the last, when it mattered most to Taylor and Mary and, hell, to everyone else, he had done far too *little*.

Nothing could save them.

Nothing could help at all.

Then he had found the half-full bottle of whiskey in his desk. He had no idea where it had come from. Maybe it, like the blind-eyed television on the desk, was a final, long-unnoticed combination gift/screw you from Coot.

However it got there, Paul dumped most of the bottle into his mouth in a series of long, hard swigs. An inch of liquid strength was all that now remained, and he stared at it.

He remembered, for a moment, what it had been like to be a good man, a good cop. He remembered, for a moment, the moment it all went wrong. The fight that he had thought would end in justice and a victory. The way it had actually ended – with the girl he'd been trying to protect coming after him, and what he had to do to stop her.

A sound intruded. Not the imagined *pop* of Jeremy Cutter's head exploding, not the much louder sound of his own gun firing, the sound so long ago and yet so very present. Paul looked around blearily, trying to place what the sound was or where it was coming from.

His gaze lit upon the window outside.

Shapes writhed in the mist. Not the fog itself, though that cloud of gray had never stopped moving, wafting this way and that across the outside of the terminal. Now, though, the movement was accentuated by the lines of darkness threading their way through the mist. Thick lines that could only be bodies.

But what *kind* of bodies?

They looked wrong; attenuated in ways that no human form could match. That could just be an effect of the fog, Paul tried to tell himself. It could be that the mist had merely refracted human shapes to an illusion of otherworldly oddities.

But if there were people out there – actual people, not aliens or ghosts or monsters – then why were they just walking around? Why not coming into the terminal or at least moving close enough to be seen clearly?

Were they lost?

Paul didn't think so. Whatever was out there, it *meant* to be out there. The things that wandered through the mist knew where they were, and what they were doing.

The sound came again, the one that had pulled him partly out of his stupor. This time he was awake and focused enough to know where it was coming from. The "dead" desk phone was ringing.

Paul realized that he was sitting on the floor, not sure how he had come to be there but dismayed at how long it took him to hoist his way up and sway toward the phone. Suddenly, answering the call seemed like the only way to find salvation. The only way to rescue not just his body, but his soul.

He reached for the phone. It clicked on, the speaker activating of its own accord. Paul's fingers, inches from picking up, now withdrew as though scalded by fire. The speaker had come on itself, and that meant it wasn't just a phone call. It wasn't the outside world, or the promise of someone coming to the rescue.

It was *them*. *It*. The Other.

The Other's voices came from the speaker. Tinny, far away, but each one clearly a different person. A sampling of humanity stitched together in a ragged patchwork that lost all its humanness in the making. "You... have... to... play... nice... with... others."

The last voice was that of a crone, a witch-voice that sounded like it might have come from some overdone B-movie of the 1950s. It cackled, then was replaced by the cooing tones of a child, the cracking voice of a teen, the sultry bass voice. "You... have... five... seconds... to... join... your... friends."

Paul's nuts turned to cold lumps, his toes felt like they were literally turning inside out. "Or what?" he asked, his lips dry, his throat packed with dust.

The Other laughed. A thousand voices, a demonic choir.

Movement caught Paul's eye. One of the dark shapes outside had drifted closer to the window. Lengthening, then shortening, the eddies and ripples of mist between it and the terminal hinting at far too much while truly revealing nothing at all.

Coot's TV – *Paul's* TV, now, and what else was he but Coot waiting to happen, Coot waiting to go mad and end his own world? – blinked to life. That was impossible, because there was still no power, there was still no *anything* but fear and mist.

But it turned on.

Static ruled the screen, a white blizzard that only gradually resolved into something slightly opaque. The static still tumbled and twirled like the fog outside, but gray darkness rose through its murk. Words formed, darker static against white, jumbled nothing.

Three words.

All.

In.

Favor.

The Other spoke from the phone. "Five... four... three..."

Shit, I'm about to get voted off the island.

The words on the TV disappeared, replaced by dark, twitching numbers that counted down in time with the voice of The Other.

Paul spun and raced toward the door that led to the lobby. He worried that he wouldn't have time to key in the numbers to unlock the door, or that he *would* have time, but would fumble the numbers in his haste.

"Two…"

Then he remembered that the keypad didn't work. He had thrown the deadbolt. He twisted at it, and now he *did* fumble, fingers sliding across metal that suddenly seemed greasy and wet.

"One…"

Fumble. Twist.

Paul glanced over his shoulder and screamed, because the thing was there, it was *right there at the glass* and oh dear Lord it was just like he feared it had three green eyes glinting on its forehead and a darkly veiled hand reaching for the glass it was coming for him and –

"Paul, you sorry *sonofabitch!"*

Paul blinked back tears. After everything, after a life that had gone so fully down the toilet, he was almost surprised that the threat to his life had started him moving. He was hyperventilating, breath stolen by a sprint of a few feet, yet into which he had put more effort than anything else he had done in years.

"Paul? You okay?"

The voice that had at first called him a *sorry sonofabitch* now mellowed into concern, and that told him who was speaking even before his confused mind managed to match the voice with a face. It was Mary. Of course it was. She was always the first to be concerned about others.

Mary stepped toward him. He knew it was her, of course, but for a moment he didn't see *her,* all he saw was three green eyes, a glow about the alien shape of a thing that should be a head but somehow was not.

"Stay away from me!" he shouted, his hand thrown up to ward off the menace. He reached for his gun, realizing too late that it wasn't there.

The vision disappeared. He was staring at Mary, and Mary alone. But the fear didn't go away. It intensified as Paul realized both how bad things had gotten. He also wondered... If he had had his gun, if it had been loaded and ready to go, would he have made the same mistake yet again? Would he have shot Mary a moment ago, if he had the means?

He thought probably yes.

"You saw it, didn't you?" said Bella, hunched in a corner and looking every bit as scared as Paul felt.

"It's real," said Paul. He looked at everyone. "It's real, I saw it."

On their faces, he saw no disbelief. He saw the *desire* to disbelieve on a few, but they had all fallen far enough down the rabbit hole that it was ridiculous to pretend they weren't in Wonderland.

"What did it look like?" said Adam. For once his stilted tones didn't sound out of place. In a nightmare, only the strange can comfort, only the unusual is at home.

Paul swallowed, pausing for breath and bringing his thoughts together. "Legs and arms like us, but three eyes." The dryness came back in a rush, and he had to lick his lips and cough before he worked up enough spit to talk again. "Three glowing eyes and this weird glowing flash in the middle and..."

"What else?" asked Adam.

"Nothing. Nothing else. The fog was too thick and they were talking on the phone and I was almost voted off the island so I just –" He realized he was babbling and clamped his jaws together so hard he bit his tongue and tasted blood in his mouth.

A click sounded. Paul turned to see that Jesús had gone to the pile of bags once owned by one Jeremy Cutter, deceased, and had thrown open the top one. Clothing flew across the floor as he quickly emptied the bag.

"Hey, you can't –" began Ken. He took two steps toward the guy, halting as Jesús turned to stare at him. Weakly, he continued, "Show a little respect, that's all."

Adam stepped forward, too, but not to voice similar concerns. He gestured toward the bags, Jesús nodded, and a moment later both were emptying the luggage onto the floor. Clothing, clothing. A few toiletries.

Adam said, "This is interesting," as he pulled out a half-dozen objects that at first looked to Paul like small books bound in human flesh. Then, as Adam opened each one, he realized what they were: wallets. Adam read from what Paul guessed were the names on the identifications inside. "Sean Templeton. Simon Moore. George Hunt. Roger Lazenby. Ethan Connery."

Mary joined Adam, craning to see around his shoulder. "He stole them?"

Adam shook his head. He showed her the IDs, then turned them so Paul and the others could see. Paul couldn't make out the individual lines of type on each card, but he had been a state trooper long enough to spot the different states of issue even at this distance.

That wasn't the important thing, though. The important thing was the face that stared back from the IDs. The same face on all of them.

"It's him," said Taylor. "All him."

Paul looked at Mary's daughter. She looked worse than anyone, as though the night had taken a particular, personal toll on her. Her cheeks were waxy, her eyes dull. She looked, Paul realized, like…

He turned away, not wanting to follow that thread to its obvious conclusion. Not with Taylor. Not now.

"Anything else in there?" Jesús asked Adam, tossing the last of the bags' contents to the floor.

Adam looked at the bag he still held, from which he had plucked the many faces of Jeremy Cutter. He shook his head. "Nothing of discernible use, either to help us escape or to figure out why we are in this position."

Paul stood. Jesús spared a warning glance in his direction as he ambled over, but Paul had lost interest in the 'banger. The moment in his office, hearing the voices of The Other come from his phone – suddenly a guy from MS-13 didn't seem so scary.

Paul held out a hand. Adam handed over the wallets, and Paul flipped each open, examining each of the IDs. "These look real," he said.

"Was the guy a spy or something?" asked Bella. Paul was proud that he managed not to jump or yelp at her sudden presence by his side.

Paul shook his head and said, "Try the laptop."

Adam looked chagrined. "I had forgotten about the laptop."

"Me too," said Jesús. He and Adam turned in circles, looking for the device.

Paul, still looking at the IDs, pointed absently in the direction where he knew they would find the case belonging to Jeremy Cutter – or Sean Templeton or Simon Moore or whoever he was – laptop after Adam used it to clock Red on the noggin.

Bella looked up at Paul with open surprise. "So you forget to retrieve your gun but you remember the laptop. What kind of dumbnuts cop *are* you?"

Paul swung toward her so hard and fast she was almost knocked back by his shoulder as he pivoted. "You don't know the first thing about me, kid, so *shut up!*"

Before, Bella had given him looks sullen and sexy, dismissive and disgusted. Now she looked at him with a grudging respect.

Even when she was in the cell and he was in the office, he realized, she had been holding the strings between them. That was how much of a nothing he had become.

Now… were the strings cut?

Maybe not. But they were definitely fraying. He wasn't so much a puppet dancing at the whim of whatever person stood before him. Before God or fate or whatever was outside.

No. Not true. Maybe I'm a bit more of a man to these people, or at least to myself. Maybe I'm coming out of whatever cave I've hidden in for all these years. But the thing outside… The Other… is definitely the one pulling the strings. Frayed or not, The Other is making us all dance.

Adam found the laptop case. He opened it, and everyone turned away from Paul's outburst to look at what he found. Even Red, hands behind him and legs splayed out on the floor in front, twisted a bit to see better.

Adam held up the laptop, a blocky thing that looked at least ten years old. He opened it, revealing a cracked, dark screen. He hit a few buttons. Nothing happened.

"It appears unusable," he said.

"Duh," answered Taylor shakily. "You busted it over the guy's head."

Adam shook his own head. "The screen is cracked but appears functional nonetheless; I suspect the crack was already there before I used the computer as a club. The rest also looks serviceable. Whatever entity has appropriated our phones and the power in this place has likely done the same to this laptop."

Bella sighed. "Let me guess: you're a computer expert. One of those idiot-savants, like in the shows. Like… what's it called… Ass Burgers or whatever."

Without discontinuing his examination of the laptop, Adam said, "I monitor and maintain security systems and high-level firewalls for various corporate entities."

"What does *that* mean?" Bella asked.

Jesús smirked at her. "It means he's a computer expert."

Paul actually liked the guy in that instant.

"Yes," said Adam. He looked at Bella for a moment. "And those shows are offensive."

"What?" said Bella, obviously confused by the jab-cross combo of Jesús snide remark and Adam's comment.

Adam took the laptop to the bench where he had earlier disassembled his phone. He moved the phone components carefully to the side, took out a larger cloth from the small pack of tools, laid it out, and started disassembling the computer.

"Hollywood either lionizes people with Asperger syndrome and high-functioning Autism, or it makes them the comic relief," said Adam. "Both are a form of marginalization. People like me appear different to you, but in our eyes *you* are the strange things. We are often smart – but so would you be if you had to memorize and practice social graces that others take for granted."

He smiled one of his odd smiles, and now Paul realized exactly *what* seemed odd about it: it was the same thing, every single time. No deviation, no variation. This was a man, Paul realized, who had taught himself how to have expressions that could be interpreted by others. He hadn't been born making the faces that so many made, but had had to figure out how to fit in with an alien species.

Adam popped the back off the laptop and started pulling out components. "Isolation is an effective motivator to excellence," he said.

Paul, impressed, said, "You do okay with it," and was surprised to realize how intensely he meant every word.

"I work hard to 'do okay with it,'" Adam said. He put honest-to-god *air quotes* around his words, and Paul stifled a laugh. Adam gave him one of those smiles, and Paul, now recognizing it for what it was – not a creepy facsimile, but a genuine if *unusual* attempt to connect – gave him a thumbs-up in return.

Adam continued plying the computer apart, speaking without pause as he did so. The work he did must have relaxed him, because his voice settled into a pleasant rhythm as he worked. "I'm not a quirky adding machine with super-observational powers. I like computers and video games because they have a structure I understand, and which never changes which means, once learned, I do not have to devote time or effort to constantly figure out what they *might mean today*. I like Star Wars okay, but I like Star Trek better because it makes more sense and I like things that make sense."

He paused, as though waiting for other to speak. No one did. "I like trivia," he continued, "because I never know when knowing a fact will turn out to be helpful in making a human connection. I enjoy hot chocolate because it reminds me of what it is like to be warm when all is cold outside. I like the color blue because it reminds me of my mother's eyes."

"What does *that* have to –" began Bella.

"Shut up," said Paul. Once again, she looked surprised. Once again, she was the one who backed down.

Adam nodded thanks and continued. "Those and a million other things mean that I am a *person*. I process information differently, but at my center, I am a lot like all of you. I am not an adding machine or comic relief. I am not a saint or a devil. I am a human. I can be angry, happy, sad, altruistic, greedy, complacent..." As he spoke, he pulled apart a pair of connectors in the laptop's guts, then replaced them. Paul didn't know what he did, and apparently neither did Adam, because he finished his list of traits with a loud, "... and surprised!"

Pictures began popping up on the screen. Obviously pulled from social media profiles, they quickly covered the laptop screen. The backgrounds ranged from snowy fields to desert sands, the activities of the subjects just as varied, but all of them had one thing in common: they were all of women.

It took a moment for Paul to realize it, but when he did there was no denying the fact: there was not a single male face among the hundreds that blipped onto the screen, hung there for a few seconds, then were covered by the other images that continued to appear.

Finally, one appeared on top, much bigger than the rest.

"What the hell?" said Taylor, glancing at Bella.

Bella's reaction was a bit more serious. "Wait, wait, wait!" she shrieked. She lunged toward Adam, grabbing the laptop away from him. Staring at the huge picture on top of the rest of them. It was Bella, nude, holding a camera up, obviously capturing her reflection at the mirror. Below was the caption, "I can't wait to see you, baby... and for you to see me."

The rest of the images flashed and disappeared. Bella's own photo did not, but it moved to the side of the screen. A series of messages, obviously culled from Facebook and Instagram, began scrolling over the laptop.

Bella read a few, then tried to use the mousepad, obviously wanting to minimize or close the image that still spread itself across the laptop screen. But nothing happened.

Paul leaned in close. He didn't care a damn about the picture, but he had spotted something that *did* interest him. He frowned at the names on the strings of Tweets and Instagram posts. One, predictably, was Bella's. The other, though…

He stared at her. "Why didn't you tell us you knew Cutter?"

"What?" she looked confused. "Why… how do *you* know him?"

Ken said, very quietly, "That was the guy who went outside. The one… the one on the bus," he added.

Bella shook her head. "No. That guy was too old. Weird hair, and –"

Her voice cut out as the screen changed. A series of images appeared. One was of a good-looking guy with a square chin, tanned and healthy. The next was of the same guy, a bit older, a bit rounder in the face. Another appeared, and another. Each was the same one, each one more sallow and older than the one before. The last was obviously Jeremy Cutter. The same man, but over time.

The first picture, the youngest one, reappeared, then shrank to a circle beside a message post:

Jeremy Cutter: Can't wait to see you, baby. You're gonna be a star.

Bella flung the computer away from her. Adam snatched it before it fell to the floor, and stared at it as more and more pictures flashed across the screen. Different women again, with text threads between them and men with many different names. Paul could see the screen still, and recognized a few - Sean Templeton, Roger Lazenby – and suspected the rest would match up to the wallets Adam had found.

And like the names, all of the posts had the same face beside them. It was Cutter. All of it, him. All of them eventually getting to the same point:

Can't wait to see you, baby. You're gonna be a star.

The screen fuzzed over, and new threads appeared. Names and faces of women:

Cynthia Coltraine: You took my money, you shit!

Dominique Pinkston: I'm going to find you and cut your dick off!

There were dozens like that, but Paul found them less horrifying than the ones with women who pleaded and begged for their "love" to come back, to just tell them what they did and they'd change and it didn't matter that he took all their money… on and on and on.

Bella had thrust the computer away from her. But she kept staring at it. Reading the same things Paul had, obviously coming to the same understanding he did: that Jeremy Cutter was a con artist, a predator who preyed on young women who wanted a way out of the lives they had and were willing to pay with money, body, soul, and even in some cases *heart* to find it.

It seemed to Paul like if it was possible for a person to actually *dissolve* into a scream, Bella was about to do it. She wailed and wailed, the sound coming louder and louder and then too loud as Paul realized screams were coming from the speakers, The Other's many voices howling in a ghastly mockery of Bella's pain.

Everyone else winced. Adam did more than that. He cringed away, then started patting his head as the scream continued, then starting shouting at her as he hit his forehead with the back of his hand. Paul couldn't hear what Adam said, but he could read the word on the younger man's lips: *"Stop, stop, stop, stop!"*

Bella didn't stop. She kept screaming for so long Paul thought she would explode. No one could scream that long, could they? But she did, and The Other's voices kept pace.

Finally, though, she stopped.

At that moment, the headlights of the bus Red had arrived in flickered, then went out.

Paul's world dissolved into a darkness populated only by screams and the sensation that the fog outside had finally made its way into the terminal. He pulled a flashlight from his belt with fumbling fingers, snapping the light on and whipping it from left to right then back again.

The light slashed the darkness, but the black was a fluid that ran back to itself whenever the light crossed it. Momentary flashes gleamed, but the darkness collapsed around it. All Paul could see were glimpses of the terror around him.

Taylor and Mary were the first ones he tried to find. They held each other, Taylor screaming while her mother clutched her close, one hand wrapped protectively around her child's back, the other holding the back of Taylor's head like Mary hoped to keep her daughter's eyes averted from whatever was coming.

Next the light captured Clarice and Ken, also holding to one another, both with eyes so wide he could see the whites as complete circles around their irises.

Bella had stopped screaming. The light found her next, curled in a tight fetal position on the floor.

The light moved to Jesús. The 'banger had Paul's gun held in front of him, and Paul had to stifle a sudden urge to laugh at the sight of the man using his gun to confront the darkness. As Paul watched, Jesús yanked a short, curved blade from inside his coat with his free hand.

The light moved on.

It found Adam, frozen in terror, half-standing, half-crouching in a posture that spoke more eloquently of terror than any book on the subject.

The light moved to Red. The madman was laughing, a high-pitched, warbling cackle that became a low, mournful *moooooo*, then back to hysterical laughter again.

And finally, terribly, fearfully, Paul swung the light to the one place he did not want to look. Perhaps as little as an hour before, he wouldn't have been able to do it at all. Now, though, he swept the beam in a tight arc that ended on the lobby windows. The fog caught the light and reflected it against the glass, creating a dull double orb in the window.

Nothing else.

Paul kept sweeping the light. Across the lobby. To the sliding glass doors.

To the *thing* that waited there.

3. Monster among them

Taylor didn't know what to do. She knew that she was terrified, she knew that it was a shock to see her dealer come walking out of Kingsley's office. She knew from the way Bella was acting that now was not a good time to do what they both had come here to do.

But Taylor *needed* it. She was hurting. It had been too long since her last fix. So when the lights went out she screamed, but not because she was afraid of what might come next. She screamed because she felt like her brain was popping out through her skull. She felt jittery and confused one moment, dull and listless the next. She kept sweating, and ants were marching over her skin with red-hot feet.

She screamed because, in the first instant after everything went dark, she was sure she had just had a stroke or something and was going to die.

Then the light lanced out. It bit into her eyes, and hurt so bad she thought she would faint. Then the light arced away and she realized it was Kingsley, shining a small flashlight around the terminal, the light moving so fast she didn't know how he could make anything out.

The light stopped moving.

The rest of the world seemed to freeze, too. Long enough for Taylor to see what the light had captured: the hunching form that pressed against the glass doors that led to the mist and darkness beyond the terminal.

Taylor had been screaming. Now she *shrieked.*

Laughter bounced through her screams. The nutjob, Red, was laughing in a way that seemed precisely timed to shove its way through the cracks in her shrieks, the moments when she drew breath, or when she whimpered, "No, no, *no*," in between wails.

The glass doors should have stayed shut. Taylor knew that. The power was out, so they shouldn't have moved without someone actively prying them apart. But they *did* move. They swung open with the dry *rasp-click* they always made. The thing outside –

(what is it it's gotta be an alien or a monster oh god oh good lord god almighty please save me i'm dying)

– lurched forward as the glass slid apart. Taylor's screams peaked, and still Red's laughter made its way around and between her screams and sounded louder than any noise she could make.

The thing outside the doors slid forward. A boneless-seeming thing, tall as a man at first but hunching over and tumbling into the lobby and Taylor knew it had to be some kind of blob some kind of space monster or alien or something that would roll over them all and eat them from the inside as they continued to scream and then –

The lights flickered on. Just an instant. Like whatever power controlled them knew *exactly* how long to permit the terminal's occupants to see in order to maximize the fear they would feel.

Bella was closest to the thing. She must have bolted at some point, running instinctively for the closest exit. Trying to escape, the way she had tried to escape her life. She had been looking for Jeremy Cutter.

She found him now, as the man's headless body tumbled forward it landed at her feet. Chunks of dark matter – coagulated blood, bits of partially-disintegrated muscle and bone – flooded out of the stump of Cutter's neck. They splashed and splutted across Bella's expensive boots, across the skin of her thighs.

Bella shrieked as loudly as Taylor had.

The body must have been propped against the doors, tumbling in as they opened. Now those doors whispered shut again, sealing the corpse inside.

The terminal's lights went out, but Taylor realized that there was still another light shining. Not that of Kingsley's flashlight, which shook as it tried to remain pinned to the headless corpse among them. No, it was the computer screen that had belonged to that same corpse in life.

The images on the screen were all of Bella. Bella at the store, Bella in bed. More of Bella nude, and one where she…

Taylor looked away, sickened, not wanting to see more. But she looked back again as the light changed and she saw that the photos had come faster and faster until they dissolved in a haze of images that flickered in and out of existence so fast they were nothing but a blur. A high-pitched whine came from the computer, growing in volume as the images increased in speed.

Then the noise just *ended*. The screen froze.

Taylor's phone, deep in her pocket where she had shoved it after looking at the first message from The Other, began vibrating. She heard buzzing sounds all around and knew everyone else's phones were doing the same.

The buzzing ended, and every speaker – phones, the computer, the public address speakers of the terminal itself – activated. The Other spoke, its many voices now jumbling over each other as they switched out, word after word.

"You're not trying very hard," said the thing. "Make your choice by five a.m., or *everyone* dies." The voices paused, and Taylor heard a strange hissing, like the sound on a record that has played to the end and now simply spins through a neverending circle of static. It sounded *diseased* somehow. "Among you hide an addict, a severe diabetic, a thief, and more."

The voice ended, the static continued. Taylor barely heard it now, though, hearing instead the word *addict*, over and over in her mind. Her mom had her clamped tight to her chest, but Taylor could look to the side and see Bella stiffen. She saw Deputy Kingsley start to look at her, then freeze.

He knows. Who else knows?

How does The Other *know?*

No answers. Too many questions.

The Other spoke again. "Maybe the question isn't who should live, but who among you most deserves to die."

Click. The speakers turned off. The static disappeared. Taylor allowed herself to breathe, thinking that at least this moment had passed; at least The Other was gone.

Then the laughter started. The Other laughed with many voices, cycling through each other and sounding not at all happy, not like people enjoying themselves. This sounded like the burgeoning hysteria of a crowd turning to laughter as the final option before the screaming began.

Everyone started talking at once.

Ken: "We have to end this before –"

Clarice: "How are we supposed to –"

Kingsley: "Nobody touch anything! Nobody –"

Bella: "Get it away, get it away, oh shit he's dead *get him awaaaay* –"

Jesús: "First person gets close to me and I'll kill –"

Taylor heard herself speak, too. Heard her voice sounding like a child as she whispered, "Momma, I'm scared."

Momma. She hadn't called Mom that since she was six.

Mom stroked her hair. "Don't you worry," she began, but whatever else she would have said was drowned out by the many voices all around, and The Other's laughter that punched holes in her mind.

"Please, stop shouting. Stop *SHOUTING!*"

Miraculously, everyone did. They turned to look at Adam, who seemed genuinely surprised at his own outburst. He even turned a bit, as though looking beyond him to see what in the world everyone was staring at.

He looked back for a moment, then stared at the computer on the seat before him. It still flickered, its screen still bright, the photos finally, blessedly, gone. Adam stared at it, and Taylor didn't think he was looking for clues. Not anymore. Just a refuge. Something to watch that wasn't the terminal or the people or anything at all. Noise on a screen.

Kinglsey turned a slow circle. Gauging everyone. "A thief," he said.

"What?" Mom asked.

Kingsley was staring at the computer screen now as well. He looked at Mom as he continued, "I knew he looked familiar." He waved at the screen. "This guy is the thief. He's a con man."

Bella was staring at the headless tangle of meat that lay at her feet. For a moment, Taylor wondered if the girl was just going to break in half and die, joining the death of her dreams that lay in a bloody mass at her feet.

Then her face hardened. "Then he got what he deserved, didn't he."

Ken and Clarice both said, "You okay?"

Bella shot them a glare so hard and ugly that it made the couple look away. "Why wouldn't I be?" she demanded.

Taylor heard herself say, "We know who the thief is, but we still have to choose."

Bella nodded. "Yeah. Right, yeah." She turned her back on the corpse of Jeremy Cutter, and suddenly there was only the same old Bella. Whatever agony she had just gone through was buried so deep in the persona she had crafted that Taylor wondered if it would ever appear again. "So one person leaves and lives, the rest of us stay and die? Any suggestions on how we make the choice?" said Bella.

No one spoke up to tell her she was wrong. The Other had made it clear: they had to choose by five a.m. That meant they had... Taylor glanced at the wall clock, knowing somehow that no matter what, it would still be working, because The Other would *want* them to know what time it was; to feel every second of their lives counting down to the end.

"Three hours," she said. "We have to choose one person who lives, or we all die."

"We could draw straws," said Adam.

Mom drew Taylor close. "No one is drawing straws for my life or for my daughter's."

"You're right," said Jesús. Taylor turned toward the 'banger. She saw him extend Kingsley's gun. Taylor didn't know a lot about guns, but she watched enough TV to know that the one Jesús held wasn't a six-shooter. It had a magazine, which meant it probably held nine or more bullets.

Enough to kill all of them.

Jesús looked at her as she thought all this. She saw his face as he recognized what she was thinking. She saw him nod. She saw him point the gun at the closest person.

At Mom.

"All in favor," he said.

He pulled the trigger.

4. Little J

Mary had seen a man shot in the head once. When she was five, Big J got in a fight in their living room with a man who came "for some business." The "business" went south and ended with a dead man on the floor, Mary screaming behind Big J's recliner, where she had taken refuge.

Big J called her. "C'mere." When she didn't, he turned a terrifying gaze on her and said, *"Now."*

She did. Big J rifled through the dead man's pockets, yanking out a wallet. The wallet had a wad of cash he shoved in little Mary's hands, then he said, "Go get me some Kools," in the same tone he always did.

She left. She picked up the cigarettes at the store, and no one commented on the strange red splotches that painted several of the bills.

When she came back the body was gone. But the vision of it remained. She woke up night after night, biting back screams for over a year, crushing them before they woke Big J. She didn't know what had happened to the body, but she knew she didn't want that to happen to her.

The face left the top levels of her consciousness after that year. After that year she rarely saw it hanging in front of her, with a gaping hole where the bullet had plowed through lips and teeth and then blasted its way out the back of the poor man's skull. When she did see it, it was usually in a nightmare, but occasionally it appeared when she was awake, walking down an alley on her way to get the Kools.

She saw it now, in the instant between realizing Jesús was aiming Kingsley's gun at her and the moment he pulled the trigger.

Mary felt a dull rush in the middle of her face. Everything felt like it was drawing toward that center spot, pulling inward and yanking her along so fast and hard that it hurt.

The pain was real, real as any bullet.

But the bullet itself did not come.

Mary blinked.

Jesús cursed, then pulled the trigger again. The hammer rose and fell, clicking down with its dry rasp on an empty chamber.

"I didn't bother coming back for the gun," said Kingsley, a wicked grin on his face, "because having it calmed you down… and there aren't any bullets in it."

Mary suddenly remembered the day after she had seen the man shot. She was a little girl. A tiny thing, really, but big enough to hold the big kitchen knife in her hand and stare at Big J – at her *daddy* – in his chair. He was asleep, a new box of Kools she had purchased sitting beside him.

That was the day the man at the store said things. She didn't understand them, but she understood the look in his eye, and when he asked her if she wanted to see some toys he had in back, she said no. He asked again. She said, "Big J will not like me keeping him waiting."

The mention of Big J made the strange, frightening light disappear from the shopkeeper's eyes.

Big J had protected her.

She put the Kools beside him, got the kitchen knife, and stared, stared, stared. Big J had protected her – just his *name* was a powerful spell. She didn't know what he did, exactly, only that it was enough to pay for Kools but not enough to get them out of this rat- and cockroach-infested place. Enough to keep him from having to work, but not enough to keep her in decent shoes or clothes. Enough to put food on the table, but usually not quite enough for her to feel anything but hungry, all the time.

Enough, but *not* enough. That was Big J.

She put the knife away. She slept. He did not wake her up to chastise her about this or that. They both slept.

Mary was never sure whether she made the right choice or not. But when Jesús pointed Kingsley's gun at her and aimed it, when he made a pithy comment – *so* like Big J, that kind of thing – and tried to hurt her, suddenly she was the little girl again.

She ran forward, screaming unintelligibly at the 'banger. Surprise, and she thought even a bit of fear, ran over his features. He jabbed out with the curved knife he still held, and she barely skidded to a stop before running face-first into it.

She was still screaming maddened, nonsense sounds. Jesús' eyes gleamed. He *was* afraid, she was sure of it. Just like the man had been before Big J killed him. Just like *Big J* was in the hours before he died – a giant brought low by a bullet and by cancer.

Would she be the one who killed, or the one who died? Big J, or the headless man?

She felt herself gearing up to run again, then felt a hand on her shoulder. Something about it downshifted everything. She turned and saw Kingsley staring at her.

"Easy, Mary," he said. Surprisingly, his calm tone did its job. She felt the madness cool, then flow out of her. A physical sensation that tingled its way down her arms and legs, flowing out of her feet into the ground.

She nodded. Paul – and suddenly she knew she would never think of him as *Kingsley* again – nodded back. He smiled a surprisingly sweet, tender smile.

Paul's gaze hardened as he swung it toward Jesús. "Put the knife down," he said in a tone Mary had never heard before.

There was an edge to it that she knew would have frightened her had she stood in its path. But she was behind it, or at least beside it, and so she swung her own best imitation of a Big-J-glare at Jesús.

He waved the knife at both of them. "I don't think so. No way."

Another person stood beside them. Ken. "You going to kill all of us?" he growled.

Clarice joined them. She tugged her shirt sleeves but stood firm.

Bella sighed and joined the line. A moment later, so did Adam. "This is what makes sense," he murmured, though she couldn't tell if he was speaking to her, to Jesús, to the others, or simply to himself.

Only Taylor did not join them.

Jesús eyed them all. She saw him calculating the odds. "All in favor isn't going to be you, you shit," she said, low but loud enough for him to hear.

He lowered the knife, but didn't drop it, and raised it a bit once more as he said, "First person to come within ten feet of me gets their throat cut."

He turned away, trying to appear dismissive and unconcerned, but Mary could tell it was an act. His control was crumbling. It made him vulnerable, but also dangerous.

Am I Big J? Or the headless man?

She didn't know. Only time would tell.

"Thank you," Mary said to the group. She tittered nervously. "I'm… a little surprised you all came to my rescue."

She looked at Taylor as she said it, just for a second. Taylor was looking away in the manner she had used since she was a little girl – the kind of looking away that told the world she was pretending it didn't exist.

Mary had been glad her daughter didn't join the line against Jesús. She didn't want that for her. Everything she had done in the last seventeen years had been to keep Taylor safe.

But Taylor *would* have come and joined the line a year ago. It was that moment, and that realization, that brought home the next moment of comprehension: something was very, very wrong with her little girl. Something had been going on for months and she was worried –

No. Not that. She's not dumb. She's too smart to get involved in… any of the things I *was involved in when I was younger.*

Whatever it was, she would talk to Taylor when she could. Later.

She looked at the group again, directing a second "thank you" to Bella, Ken, Clarice, and Paul.

Bella shrugged, trying to look nonchalant and totally failing. She looked pleased with herself, and Mary wondered what kind of life the girl had suffered that she could turn out so desperate to get away, yet so hard she threw away her pain – or at least buried under a thick layer of bad attitude – as though it had never existed. "What does it say in the movies?" said Bella. "All for one and one for – hey!" she interrupted herself. "Where's the makeup bitch?"

Mary looked around automatically, as did the others. Where *was* Shelly? She wasn't in the line of folks who had stood up to Jesús and didn't appear to be anywhere in the lobby.

Even Taylor and Jesús were looking around. Red, of course, began to laugh.

"Where'd she go?" murmured Ken.

"*When* did she go?" said Paul.

That was a good question. Mary tried to think when she remembered seeing Shelly last. There was the whole Shelly/Bella showdown – wasn't *that* a grand moment? – and then… was she in the lobby the first time the lights went out? What about when they found Cutter's wallets? When they tried to look at Red's wallet?

Taylor said, "Did she get out somehow? Escape?"

"How?" demanded Bella. "We've been straight-up in front of the door this whole time." She glanced at the door when she said it. At what was left of Jeremy Cutter. No emotion showed on her face as she did.

Paul swung his flashlight around, trying to find the missing woman. The beam cut through the lobby, sending bits of light into corners while still somehow conjuring even deeper shadows.

Mary felt for her phone. She thumbed the home screen. The screen brightened, but the usual home screen didn't appear. Just a blank field.

She tried what she wanted to do anyway, swiping up on the screen, and was surprised to discover the screen that offered her a flashlight option appear as usual. She clicked it.

The others were keying on their phone flashlights as well. Paul's own police-issue flashlight slashed the air, but the phones illuminated pale, weak orbs around their owners. Everyone's face fell into shadow as they held their phones forward and out. It was like being in a commune of wraiths who had all lost their contact lenses.

Mary stifled a giggle. Laughing wasn't a good idea now; not just because it was inappropriate to the situation, but because she felt as though laughing might open a deep hole inside her. A roiling darkness so bottomless and profound that she would never climb back up even to the poor light of this place.

Mary cast her pale glow around. Looking.

She shouldn't have been the one to find it. She was farther than some of the others. The light on her five-year-old cell was much dimmer than the others in the room. She was older than most of them, and her night vision wasn't the greatest.

But she was Big J's daughter. She was the one who saw the bodies. She saw this one.

She saw Shelly.

Shelly was dead, laying across the baggage carousel, her eyes closed, her skin a vile shade of gray. Her scarf had been caught up in the overlapping pieces of metal that spun around the carousel. The material must have been drawn below one of the plates, obviously yanking tighter and tighter until it strangled the woman.

The lipstick she had so recently applied was garishly bright against it, making it seem like they were staring at a vampire right after feeding.

Mary had seen a man get his head blown off. She had seen Big J, dying by degrees and then all at once. She had seen others die, too. Never like this, though. Not with a face so gray and so bright in turns, so waxy and so gaudy.

Someone gagged.

"How did it get inside without us –" Mary began.

"I don't think it did," said Paul. "Looks like she did it herself. Otherwise we'd have heard something. It was only twenty feet away."

"There was no electricity," said Adam.

Ken shrugged. "There has been when The Other *wants* to use electricity – like with the doors or the lights or even the computers and phones. It wanted the mechanism to work for… this." He gestured at Shelly, then glanced around. "Otherwise she would have struggled and there's no way we would have missed it." He pointed at the doorway between the baggage area and the lobby. It was small, but the view to the lobby was unimpaired and easy to see – a straight line of sight. "It was only twenty feet away, so she had to have been okay with what happened."

Mary noted that the two men had shifted their choice of pronouns – earlier in the night it had been "him" or "them" or "some guy." Now it was *it*.

It had changed the power.

It had allowed Shelly to strangle herself.

It had watched… and *it* would watch as the next one of them died, too.

The Other was outside, but it saw in here. It saw everything. And she sensed it was laughing.

"Why would she do that?" said Adam.

"Because she knew she wouldn't make it," said Clarice. "And she wanted out." She was pulling almost frantically at her sleeves. Ken's hand snaked out, but not fast enough to stop her from yanking one of the sleeves up and down and up and down – high enough for Mary and anyone else who was looking, to see the line of hazy scars that crisscrossed Clarice's wrists. Faded, looking almost like the gauze and bandages that surely must once have covered the wounds when they were fresh and new.

"At least this way she got to choose how she'd go," whispered Clarice. Mary heard a strange *need* in the woman's voice. She wondered if, had Clarice thought of it, they might be finding her the way they found Shelly.

Ken drew his wife to him. He pulled her out of the baggage area. The rest of them went as well, Mary following last. She spared a quick glance at Shelly and thought she saw a spasm pass through the woman's body. A death-twitch that made Mary turn quickly away and resolve not to look again, not to even look in that general *direction* again.

A gasp pulled her quickly forward. When Paul said, "What the hell did you –" in a panicked voice, Mary shoved to the front of the group, suddenly certain she would find Taylor there, dead as well. Maybe hanging from the ceiling, maybe having contrived to kill herself by beating herself to death with a chair.

Neither outcome proved true. Though there *was* another body: Red lay against the seats, slouched a bit lower now as the pressure that had kept him upright beat out of his throat, which had been slit from ear to ear.

No one made the slightest move to help him or try to save him. They watched as he died, and Mary knew it wasn't cruelty. They weren't trying to kill him, but a single glance told even the most innocent or unlearned that the cut Red had suffered was fatal.

Red's feet twitched a final dance against the floor. A sudden stink filled the room as his bowels loosed. His eyes closed and he slipped to the side, fully an inch of his face dipping below the thick pool of blood around him.

Jesús wiped his bloody knife on a cleanish patch of Red's trousers, then looked at the rest of the group. He smiled his shark's smile. "I suggested that the new guy volunteer to stay." The grin widened. "He agreed." And the grin cranked open still further as he said, "All in favor?" and raised his hand.

"You monster," whispered Clarice.

"Monsters in your midst," agreed Jesús, and for some reason Mary didn't think he was talking about himself, or even about The Other.

That scared her. What other monster could there be? The fear drove her back to anger. She wasn't Big J. She couldn't blow a man's head off, or twist his head around so he was looking at his own ass, the way she had also seen Big J do once.

But maybe she was *Little* J. Maybe she could get rid of this one person. By direct violence? Maybe. She'd done things she wasn't proud of in her life, and some of them had been most direct indeed.

But not yet. Hopefully not ever. She had left that life, that old self, behind. She hoped.

"Why don't you just *leave*?" she demanded. "You already said you wanted to go, and you're obviously a tough guy, so just get out of here!"

"I thought I would kill you all when it was easy. Now it's more complicated," said Jesús calmly. He stood, the knife in an easy, ready grip at his side. "Besides," he added, shifting his gaze to the fog that hung outside, writhing beyond the glass, "I don't know my enemy."

5. All the little ants

Everything hurt. The ants that crawled on Taylor's skin were now burrowing inside, deeper and deeper. Everyone had turned off their phone flashlights and now there was only the glowing mist and the occasional glint of Kingsley's flashlight as he snicked it on and off like he was reminding himself how it worked, which was a good thing because if the lights had all stayed on Taylor would have started screaming.

She almost *did* scream when Kingsley stood at one point and opened the doors to his office and the ticket office, wedging wadded-up paper under each as a makeshift doorstop. She understood why he was doing it – no one wanted any more surprises – but the sound of the paper squeaking against tile as he wedged it under each door made her brain feel like it was melting.

A few minutes after that, Kingsley clicked on his flashlight and walked back and forth with it like a cop pacing out his nightly beat. Taylor cracked an eye. She had to admit that he looked different. He looked stronger. No, that was wrong… he looked *more*. That was better, yeah, that was it. He looked like *more* than he had been a few hours ago.

Jesús was a psycho, Adam was weird. Ken and Clarice alternately looked strong and weak. In spite of everyone seeing her naked on the screen and knowing she'd been taken for a ride to nowhere by a conman, Bella had thrown off her momentary agony at finding out her meal ticket intended to make a meal ticket of her, and had returned to status quo: bitch – though, granted, a bitch that Taylor needed.

Mom, of course was still Mom.

Everyone was the same. Or if changed, then the changes were just variations on what had already been there before.

Except Kingsley. He looked like he had changed in some fundamental way. Taylor wasn't sure if she liked it or not, but knew that if she had met *this* version of him, she never would have shown up to the terminal looking for a score. That was something you did when there were no cops around, or when the only cops were fat, lazy lumps who did not give two shits in a storm.

That wasn't Kingsley. Not anymore.

She glanced at him. His flashlight wasn't hurting her eyes as much as it had a few minutes ago. Maybe she was getting over this hump. Maybe she could do without.

She looked at the wall clock. 3:49 a.m. Well after the next bus should have come and gone. Well after *someone* should have shown up.

The ants burrowed a bit deeper at the thought. Biting, clawing, chewing their frantic way into her body. She stifled a moan. She could feel herself shaking.

She looked around. No one was watching. Kingsley was pacing, most of the rest of the people were staring into space. Adam was playing a GameBoy, which struck Taylor as absurdly unfair: how come *he* had access to his drug of choice, when Taylor was strung-out and hurting? How come The Other was accommodating *him*?

Kinglsey made a noise. He moved closer to the glass. "What the..."

"What is it, Paul?" asked Mom.

Kingsley glanced at her. "I thought I saw something. Blue flashes."

Clarice stood. "Is it a squad car maybe?"

"Maybe," said Kingsley, in a tone of voice that screamed he was lying.

He stood motionless at the window. He flicked his flashlight outward, trying to look beyond the terminal. The fog caught the glow, spread it out, rendered it into a useless nothing.

Everything was a useless nothing.

Taylor looked at Bella. The girl was looking out the window, too, but seemed to feel Taylor's gaze on her because she turned and locked eyes with her.

Taylor stood. Mom was on her instantly. "Taylor, what are –"

"I'm going to the bathroom."

Mom's eyes darted back and forth, fear fevering them and making them into tiny embers in the dark. "Then I'm coming with you."

"Why?" said Taylor. She concentrated everything she had on hiding her discomfort from her mother. She nodded out the window as she said, "It can come in any time it wants." She looked at the headless corpse of Jeremy Cutter, which lay where it had first tumbled in. The blood had darkened around it, becoming a sticky-looking pool of tar in the blackened lobby. "It can *kill* us any time it wants. Or we just take ourselves out of the equation," she added, nodding toward the corpse in the baggage area.

Only she didn't finish the last sentence. She got as far as "of the equa –" and then felt like she was going to swallow her tongue.

Shelly Sherman, Mary Kay Beauty Consultant, talker, suicide… was staring at her.

Taylor *screamed*. Mom had been sitting on a chair nearby, but now she erupted to her feet, getting between Taylor and the corpse that stared at her with eyes wide open. "What?" shouted Mom. "What is it, sweetie?"

Taylor shoved her mother out of the way. "Shelly! She –"

Again, her words ended mid-sentence.

Shelly's eyes were closed, the same way they had been since the body was found. The ants were digging deep, making the dead move, making the living seem like shades.

"She… she…" Taylor heard her words drift to nothing. The ants were eating them, too. Eating everything.

"What was it?" asked Mom. She looked into the baggage area, blanching as she saw Shelly's –

(eyes closed eyes closed her eyes are closed when do I *get to close my eyes they hurt everythinghurtseverythinghurtsHURTS)*

– body. She reached for Taylor. "What did you see, baby?"

Taylor shoved her mother's hands away. "Nothing." She took a step toward the bathroom. The ants were digging into her spine, trying to keep her from walking a straight line.

"Honey, don't –"

Taylor didn't turn back as she snarled, "Any way you cut it, we're screwed. So if I'm going to die, I'm going to do it without pee running down my leg."

"Wait," said Kingsley. Again, Taylor was struck at the difference in the deputy's voice. Even that single word packed more of a punch than she had ever heard from him before. She turned as he held out his flashlight. "Take this," he said.

She did. Held it out in front of her. Her eyes flicked to Bella as she turned, catching the other girl's eye, making as subtle a nod as she could toward the bathroom.

Then she had her back to the company. A few painful steps to the women's room.

She barely made it inside, barely managed to wait until the door had closed behind her, before spewing in the sink. There wasn't much to it – she couldn't remember what or when she'd eaten last – but it hurt coming up. Acid bile scorched her throat. She savored the feeling. It drove the ants away, if only for a moment.

"Oh, shit," she said to herself, not sure if it was the agony and fear of the night that gave her the words or the ecstasy of a moment without bugs crawling inside her.

Either way, they came back. Harder and faster, chewing deeper than before. Taylor dry-heaved into the sink, the smell of vomit thick down there, the feel of the air in this place thick on her sweaty face.

"Not doing so good, eh?" asked Bella.

Taylor looked up at the reflection of Bella in the mirror. The other girl looked nearly like always: cocky, hands at hips, boobs out so far they looked like a parody of sex.

Usually there weren't blood and skin and other, darker things splattered on her boots and knees and thighs. But beggars couldn't be choosers.

"I need some," said Taylor.

"You got the money?" asked Bella.

"What do you need it for now?"

Bella's eyes went so cold they made Taylor shiver. "What's that supposed to mean?" When Taylor said nothing, Bella said, "I need the money for *myself.* Now you got it or not?"

"In my purse."

Bella didn't move. Waiting. Taylor looked away, staring at her mess in the sink as she said, "I don't know where it is."

Bella made a sound of disgust. "You want my product, but forgot to bring the money? I'm not a charity."

"I didn't forget it. I lost my purse."

Taylor thought about it as she spoke. Was that true? She couldn't remember. The ants were eating her memories, her brain.

Did I bring my purse?

I must have. When did I lose it?

The answer was the scuttling chitter of feelers and mandibles and chitinous legs.

"Then find it."

"What?" said Taylor. She'd already lost the thread of the conversation.

"You lost your purse? Then find it."

Taylor felt tears jewel her eyes. "Please, Bella. I brought enough to hold me over, but it was in my purse, too, and – can't you just…"

She looked at Bella in the mirror, unable to turn and face the girl's actuality. The reflection was bad enough. Bella's arms crossed over her boobs – she looked like a T-rex hugging a pair of beach balls, and incredibly, Taylor laughed.

That didn't help the moment. Bella's expression hardened even more. "Look, it's been a shitty night. I was supposed to blast through, grab a last bit of cash…" Her words petered out for a moment and a flash of pain came over her before the eyes hardened again. "I was gonna blow this place. Just take the bus to L.A. and never look back. Only I can't because aliens want us to choose which one of us gets to live, which we can do by vote or just by killing each other. So your… problems… aren't…"

Bella's voice drifted away. It had started to disappear as Taylor straightened, which she did – painfully – at the words "by killing each other."

Taylor turned. She stared at Bella. Bella was staring back, her eyes no longer bitchy or crafty. They looked dangerous.

The ants were still on fire, still burning *her*, but Taylor knew she could use that fire, could harness it for a moment for the violence she felt in the air. She realized she had lifted Kingsley's flashlight. It wasn't one of the super-heavy-duty ones some cops had, but it had a good heft. It would make a decent club.

Certainly good enough to kill Bella.

Bella's eyes darted left and right, clearly looking around for a weapon. Taylor wouldn't let her find one. Not with the ants doing their damage. She took a step toward Bella. She could kill the girl, she knew.

The ants were telling her it was okay.

Demanding she do it.

She would beat on Bella until the other girl told her where the drugs were. Then…

"All in favor," Taylor said. It came out as a dry croak, a voice she didn't recognize as her own.

Real fear appeared in Bella's eyes. Then relief as the door swung open and Taylor's *mother walked in*. She didn't notice what was happening, a full head of steam preloaded and driving her into whatever stupid thing she had prepared. "Taylor, are you –" She stopped, finally noticing the tableau she had blundered into. "What's going on?" she said.

"Christ," muttered Taylor. All the fight dropped out of her at the sight of her mom. "Mom, can't you just leave me alone for five seconds?"

Mom blinked, looking from Taylor to Bella, back again, and back again. She looked like a bobblehead. "I'm sorry to *inconvenience* you," she said, a bit of fire creeping into her voice, "but –"

Bella turned on her heel and pushed past Taylor's mom. "Your daughter's a psycho," she spat as she walked out.

Taylor couldn't read Mom's expression as she stared at Bella, but she worried it might be suspicion.

Every once in a while, Taylor started to suspect Mom wasn't quite an idiot. Slow, boring… yeah. But dumb?

Taylor flinched as Mom stared at her. "What?" she said sullenly.

Her mother crossed her arms. Like Bella, she looked a bit like a T-rex. But not a cartoony one with ridiculous boobs – a straight-up carnivore, hungry and mean. "You said you had to go to the bathroom." She nodded at a stall. "So go ahead."

Taylor stared. Waited. "You mean it," she said incredulously.

"Damn right."

Taylor threw up her hands. She went into a stall, slamming the door as she did. "I'm peeing now," she called, and added a grunt for good measure. "Are you happy? Do you have a treat for me going in the big-girl potty?"

Mom didn't answer. Taylor finished and left the stall just as Mom left the bathroom.

She felt alone.

She felt tired.

The ants burned…. burned… *burned.*

6. Because they could

Bella didn't know what else could go wrong. In the space of a few short hours, Going Places had shifted to Stuck in a Cell, and now the whole thing had become Gone To Shit. Present tense had become past tense, and Bella did okay in English, so she knew what those meant: she wasn't happening, she had already *happened.* She was a has-been before she ever was.

As she left the bathroom, she saw Adam. The weirdo still hunched over playing his GameBoy, and wondered: The Other controlled everything in here, so why did Adam still get to play his game? Nothing else worked, so why that?

And why would he want *to? I mean, who even* has *a GameBoy, let alone playing it while the world disappears and my career ends?*

The sight of it, the guy playing quietly, calmly, infuriated her. She marched over to him, hovering. He bent slightly away, obviously not liking the intrusion into his space. That made her even angrier; what kind of guy *didn't* want her near him?

"You know we're going to die, right? You should do something more than just play your stupid game."

Without looking up, Adam said, "What do you propose? Complaining endlessly?"

Before she could answer, the sound of cracking plastic drew her attention. She turned to see Ken ramming his elbow through the front panel of a vending machine that stood against the wall near the bathrooms. He pulled his elbow back, carefully unwrapping the jacket he had bound around it. Plastic sheared away and several large pieces clattered to the floor. It was a bright, almost *happy* sound.

That burned Bella. Everything *sucked*, so happy sounds were not allowed.

More than the sound, though, it burned her to watch the guy hand his mousy wife a water that he pulled out of the machine. He got another for himself, and none for Bella. He didn't even *look* at her.

The machine held both drinks and snacks, and after Ken swigged some of the water he had grabbed, he pulled a few Pop Tarts out of the thing's guts. He handed one to his wife, then he and Clarice moved away as others in the lobby drifted over to find their own version of apocalyptic fast food.

A blue flash glinted in the fog beyond the windows. Everyone stopped moving. Staring. Waiting.

Nothing more appeared.

"Maybe it's the government," said Ken. "Doing some kind of weird study."

"No government could do this," said Clarice. "Even if they wanted to, it's too big. They couldn't hide it."

"So it's aliens?" asked Ken. He looked at Bella as he said it and actually *smirked*. She wanted to kick his teeth in.

"You don't believe in aliens," said Clarice.

"You should," said Adam. He was still playing his game, but he began speaking, a steady stream of words coming in his weird, upsy-downsy way. "Given the size of the universe, the probability of a civilization developing on another planet would have to be less than one in ten billion trillion for us to be the first *developed* alien life. Let alone undeveloped life, which is a statistical certainty. Not to mention the fact that there are numerous legitimate scientists who believe they have found evidence of extra-terrestrial life."

"Bullshit," said Bella, suddenly interested in spite of her desire to simmer and be gorgeously, sexily angry.

"Not bullshit," said Adam. "In October of 2016, a respected professor at Penn State University stated that star KIC

8462852 displayed blinking patterns consistent with the creation of a Dyson Sphere."

"What's that?" asked the deputy, who had been scrounging for his own get-fat-quick nutrition in the machine. Now he had a Snickers bar in his hand, which he unwrapped with all the class and subtlety of a gorilla handling a banana with chopsticks.

"A Dyson Sphere is a construct which scientists believe could be built to harvest a star's energy. *Built*," Adam added, emphasizing the word in a way that sent chills down Bella's spine.

What things *would build something that could harvest a star's energy?*

And are they outside?

She looked out the window, expecting to see a line of green-eyed things or more of the blue flashes.

She saw neither.

Adam continued. "Since 2008, NASA's Kepler Spacecraft has located over four thousand planets which could have held life. And one planet in particular – GJ 1132b has an *atmosphere*. An actual blanket of alien air that many believe likely supports current life."

The door of the women's bathroom clicked. Taylor came out. A moment later, so did her mom.

Bella locked eyes with the roly-poly woman and saw that Mary *knew*. She might not know the exact details, but there was something in her gaze that told Bella she was aware on some level that her daughter was using, and equally aware where her supply came from. If Mary had her way, Bella would be voted out – or shoved out – into the fog, to turn into a headless wonder like the sack of meat –

(He doesn't even have a name, I never knew him, never knew him and he didn't matter at all.)

– in front of the doors.

Taylor held out the flashlight she had been using toward Kingsley, who had finished his Snickers bar. He shook his head. "You keep it," he said.

A moment later Ken asked Adam, "So you're saying that the things out there are extra-terrestrials? Then why would they do this? Why the mind games?"

Adam shook his head. He grimaced as his game made a sad little beep – he must have missed a score, no doubt lowering his Dork Quotient by a full ten points.

Idiot.

Bella thought it, but didn't say it. Because idiot, weirdo, whatever – Adam was talking about something concrete. Bella didn't know if it was aliens out there (though she thought it likely at this point), but if it was then Adam seemed to be the guy who knew about them. Maybe he could get them out of this.

Adam shook his head again and said, "I am not saying it is aliens. Only that it could be. As for the why… that is what any culture does when encountering a new one. They test defenses. They try to know whether the other – us, in this instance, though I find it interesting that whatever is doing this to all of us refers to itself as 'The Other' – is friend or foe."

Kingsley shook his head. "That makes no sense at all."

Adam actually looked up for a moment, obviously getting wood off this conversation. "It does. And even if it did not, a truly alien race *would not* make sense to us, would they? That is the definition of 'alien' – something so strange and foreign as to be nonsensical. Incomprehensible." He turned wide eyes toward the lobby windows. "The unknown must always be feared. Survival demands it."

The GameBoy whistled a few descending notes: game over. Adam looked back down and started playing a new game. "So yes, it could be aliens, just as it could be a government."

Clarice shook her head. "No, governments can't – they *don't* –"

"But they do," said Adam. "The SADF –"

"SADF?" asked Bella.

"South African Defense Force. The Army of apartheid South Africa."

"Apartheid?" she said. "What's th –"

"Shut up, kid," said Kingsley. Bella surprised herself by complying. The world had shifted. Down was up, and big, luggy deputies were bossing her around. Kingsley looked back at Adam. "Go on."

Adam nodded. "The SADF performed sex-change operations, chemical castration, electric shock, and other medical experiments on homosexual soldiers in an effort to 'cure' them."

Bella's eyes went wide. "So they cut off their –"

"Shut *up*," growled Kingsley.

"*Callate*," added Jesús.

Bella looked from one to the other. She would have bet her life on Jesús coming out on top in a fight between him and the cop. But the world kept tilting and she was no longer sure. All she knew was that she was suddenly, surprisingly, afraid of them both. She nodded. "Sorry."

"There's no way that's true," said Clarice. "It can't... people aren't..." She pulled at her sleeves.

You should know better, baby. Someone who's been hacking at herself, causing pain rather than face the world, should know how messed up people are.

"It is not only true," said Adam, "it is well documented."

"That's disgusting," said Clarice.

"No." He paused his game and looked up, taking in each person's gaze in a rare moment where he was apparently so into what he was saying it didn't bug him to look everyone in the eye. "What is disgusting is that the head of the study was in private practice as a surgeon at the time – and not in South Africa. In *Canada.* Polite, developed, culturally sensitive Canada. He was a Clinical Professor in the Department of Psychiatry of Calgary's Medical School until *2010."*

"You're kidding," said Kingsley.

"No." Adam shook his head. "I do not kid."

"But that was South Africa," whispered Clarice.

"Yes," said Adam. "But the U.S. government has been party to other such 'experiments.' In the 1940s, the United States and Guatemalan governments infected numerous impoverished Guatemalans with syphilis in order to study possible 'cures.' No one was ever cured, and the leader of the study went on to research the effect of leaving syphilis *un*treated for as long as possible. The subjects this time were United States citizens, mostly poor black men. The study continued through 1972."

Bella blinked. Adam's voice had risen in volume and confidence, and it seemed almost like… was it getting brighter around him?

In the next moment, she forgot the question as Kingsley said, "That is some scary shit."

Quietly, Mary whispered, "People can't be like that. They aren't so cruel. So *evil.*"

Bella knew bullshit when she heard it. Mary didn't believe what she was saying.

Though you didn't know the bullshit when you heard it from him.

She shoved that thought deep, into a place she hoped she'd never find it again. Past was past. She was still destined for greatness. *That* was the truth.

"Hitler was no Mother Theresa," said Ken thoughtfully.

"Hitler was a *person,*" said Mary. "I'm talking about *people*. Some are bad, sure, but mostly –"

"There are other instances," said Adam. "In the 1950s, the CIA paid Dr. Donald Cameron to run Subproject 68, better known as MKUltra."

"I heard of that one!" Bella crowed, happy beyond reason to be able to say it. She looked around, embarrassed and angry at how many of the people in the lobby looked surprised at her statement. They thought she was an idiot, she realized, and the realization burned. "What?" she said. "I watch Fox News. I know stuff." To Adam she added, "But the MKUltra stuff is just a conspiracy thing. Tinfoil hats and Illuminati."

No one's expression changed. She wondered how many people thought she was an idiot. Not just in here, but in *general.*

Jeremy sure did.

"Again," Adam was saying, "MKUltra is a well-documented reality. Its purported goal was to discover methods of mind-control and information extraction. The subjects were not criminals or evildoers. Just people with anxiety, depression, or other personality 'disorders.'" For the first time, Bella saw a solid, easily discernible expression on the guy's face: *hatred.* "People like me," he said.

"What happened?" asked Taylor.

Bella waited for someone to tell *her* to shut up. But apparently they all thought the junkie rated higher in conversation skills than Bella. That stung. Bad.

She saw Taylor's hand shaking. Thought about outing her. What would everyone think of Miss Perfect then?

"Shhhh, baby," said Mary. "Don't. We don't need to know that." She shifted her gaze to Adam. "Is this really helping?" she asked.

"Let him talk," said both Ken and Kingsley in unison. Clarice pulled at her sleeves but nodded. Even Jesús looked interested.

Bella felt like this was all a dream. It *was* getting brighter in here. That meant she was going to wake up, right? Right?

"MK Ultra's 'researchers,'" said Adam, "tested sensory deprivation, torture, isolation... Simply put, they created madness. The subjects forgot how to talk, suffered serious amnesia, and worse."

"*Our* government did that?" asked Clarice.

"Hon," said Ken. He pointed at his face. "You know what they did to my great-grandparents. It wouldn't be the first time."

"All sides did it," said Adam. "During World War II, Japanese Surgeon General Shuto Ishii vivisected POWs, forced women to abort their own babies... and the Allies used his research as a springboard into modern biostudies."

"Stop," whispered Mary.

"In 1999, a federal judge approved a four-million-dollar settlement to families of numerous black men who had inoperable tumors. They were used as guinea pigs in a study funded by the U.S. Military, in which they were irradiated with the equivalent of 7,500 X-rays."

"Stop," Mary said again. Bella felt herself mouth the word, too.

Adam rolled right over both of them. "Sick of the government? In 1989 the CDC joined with Kaiser Pharmaceuticals of Southern California. In a study in which as many as 1,500 infants were given an experimental, unlicensed vaccine. The parents were not told, and the infants were mostly children of poor minorities."

The light in the terminal brightened.

Wake up. Wake up, Bella, wake the hell UP*!*

But the dream continued. The nightmare deepened as Adam spoke.

"1994: twenty-three schizophrenic inpatients at the New York Veterans Administration are taken off meds and given amphetamines instead, to see what would happen. 1988: New York City foster children are unwitting human subjects in experimental AIDS drug trials which some believe are still ongoing."

"Stop!" Mary screamed. "Just *stop!*"

Adam didn't. Maybe he couldn't, just like Bella couldn't stop herself from listening. "But none of that is the worst," he said. "According to declassified papers, the CIA gave unsuspecting people LSD and watched while they had sex with CIA-paid prostitutes in brothels owned and operated by the CIA. Agents watched the sex acts on the other side of one-way mirrors."

"How is that worse than vivisections?" said Bella. Before anyone could make a comment she jutted out her lower jaw and added, "I know big words, too, you know."

"Because," said Adam, "when the 'studies' came to light, no one could really explain why they did it." He shook his head. "They did it because they could."

It *was* brighter. But it was still a dream. And just as in any dream, Bella felt like she couldn't control herself. She turned her head, looking out the lobby window. Everyone else turned as well, the dream-sensation heightened by the sight of them all looking like they were puppets on a single string.

The fog *was* glowing brighter, and as Bella gazed into the brightness, the sense that this was a dream burned away. She wasn't in a dream. She was in a nightmare. A light bright enough to expose who and what she was: a fraud. A fake. A *nothing*.

Within the fog's depths, lights began flashing on and off. Muted bursts that actually made Bella think of the dim lights of the cell phones the people in the terminal had held up to ward off the dark.

Maybe they have cell phones. Wasn't that a line in a movie? "Alien phone home?" Something like that?

She giggled. Laughed. Couldn't stop.

The laughter ended when her phone buzzed.

Oh shit, they're not calling home. They're calling us.

She pulled out her phone.

The Other: choose
choose
choosechoosechoosechoose
choosechoosechoosechoose
who dies

The departures/arrivals sign turned on again, words scrolling across it in blood-red letters:

Choosechoosechoosechoosechoosechoosechoosechoosechoosechoosechoose choosechoosechoosechoosechoosechoosechoosechoosechoose...

Then the words blinked out, replaced by a macabre parody of the sign's earlier, normal posting:

Current Time: 3:55 A.M.
ALL DEPARTURES DELAYED INDEFINITELY
5:00 A.M. DEADLINE – ON TIME

The "ON TIME" blinked on and off, a winking eye. Then the lights on the sign jittered. The words sliced in pieces, silent static covering the screen.

"Coot," Kingsley whispered. Bella glanced at him and saw him standing slack-faced, staring at the static like it was the answer to everything. She didn't understand what he was saying, but she didn't like the look on his face or the slackness of his mouth as he said it again: "Coot. Full Coot."

The static disappeared, replaced by numbers:

1:05:00

Then those numbers shifted:

1:04:59

All the phones turned off. Not just the messages that Bella could see on the screens held in death-grips by the others, but the screens themselves. Adam grunted in sudden dismay as his GameBoy turned off as well.

The flashes outside the terminal winked out.

Ken grabbed his wife, who was making weird, panting sounds. "Calm down," he said. "Breathe. Just –"

"Do… you… *know*?" shouted the many voices of The Other, the words coming from everyone's cell phones and the terminal's speakers. "Do… you… *KNOW*? Do you know who sits beside you? Have you chosen a sacrifice?"

And suddenly the things were closer than ever before, dark smudges in the gray fog, green eyes hanging in triplets everywhere outside. Bella tried to count them and couldn't. They were moving among each other, the darknesses seeming to merge and then split, to join and tear apart. The blue lights reappeared, and began to dance, flashing on and off in rhythms that had no apparent pattern, yet somehow spoke of dark, angry purpose.

"Look!" shouted Bella, though everyone was already looking. But the kind of thing happening now – *someone* had to say something. *Someone* had to bear witness.

"They're getting closer," whimpered Clarice. "They're getting closer." She started sobbing.

Ken gathered her to him, and Bella felt a bright stab of guilt: why didn't anyone hold *her*? For a single, terrible moment she allowed herself to wonder if perhaps the world wasn't there for her gain. Maybe it didn't even *care*.

Just like he didn't care. Not really.

She tried to push that away again. She failed. For a moment she knew that the life she had chosen would lead only to ruin – and certainly never to the touch of a man so in love with her, like Ken was in love with Clarice.

The blue lights outside disappeared. One trio of green eyes followed suit at a time until only one set remained, directly in front of the lobby windows, but as always far enough away that the fog created a wraith of whatever form the thing outside had taken.

The last trio of green lights flashed, like the thing was languidly blinking. Then they winked out.

The terminal speakers clicked. The Other spoke again, its words spaced far apart as it switched from voice to voice. "Only… one… hour… left." A long, long pause followed, and then a little girl's voice said, "Tick-tock," and laughed. The laugh was the kind you would expect to hear at Christmas. A bright, happy thing – but in the darkness of the terminal the brightness of it didn't warm Bella. It made her cold to the soul.

The speakers clicked as an audible sign-off. The Other was done speaking, but Bella heard the last word, the child's voice, echo in her mind. "*Tick-tock*."

Darkness everywhere.

The only illumination was the clock, silently counting down…

… the flashlight Taylor still held…

… and the soft, mocking glow of the fog…

7. The sense of things

Adam S. Miles fixates on some things. It is called perseveration, defined as an abnormal insistence on sameness, an inflexible adherence to routines. He relies on certain things: he must have donuts every Thursday, Friday, and Saturday morning. He hangs his shirts up facing the same direction in his closet. He owns only black ties – three of them, identical.

This is one of the reasons he enjoys Tetris: it is repetitive, calming. It allows for mental engagement, but at its core it is the same ones and zeros, the same program iterating in what seems to be infinite variety but in reality is randomized outcomes created by the same input.

He has been thinking repeatedly about the words The Other spoke earlier, in their many voices. So it is frustrating to hear them replaying in his mind, saying over and over the words, "You're not trying very hard. Make your choice by five a.m., or *everyone* dies. Among you hide an addict, a severe diabetic, a thief, and more. Maybe the question isn't who should live, but who among you most deserves to die."

Adam S. Miles has heard people talk about the value of life – often in conjunction with arguments why people like him would be better off not being born. That is ridiculous. But the idea that there are those who give less to society is true, he must admit. And there is also this: actions have consequences. Being born is not, he believes, the responsibility – or the blame – of the child. But the child makes decisions that do determine what he or she gives, or takes, from the world.

"Maybe the question isn't who should live, but who among you most deserves to die."

He hears it again. It is reproduced perfectly in his mind, and the perfection of it is upsetting. He does not like The Other's voices. One throat making them all? Many throats joined somehow? Adam S. Miles does not know, but knows that none of the voices are his friends.

Which does not mean they cannot speak accurately.

"Maybe the question isn't who should live, but who among you most deserves to die."

The words shift. They become the words The Other *just* said: *"Only one hour left. Tick-tock."*

Adam S. Miles looks at Jeremy Cutter's baggage. It hangs open nearby, its contents strewn across the floor of the lobby.

He spots the bags of Shelly Sherman nearby. He looks at his phone, but it is off and will not activate when he presses the button for the home screen. Nor will it brighten when he presses the power button.

He knew it would not work as a phone, but hoped he could use it as a flashlight. Apparently The Other has cut off that avenue of illumination.

The fog is glowing brighter than it did, but not enough for him to continue doing what he started earlier: finding out what links the passengers; what they have in common and why they are all here.

He digs blindly through his small bag of tools until he finds a slim cylinder. He clicks the button at one end and a small but bright beam activates on the small light he uses when he has to look inside a computer's guts.

He goes to Shelly Sherman's bags and begins going through them.

Nearby, Ken Nishimura is holding his wife as she quietly cries. For some reason, her cries do not bother Adam S. Miles. They are a sad sound, but a normal one. He often does not understand facial expressions, but he knows what crying means: Clarice Nishimura is sad.

Adam S. Miles continues looking through Shelly Sherman's things, hoping to find something that will make all of them less sad. Or at least give someone among them a better chance to survive this.

Preferably him. He does not want to die.

"She's *dead,*" says Ken Nishimura as Adam S. Miles searches Shelly Sherman's things. "Can't you let it go?"

Adam S. Miles has found nothing but clothing so far. A great deal of it is underwear, which surprises him for some reason. How many changes of underwear does she need?

He moves to the next bag, and as he does he says, "The Other asked, 'Do you know who sits beside you?' It was right in its assessment that there was a thief among us. Jeremy Cutter was a thief, that much is certain from the contents of his luggage. Perhaps knowing who the others are will help us somehow."

"What?" said Deputy Paul Kingsley, "You think they gave us a helpful hint or something?"

Even Adam S. Miles can tell Deputy Paul Kingsley is being sarcastic. He shrugs. The bag he has opened is crammed full of makeup things. "Perhaps. Or perhaps there is a commonality. There has to be a reason for all of us to be going through this. There has to be a –"

"No. Stop, just stop, just –" begins Ken Nishimura.

His wife shudders and makes one last sob. She stands away from Ken Nishimura, which makes him stop whatever he was going to say.

Clarice Nishimura moves closer to Adam S. Miles. He wonders if she is going to physically try to stop him from continuing his search. He hopes not. He did not like the last fight he had, with Terrence Jonas Inglebrook (though he has to admit that hitting him with the pipe felt good) and he does not want to be in one now.

Instead of reaching out to stop him, though, she takes another of Shelly Sherman's bags and opens it. "Hon?" asks Ken Nishimura.

Clarice Nishimura is pulling things out of the bag. More panties which makes Adam S. Miles *really* wonder what kind of person Shelly Sherman was. "He's right," says Clarice Nishimura. "We have to know what's happening if we want to have any chance at all. Who we are is as good a place to begin as any." She moves on to another bag.

Shelly Sherman had a lot of bags and *a lot of panties.*

"We know about the thief," Clarice Nishimura says. "What were the others? Diabetic and…"

"An addict," says Mary the ticket lady. She spares a quick look at her daughter, who does not look at her mother, but at Adam S. Miles.

"Why would they say that stuff?" asks Taylor, whose last name and title Adam S. Miles do not know, which bothers him so he decides to think of her as Just Taylor.

"'Maybe the question isn't who should live, but who deserves to die,'" says Jesús Flores. He is staring at Red's corpse.

Ken Nishimura looks there, too. Then he stares at Jesús Flores. "No. that's not for us to decide."

Jesús Flores points his curved knife at Ken Nishimura, which makes Adam S. Miles focus on what is happening. He does not want to fight Jesús, but he can see Deputy Paul Kingsley lean forward, and knows if the police officer attacks Jesús Flores, then Adam S. Miles will jump in as well.

Jesús Flores is dangerous. He is *not* someone who deserves to be chosen. "All in favor" should *not* be him. That would make no sense.

Adam S. Miles likes things that make sense.

Jesús Flores smiles so widely Adam S. Miles wonders if it hurts him. "It is *exactly* for us to decide," says the tattooed man. "Just because you don't have the *cojones* for it doesn't mean the decision won't be made. Not by you, *maricón*. But someone is going to do it."

Clarice Nishimura straightens, pulling something out of one of Shelly Sherman's bags. "Here," she said.

She holds a manila envelope. Adam S. Miles swings his penlight over, aiming it at the envelope. Clarice Nishimura smiles at him, then turns it over.

The manila envelope is thick, but other than the words, "OFFICES OF PETER DENNEHY, P.I.," stamped on one corner, it is devoid of decoration.

Clarice Nishimura opens the envelope. A picture falls out. Adam S. Miles picks it up, looking at it. It shows a girl playing on a playground. He thinks she looks to be around eight years old. She is beautiful, with the same blond hair as Shelly Sherman has, and a similar angle of chin and cheek. He turns over the picture, noting it says a single word on the back.

Ken Nishimura has approached, and is looking at the photo as well. "Who's Michelle?" he asks, reading the word.

Clarice Nishimura has something in her hands: a pile of papers she must have found in the envelope, which now lays discarded nearby. She angles the papers to take advantage of the light Adam S. Miles holds. Just Taylor is also pointing her flashlight at them now. "It's her granddaughter," says Clarice Nishimura.

"Why have a file on her granddaughter?" asks Bella Ricci.

Clarice Nishimura is flipping pages as she reads passages out loud. "Shelly Sherman… history of drug and alcohol abuse… incarcerations for resorting to illegal means of getting drugs including –" Clarice Nishimura's eyes bug out a bit. "Burglary and *prostitution*?" she says, and glances toward the baggage area for a quick second before going back to the file.

Bella Ricci whistles. "Never would have pegged her as the party type."

Adam S. Miles thinks she is trying to make a joke. No one laughs.

Clarice Nishimura reads on. "Last time she was arrested, Shelly was pregnant. No father known. She put the child – a girl named Ellee – up for adoption. Looks like Shelly tracked her daughter down just in time to miss the funeral." She flips a few pages. "Car accident."

"How sad," says Mary the ticket lady.

Clarice Nishimura looks at some pages. She frowns, then flips to the back, looking at what looks like a court filing. "Since the funeral, Shelly's been trying to arrange to take custody of the little girl – her granddaughter."

"That can't have been easy for someone with her background," says Deputy Paul Kingsley.

"But she got it done," says Clarice Nishimura. A few more papers shuffle through her fingers. "Reading between the lines, it looks like a *lot* of money changed hands to make it happen."

Adam S. Miles reads now as well, peering over Clarice Nishimura's shoulder to do so. "She was going to meet her at the hotel in town in the morning." He looks at the body in the baggage area. He is not happy she died, but the sight of the body itself does not bother him too much. Not like the headless body of Jeremy Cutter, or Red's bloody corpse with its death-smile on the face and gory second grin on the throat.

Shelly Sherman does not have a smile. Her tongue pokes out a bit, which Adam S. Miles supposes must happen if you are strangled with your own scarf in a baggage carousel. "She must have been waiting for the early morning transit bus, then was going to meet her granddaughter."

"She almost made it," says Clarice Nishimura.

Movement draws Adam S. Miles' attention. He sees Mary the ticket lady, moving toward Just Taylor.

Adam S. Miles has noticed Just Taylor through the night. She was a beautiful young woman when he first saw her. The night, however, has taken its toll. She has looked paler and paler as the night progresses, and now her skin has a greasy tint to it and she is shaking.

He decides to change his thinking of her, which is hard but he can do it when necessary. Instead of Just Taylor, he thinks of her now as Taylor the possibly sick girl.

Mary the ticket lady tries to put her arm over Taylor the possibly sick girl's shoulder. Taylor the possibly sick girl shakes her away. She spares a look at her mother that Adam S. Miles is sure is one of anger.

He looks away, uncomfortable. Back to the picture of the little girl. "Anyone else know anything about this girl?" No one speaks. "Anyone use this private investigator?" he asks, pointing at the manila envelope. Again, nothing. Deputy Kingsley shakes his head. "So that is not a common point," says Adam. He puts his hands on his hips and says, "What about birthdays? Places we lived or places we were born or –"

Jesús Flores erupts into shouting. "This is a waste of time! You think evil always has a reason? No, evil *has no reason*. It does not happen to tempt or to teach. True evil simply *is*, and it happens to any who find themselves in its path when it chooses to strike." He stops and weaves a bit, as though suddenly dizzy. He frowns, looking as though he is concentrating. Then he turns on his heel and marches back to the place he was sitting when the night was normal and the lights were on and there was no blood on the floor.

Jesús Flores gets to the seat but does not actually sit down. His body goes rigid and he says, "Which of you took my bag?"

No one answers.

Jesús Flores turns around, pointing the knife he holds in a slow arc that takes in the night's survivors. "I'm going to say this once: you will give me my bag. Do it now, and I will freely forgive."

No one answers.

"Fine," says Jesús Flores. In a single, dancing move that is almost too fast for Adam to follow, he slides across the terminal floor, grabs Mary the ticket lady, and spins her around. Her eyes are wide and she opens her mouth to shout, but closes it again as Jesús Flores' knife slides into the hollow below her jaw.

"Mom!" shouts Taylor the possibly sick girl.

Mary the ticket lady groans as Jesús Flores roughly roams his hands around her body. He is frisking her, looking for his bag or whatever is in it, Adam S. Miles supposes. "Stop," says Jesús Flores to Taylor the possibly sick girl when she is about three feet away. Without removing the knife from Mary the ticket lady's throat, he says to Taylor the possibly sick girl, "Now you. Get over here."

Taylor the possibly sick girl does not move. She looks at Mary the ticket lady and mouths the word, "mom."

"Neither of us have –" begins Mary the ticket lady.

"Now!" screams Jesús Flores.

"No!" shouts Mary the ticket lady while her daughter at the same time screams, "I don't have your bag!"

"Then you have nothing to hide, *chiquita,*" says Jesús Flores. "Don't make me –"

At that moment, the dizziness that struck him a moment before apparently hits him again. He slumps to one side. Not long, but Mary the ticket lady elbows him in the stomach. Jesús Flores' breath explodes and he reels, allowing Mary the ticket lady to escape.

That surprises Adam S. Miles. Shelly Sherman was a prostitute, Mary the ticket lady has some street fighting skills. What other secrets hide here?

Jesús Flores grits his teeth, forces himself upright, and takes a shaky step toward Mary the ticket lady.

Ken Nishimura steps forward, angling to get between Jesús Flores and Mary the ticket lady. Jesús Flores kicks him high in the chest – his suit must be specially tailored to allow this kind of movement, because Adam S. Miles notes it does not rip.

Ken Nishimura, who managed to stay mostly upright even when his nose was broken earlier, now collapses. "Ken!" Clarice Nishimura shouts. She lunges toward him, but stops as Jesús Flores waves his knife at her, then drunkenly frisks Ken Nishimura as the other man groans on the floor, his arms clapped across his sternum

"*Nada. No hay nada.* Not here!" shouts Jesús Flores, and for a moment Adam S. Miles is sure he will slit Ken Nishimura's throat. That would make Adam S. Miles sad, because he thinks Ken Nishimura is a pretty okay guy.

It would also, admits a small part of him, deep inside, make him a little bit happy. Because that would make Adam S. Miles a little bit closer to being the one left when everyone votes.

Just as Adam S. Miles is sure Ken Nishimura is about to die, his wife draws Jesús Flores' attention. She steps forward, holding up her arms. The scars on her wrists and forearms seem to glow a vivid white. "Just don't hurt him," she says.

Adam S. Miles does not understand what is happening for a moment. Then Jesús Flores growls and stands, frisking Clarice Nishimura as roughly as he already did with Mary the ticket lady, and Ken Nishimura.

It could be Adam S. Miles' imagination, but it seems to him that Jesús Flores lingers on certain spots. Breasts, buttocks.

Adam S. Miles knew the tattooed man was bad news. Now he knows the man is *evil.*

He will not be the one at the end. That would make no sense. I have to make sure he is not the final one when we determine who lives.

Ken Nishimura reaches for his wife, though Adam S. Miles does not know if it is to try to stop the bad man or because Ken Nishimura wants a trained nurse to examine his chest. Either one would make sense, under the circumstances.

Jesús Flores finishes his frisk, and Clarice Nishimura bolts away from him, rushing to her husband. Ken Nishimura winces as she helps him sit up. "Are you okay?" he manages to say.

"I'm fine. Fine. Fine," says Clarice Nishimura. She repeats it the same way Adam S. Miles sometimes repeats things when he is perseverating. "What about you?"

"I'm okay," says Ken Nishimura. He stands, slowly, grunting and groaning as he does. One arm is clasped across his chest. "I think he broke a rib."

Jesús Flores looks at Adam S. Miles as Ken Nishimura stands. The bad man seems to discount Adam S. Miles, apparently deciding he will *not* have his bag and so not worth spending time frisking

Adam S. Miles rarely is thankful that others think of him as a "retard" or "slow." This is one of the few times he *is* grateful. Jesús Flores turns back to Taylor the possibly sick girl. Mary the ticket lady stands between her daughter and Jesús Flores, her arms thrown wide as though to embrace him. But that is not what she is saying, is it? She does not want to hold Jesús Flores, only to hold him *away* from her daughter.

Jesús Flores steps toward Mary the ticket lady. "If she doesn't have my bag," he says, "then there's nothing to worry about. But if you don't get out of my way, then you'll have a *lot* to worry about. For a little while. Then you won't worry at all.

Your daughter will still get searched, but she'll do it while watching you bleed out. *Comprendes*?"

"Mom? What –" says Taylor the possibly sick girl, her voice low and husky with an emotion Adam assumes is fear.

"Muévate," says the tattooed man to Taylor the possibly sick girl. "Move!"

"Over my dead body," says Mary the ticket lady.

"If you insist," says Jesús Flores.

Surprisingly, Deputy Paul Kingsley moves forward, placing himself firmly in the path of Jesús Flores. "No," he says. He pulls a club from his belt and holds it out. He stands taller than he has up until now, tall enough that he seems to give Jesús Flores a moment's pause.

But only a moment.

"Bad move, *amigo*," says Jesús Flores.

"Why? Because you're *Mara Salvatrucha*?" asks Deputy Paul Kingsley. "Yeah, I know what that tattoo means. Same as I know what those teardrops are supposed to mean: it's the number of guys you've murdered – or maybe the number of times you got made into someone's bitch in prison." Jesús Flores growls and steps forward. Deputy Kingsley holds his ground. He points with his nightstick. "But you know what? I don't care. Maybe you're a scary dude most of the time, but tonight, in all this," he says, gesturing outside at the fog, "you're just one more rat in the maze. So back – the – hell – *off*."

Jesús Flores gathers himself to rush Deputy Paul Kingsley. Again, Adam tenses, readying himself to jump into the fight as well. He would not fight Jesús Flores on his own, but if everyone else joins in it is good odds. It makes sense.

Before Jesús Flores pitches himself into his headlong attack, he suddenly reels dizzily to the side. He stumbles over some of Shelly Sherman's bags, almost going to his knees but managing to right himself at the last second. He straightens, lunges, swings his knife.

Deputy Paul Kingsley dances backward with surprising grace, which is good because Jesús Flores' knife flashes out only inches away from Deputy Paul Kingsley, and the police officer barely avoids evisceration.

"This is your last chance," says the tattooed man hoarsely. He is not panting, exactly, but taking small, gasping breaths. He looks like he is trying to decide whether to commit further mayhem or simply pass out.

Suddenly, Taylor the possibly sick girl shoulders her way past Mary the ticket lady. "Taylor, don't –" begins her mother.

Taylor the possibly sick girl says, "My purse is missing, too. I didn't take your stuff." She turns out her pockets, showing they are empty, then gestures at everyone else. "I don't think anyone did."

Adam S. Miles understands. He understands that she is saying The Other did it. And perhaps she is right. He does not know, but he suddenly fears…

He turns. He sees – or rather, does *not* see – exactly the thing he feared. "My games!" he shouts.

The GameBoy has been sitting on the chair he was sitting on earlier. On the chair beside is where he always sets the soft case that holds the GameBoy and several of his favorite games. Tetris is his very favorite, but he does enjoy others from time to time. The games each have a designated sleeve, all of them visible when he opens and unfolds the carrying case.

The games are not there. The sleeves are not there. The *GameBoy* is not there!

"Missing, where is it, missing, where is it?" he says, and his voice rises to a high pitch. He does not like his voice when it sounds like this, but he cannot change it right now. "Castlevania

II, Final Fantasy III, Tetris –" He spins around, and wonders if he looks angrier than Jesús Flores did.

"Which of you took them?" he screams.

The others have moved to their own bags. Mary the ticket lady pats herself down – odd considering Jesús already did that – and says, "I'm not missing anything."

"Me neither," says Ken Nishimura, who has moved painfully to his bags and now has them open in front of him.

His wife is doing the same, and says, "My stuff's all here, I think." She sounds shaky but is not screaming or panicking or crying. That is good.

Adam S. Miles *does* feel like screaming and panicking both. Not good. "Where – where…" he gasps.

Bella Ricci and Taylor the possibly sick girl share a look, and Bella Ricci shrugs. "Everything on me is still on me," she says.

"Are you *missing* anything?" Taylor the possibly sick girl asks, and even Adam S. Miles, still in the grips of pre-panic, can tell she is speaking oddly.

"I have everything on me that I had on me a few minutes ago," says Bella Ricci evenly.

Taylor the possibly sick girl frowns. She slouches a bit, but turns to Jesús Flores. "That's what I was going to say." She points at the headless body near the front doors. "The 'thief' is already *dead*, and he doesn't have anything of ours – we would have found it when we searched his stuff. So that means those things out there did it. To push us." She juts out her chin at Jesús Flores. "Or maybe it's evil, so there's no reason for it, like you said." She turns to Adam S. Miles. "Maybe it's alien, so we just can't understand it at all, like you said." She turns a slow half-circle, looking at everyone who is left. "Either way, the problem isn't in here. It's out there. We're doing what it wants. It's pushing us around, and we're going to end up just killing each other."

Jesús Flores looks like he is genuinely considering this. Adam S. Miles barely cares. He is going through his bags. The games are not there, the GameBoy is not there – of course they are not, why would he put them there when he *never* puts them there – but he cannot stop going through his suitcases over and over.

Jesús Flores stumbles toward the vending machine in the corner. He reaches in the hole made by Ken Nishimura and withdraws a Twix bar. He opens it with loud crinkles, then slowly eats.

"You're the diabetic," says Clarice Nishimura. "The bag has your insulin."

By way of answer, Jesús Flores points his knife at her. "I *will* find my bag," he says.

Ken Nishimura groans suddenly, clutching at his chest with one hand, his side with the other. Clarice Nishimura draws him to a chair.

Adam S. Miles cannot find his games. They are gone. If he lets himself think on that too long, he will go crazy. So he has to do something else. Has to look for commonalities. For some reason they are all here, because though he spoke of the inscrutable nature of true alien life, he cannot believe that is the case. There has to be some sense here, some purpose. Sense – the ordering of unordered things, the putting to rights that which has fallen to chaos – is one of the things that relaxes him.

He reaches out for Ken Nishimura and Clarice Nishimura. "Wait," he says. "Do not sit down. It makes sense to continue to look for clues that –"

Ken Nishimura just sits, moaning and grimacing in pain as he does. His wife grimaces, too, and says quietly, in a voice

Adam S. Miles suspects is meant only for her husband, "Don't do that again. I can't... I can't lose you."

Adam turns to his bags. Considers whether to look for his GameBoy and his cartridges again. This would be a time when it is a crutch of the kind he does not need, so he decides against it. But he *does* need to move. To do something.

"It makes sense to continue our investigation," he says.

He starts looking through Shelly Sherman's bags. Then, he knows, he will examine the bags of Jeremy Cutter. They have already been looked through, but perhaps something has been missed.

Adam S. Miles has to continue. Stopping will allow him to think of what is happening, and that will drive him mad. There is too much to focus on, too much information – at the same time, and none at all. Impossible. Nonsense.

So he keeps looking through the bags. He cannot stop.

He has to make sense of this.

The sense of it... is all he has left. Randomized events may occur, but life is best when he can find the underlying sense, structure it to his convenience, then push it in a way that the blocks all line up and the game continues. He gets high scores in Tetris that way, but it is more than that.

Ultimately, finding sense has been his key to success. And now he knows it is even more than that. Now it is the key to his survival.

8. Peaceful lies

Big J was back.

Mary knew it was ridiculous, but that was how she felt: like she always did in those moments right before Big J woke up and decided what ring of Hell he would send his daughter to that day. He always snuffled and snorted, great gasping snores that broke in irregularly, coming faster and faster as he surged toward the waking world.

Then, always, one of his own snorts would wake him. He would look around. He would see her there if she was unlucky. When she *wasn't* there, "unlucky" didn't begin to describe it. She knew from an early age she was expected to be around when he was awake, and to take care of him in ever-increasing stages.

She worried a bit about that. Because sometimes when Big J beat her, there was a look in his eyes that mirrored that of the grocer who had invited her into the back room. Sometimes, she worried if the "help" Big J required of her would find ways to become even uglier.

But she didn't know. So she attuned herself to wait, to hear the call of his rising, to be there when he opened his eyes and said something.

She felt like that now. Something was waking up.

Something was *coming*.

She reached for Taylor. She couldn't believe it earlier, when Taylor clutched at her like she mattered, like it was just them against the world again.

She couldn't believe, either, the understanding that had begun to force its way into the upper levels of her mind.

Her daughter was gone. At least, the Taylor she had known was gone; the daughter Mary had thought she still had –

all evidence to the contrary – was no longer in existence. She had a daughter, yes, but it was a creature who had grown and become something different than Mary had believed; certainly different than Mary had hoped.

Still, there was that embrace. That moment when Taylor clung to her.

Mary wanted that moment back. So even though she knew it was the wrong thing to do, even though every instinct she had screamed at her that trying to recover that moment would only push it further away, she reached for her daughter. The instincts screamed, but the *need* she had was simply too great.

The instincts were not smug. They did not cross invisible arms and say, "I told you so," when Taylor shoved Mary's hand back and shouted, "Don't touch me!"

The instincts were part of Mary. So like every other part of her, they broke a bit inside.

Taylor had been shivering. Her face was dripping with sweat one moment, bone dry the next. Mary knew what she was seeing, but didn't want to admit it so she pushed it away.

We can get out of this. I got us out of the hood, so I can get us out of this.

A lie. But it helped her in this moment, so she believed it so thoroughly that no other reality could sink in. The lie was armor. The lie made her reach for her daughter again.

At least this time Taylor didn't shout. She took a huge breath, gasping it out in snuffling bits.

Snorts. Like Big J. She's becoming what I tried to keep her from. Becoming him… or maybe just one of the people he supplied. The headless man that Big J killed.

Then Taylor leaned pointedly away from Mary. "Just give me some space," she murmured.

Mary saw but chose not to see the moment when her baby leaned away from her, and toward Bella.

Is Bella *the Big J in the room?*

She didn't think so. Bella was obviously a hardened kid, but did she rise to that level? No. Impossible. Big J was dead and gone, and there couldn't possibly be another one like him.

Certainly not me. Certainly not Taylor.

But that wasn't exactly true, either, was it? Because hadn't Mary herself committed more than a crime or two? Hadn't she been willing – for a while at least – to hurt people if it got her a bit closer to the next dollar, the next score, the next moment where she could buy her way out of the life she hated?

No. I'm not Big J. Taylor *isn't Big J.*

(You're lying.)

She looked around, trying to find something that she could cling to on a night where she felt like she'd lost the entire life of protection she had tried to build for her family. She spotted Ken and Clarice. They had leaned close – they had been so close, all night, barely ever more than a foot or two from one another! – and were whispering to each other. Different whispers than earlier; no honeymoon eyes or loving caresses with that hint of sex that drips from the newly married and still happy. But the love was still there.

Mary needed that. She needed to feel it, if only reflected from another source.

She walked toward them. A few feet away, Ken noticed her. He surged to his feet, arms wide, his wife behind him. "Get back, or –"

Clarice looked at Mary. Her eyes flitted to Taylor, then back again, and Mary thought she saw a kind of recognition in the other woman's eyes. A shared moment of pain.

"It's okay, Ken," she said. She pulled her husband back, the sleeves on her arms rising again to show her scars. She saw

Mary notice and visibly resisted the impulse to pull at her sleeves, gesturing instead at the seat beside her. "Take a load off," she said.

Mary did. She had her own hands clutched in her lap. She stared at the darkness of her skin, shadowed in the greater darkness of the night all around. She wondered if she might disappear into the night. Just melt away and be gone.

"I'm so scared," she whispered, and knew it wasn't just the The Other that scared her. Maybe it wasn't even what scared her most. She looked up. Searching the way she had a moment ago, looking for something real and true and *good*.

Something sparkled. Mary grasped the light, holding to the brightness as she pointed at the ring on Clarice's finger. "That's lovely," she said.

Ken laughed, a humorless tone with surprising edge to it. "You want to talk *jewelry*?" he said.

Mary looked at the sign on the wall. Still counting down. 48:27… 48:26… 48:25… "Better that than start voting," she said.

Clarice nodded and sat forward. She would play along, Mary saw, and wondered if that was the recognition she had sensed: the need in both of them to hide from the reality of the moment.

Clarice held up her ring, looking at it. Even in the gray light of the fog and the occasional whip-blade of the flashlight Taylor still held, it managed to glow. "It is beautiful, isn't it?" she said. "The lady – Shelly – commented on it earlier, too. Even the police officer." She laughed quietly. "When Ken showed it to me, I thought he'd stolen it. It's a bit much for a guy who works at an accounting firm that mostly consults for public defenders on cases where the accused can't even afford to pay their own costs."

Ken looked supremely uncomfortable. "Honey, she doesn't want to hear all this…"

Mary nodded. "Yes. I do. It's nice. Nice to… forget…"

"He told me the story and I almost *died,*" said Clarice. She nearly shouted the last word, the way one does when telling a story for the fiftieth time… and still enjoying it. She held the ring before her eyes, close enough that it probably blocked most everything else.

Mary understood that. Sometimes you *needed* to shove something beautiful up close, so you could pretend that the beauty was *all* there was. "What's the story?" she asked.

"It was his grandmother's," said Clarice. "And I finally got to wear it myself yesterday." She didn't drop her hand, but her voice changed as she said, "Hopefully I'll still be wearing it tomorrow."

She looked at Ken with something like worship. He had looked uncomfortable, and now looked like whatever was six steps past that. He cleared his throat and looked away. His gaze settled on Adam, who was still rifling through bags. "I'm gonna go help him." He smiled at Mary. "Don't let her talk about the honeymoon," he said.

Something in his eyes said that was *exactly* what he wanted Clarice to talk about, and as he moved off Mary wondered what it was about the ring he didn't want to think about.

But he was entitled to his secrets, wasn't he?

Weren't they all?

Mary watched Ken go to Adam and join in the Great Luggage Toss. A moment later, Taylor joined in. Mary had no idea what they were looking for, and suspected none of them knew, either.

Bella waded into the fray. She took one of Shelly's bags, dumped it unceremoniously on the floor, and began pawing through its contents.

Mary didn't want to look at Bella, or address the thoughts –

(if she hurts my baby i'll kill her if she's big j i'll kill her)

– that kept running through her mind. She turned back to Clarice and said, "You're on your honeymoon?"

Clarice nodded. She was watching Ken with open adoration. "His grandparents' honeymoon, actually." Off Mary's confusion, she laughed a bit and said, "They met at an internment camp in Utah, where they were married. Their honeymoon was a trip from there to Los Angeles after they were released, and Ken wanted to follow the same route they took." She looked at her ring again, smiling, obviously lost in the memory of only a few hours before. "His grandmother didn't have a ring until she'd been married for thirty years, when Ken's grandfather gave her this one. Both of them are gone now, but they left the ring to Ken, to give to whoever was lucky enough to catch him." She looked at Mary, suddenly radiant as she said, "And that was *me*."

Mary reached out. She took the other woman's hand and squeezed it. Not the one with the ring, because neither of them wanted to cover that light right now.

"That's sweet," she whispered. Then she let go of Clarice's hand and said, "Though I still don't know if it's enough to make a Greyhound Honeymoon worth it." She grimaced. "Too many sticky seats. And the bathrooms in the buses certainly aren't romance-inducing."

"I'll admit, neither of us signed up for the Alien Encounter Package," said Clarice. She rubbed at her arms, and when she saw Mary notice, she slowly, deliberately, drew up the sleeves on her shirt. She rubbed her hands over the scars, tracing them. "I had a bad childhood. Made hers," she said, nodding toward the back of the terminal, to the baggage area and the body there, "look ideal." She rolled the sleeves back down just as deliberately as she had pulled them up and said matter-offactly, "Ken rescued me. I'd never met a good man before. Not *genuinely* good. That was what made me fall in love with him. It's what saved me."

A dark, jagged laugh cut through the hints of normalcy, the gauzy haze of a moment's contentment. Mary and Clarice looked at the source: Jesús was finishing the candy bar he'd been slowly working on. He still looked sickly, weak. He still looked dangerous, too, and as they watched he ran his knife over his own wrists. Not to cut them, just mocking Clarice.

She shrank into herself a bit, but managed, "I'm sure *you* believe everyone is evil to the core."

"People who are evil to the core usually do," Mary agreed.

Jesús shook his head. "I believe people are just people." He glanced at Red's body. The eyes stared, sightlessly accusing the world that had ended him. "And all people, good or bad, walk a path surrounded by shortcuts. Most of them take one – *for a good cause,* of course," he said, his lips curving into a derisive smile. "But once taken, the shortcuts *become* the path."

In the next instant, Jesús went from a laughing, shaky form in the darkness to a wide-eyed monster. Fear was in his eyes, loud and clear, and that scared Mary almost as much as the fact that he rose to his feet and screamed at everyone, *"I WANT MY BAG!"*

He swung around, knife flashing a deadly arc. People darted out of his path as he lunged back and forth. Mary couldn't tell who the man was attacking. Maybe he was trying to cut his own disease to pieces. But anyone who got in his way would pay the price.

Jesús dove at Adam, who had wandered too close while tearing through the bags in the terminal. Adam yipped and danced away, barely avoiding the blade as it slashed the darkness.

"My bag!" shouted Jesús. "Now! Give it..." His lunges became more and more drunken, and finally he leaned against the wall near the ticket office. He slid slowly down. "My bag. Give it..." He sobbed as he tumbled the last few inches, hitting the floor hard and almost tumbling all the way down to his side. He righted himself at the last second, wiping his forehead with the back of the hand that held the knife, then jabbing the knife a few times in the air. "Please..." he said.

Mary watched him.

People had died. Jesús *was* dying, right before them. And though she didn't mind that, not one bit, she minded how much lack of caring she could find right now.

Let him die.

Let them all *die. Just Taylor has to live.*

That's the end. That's how it turns out.

All in favor.

It's gonna be Taylor. She's my little girl.

9. No more ants

Taylor skidded away from Jesús, same as everyone else. But unlike the others, she was only afraid for a split-second. Because in the moment she ran away, twisting to avoid the blade that hacked at everything and nothing at all, she saw something. The most beautiful, glorious thing she could imagine.

Her purse.

It was back in baggage claim, near the body that rested on the carousel. Taylor and the others had been in there – so close she could have *touched* her purse. None of them had seen it, though, because they had been so focused on the dead body that none of them would notice the bag on the floor not two feet from Shelly's corpse.

But Taylor noticed now. She noticed the purse, and noticed that everyone else was watching Jesús.

She ran for the purse.

The closer she got, the more her skin crawled. She had the sudden feeling that Shelly wasn't really dead – not all the way, at least. Taylor would reach for the purse, then Shelly would reach for her and that would be it. That would be the end of Taylor.

She stopped for a moment. Then the ants dug in deep and hard. They burrowed into the parts of her brain that reminded her what was in the purse, and how very much she needed it.

She darted out a hand, snatched the purse, then ran.

Jesús was playing along as perfectly as if they had planned this moment, because he slumped near the ticket window. Everyone watched him there, and that meant their backs were turned both to the baggage claim and to the bathrooms.

Perfect.

Taylor slunk out of the baggage area. She saw Kingsley move toward Jesús, his face hard as he said, "You better calm down before I –"

Kingsley shouted as Jesús whipped the knife. The deputy evaded most of the attack, but not completely: Taylor saw a gash appear on the arm of his shirt, a thin line of blood trickling through the fabric.

"Can't you do anything, you fat ass?" shouted Bella.

Apparently that touched something off in Kingsley, because he suddenly rounded on Bella. "Hey, I was busting guys before your mother started turning tricks at the gas station, and *way* before you were sending your gross little sex pictures to some guy who probably didn't even know your name."

Bella's eyes went so wide that Taylor flinched. "I'll *KILL YOU!"* screamed Bella.

That was the perfect moment for Taylor to complete her escape. To open the door to the women's bathroom, make sure it closed silently behind her, then head to the closest stall.

She went in, already digging through her purse as she sat on the toilet. She still had Kingsley's flashlight –

(Stupid, I should have put it down so no one noticed the light disappearing but oh well.)

– and aimed it at her purse.

There.

She pulled out the syringe. The tubing. There wasn't much – she'd told Bella the truth about being at the end of her rope, supply-wise. But there was a bit. Hopefully enough to satiate the ants, to put them to sleep and let Taylor dream her way through the rest of this insanity.

She pulled up her shirtsleeve and tied the tube around her arm. Slapped the crook of her elbow. She slid the needle home, and couldn't even feel the pinch.

She pushed the plunger down. Surprised at first, because the liquid in the syringe suddenly looked wrong. But she knew that was just the night, the darkness, the dancing light of Kingsley's flashlight. This was the stuff. She knew it was, because the ants were already slowing down. Quieting.

Too quiet?

Something was wrong.

Taylor felt the ants still. Not satiated or content. They felt *dead*.

She felt herself tumbling into a dark hole. She stood, swaying into the walls of the stall that suddenly seemed on the verge of collapse around her.

The ants were silent. They weren't asleep, they weren't dreaming, and neither was Taylor.

She stumbled toward the bathroom door and as she stumbled she felt herself falling.

The ants were silent. It was what she had wanted. But now she knew there were worse things than ants biting into your skin, your mind, your *soul*.

Worse things beyond the night. Beyond the dark.

Taylor stumbled, tumbled, fell into an anthill deep below the ground of reality. And found a hall of dead, dry things that clutched at her and pulled her to them made her into themselves.

10. I'm going to do it for you

Paul had barely felt the cut when it landed. Jesús' blade felt like it had carved into him at a molecular level. So fast and so sharp that he didn't feel it at first.

A second later, though, the pain hit: a bright, burning line on his forearm. The sudden agony of it fed into the rage he was channeling. He poured it out at Bella, who probably deserved it… but Paul knew he would have tried to punch Ghandi in that instant. He wanted to hurt something, and in his pain and fear he didn't much care what. He screamed the worst thing his mind vomited up from his own pain, screaming at Bella, finishing with the words he knew would pain her: "… and *way* before you were sending your gross little sex pictures to some guy who probably didn't even know your name.""

"I'll *KILL YOU!*" Bella screamed.

Paul screamed right back. The changes he'd felt over the course of this mad night continued. Sometimes he felt small and insane, like Coot must have felt. Sometimes he felt stronger than he had in years, though he didn't know why.

Now was a strong moment. "With *what*?" Paul shrieked at Bella, turning away from Jesús to get right up in the snotty kid's face. "I've never used any of the shitty drugs you peddle, so how could you possibly –"

He stopped. Bella had shrunk away from him, her arm going up as though to shield herself from a blow she knew *must* come. On her face, expressions of fear and contempt warred for supremacy.

It was a set of emotions he had seen before, on the face of the girl he killed, the moment before she died.

He turned to look at the rest of the group, the rest of the *survivors*, and saw the same looks on their faces as the one on Bella's.

He stopped himself in the middle of his sentence, the words fleeing before the power of that moment. He was nothing to them. That was okay, he supposed… except it wasn't. Not when he saw that look in Mary's eyes.

"You all think I'm a joke," he said. "Someone who disgraced his way to the bottom. But you know why I'm here?" He took a step toward Mary, reaching out not in anger or despair, but simple pain. He had never reached out like this before.

She reached out, too. Just a bit. Didn't take his hand or even touch him, but the contempt he saw in her eyes diminished a little.

"You know why I carry a gun with no bullets, and I drink away my days at this shitty place?"

Again Mary's hand twitched upward. Again she didn't touch him. But she came closer, and Paul wondered in that moment what would have been different if he'd reached out like this earlier. If he'd shown himself to her sometime before this horrible night.

"Paul, it's fine," said Mary. Her voice was tender. "You don't need to –"

"I'm here because a fourteen-year-old kid came at me with a double-barreled shotgun when I tried *to put her pimp in cuffs* after he was done beating her. I was trying to save her, and I killed her instead." Paul almost sobbed, feeling the memory hit him. He forced a deep breath, then waved his hand at the terminal windows, at the *un*world beyond. "I'm here because I couldn't stand to see what was out there anymore." He looked at his own hand. It held nothing. Just empty.

Like me.

"I knew I'd see the same stupidity in here," he said, and laughed a bit. "But I hoped I'd see enough people just passing through that… I don't know… they'd be better. I mean, whoever

I saw would be traveling. And people travel so they can go to good things, so that meant the people I saw would be happy, wouldn't they?" He gave another tittering laugh, dismayed at the sound of it but unable to stop. "Just playing the numbers, you know? But the only thing I ever saw was more selfishness and pettiness and spite." He opened his hand, slowly extending it toward Mary. "The closest I ever see to something I *want* to see, Mary, is how you treat your daughter."

He felt his eyebrows go up when he said that, surprised that he had found it in himself to allow the honesty of the moment. He saw Mary's surprise, too, and knew that he was going to crawl into himself when she inevitably, *rightly*, laughed in his face.

She didn't, though. She smiled. It was probably the first real smile he'd seen tossed his way in years, and certainly the first one she had given him. He didn't begrudge her that. He had earned every bit of her dismissiveness, her suspicion, her fear. But he didn't want it anymore. He didn't want any of those things.

Most of all, he didn't want to be Coot. He wanted to be what he had been: a good cop, a good man.

"I just thought you should know," Paul said. "You and Taylor are the only reasons I didn't go Full Coot." He laughed at the confusion on Mary's face, knowing she wouldn't understand that last, knowing that he would tell her if she asked. But whether she asked or not, she knew this: he wasn't the person he had been. He was more. He was the man who watched her without hatred, but with the admiration borne of a soul that knew what evil looked like.

"You're not evil," he said quietly. "The whole world, but not you or Taylor." He smiled. "You've done good by her, you know?"

Mary looked embarrassed. Her cheeks flushed so bright they seemed to light up the darkness –

(and it is dark, why is it so dark, something wrong about that...)

– and she looked at her feet. Then she looked up and frowned. "Wait." She looked around and Paul realized what she was looking for at the same moment. He realized what had bothered him about the darkness: his flashlight had illuminated the place, if only a bit. It had disappeared some time ago. Now he knew where it had gone.

Mary figured it out at the same moment, and both said the same thing at the same time: "Taylor?"

Taylor was nowhere to be seen. "I'll check the back offices. You check the bathrooms," he said to Mary. Jesús was still making muffled, mewling noises behind them, but suddenly the *Mara Salvatrucha* member mattered less than nothing.

Mary nodded, but neither of them had a chance to take more than a step before the door to the women's bathroom slammed open. Taylor came out, and Paul would have pulled his own eyes out to save Mary the sight of her daughter tumbling onto the floor. The tube on her arm made it easy to see what had gone on in the bathroom. The look on her face made it even easier to see that something in there had gone dreadfully wrong.

"Taylor!" Mary screamed. She ran toward her child, and Paul followed as fast as he could.

Taylor stopped slide-stoop-falling for a moment. She turned her face toward Mary, but Paul could tell instantly she wasn't seeing her mother. Probably not much of anything. Her eyes widened, and she said, "Mom? It'sh kinda... shtrange..." in slurred, thick voice.

She fell, the flashlight she had been holding plummeting to the floor. The light hit the cheap tile and bounced, clattered, rolled. The light spun, disorienting Paul. He heard the others scream as though the light might hurt them somehow.

Taylor drooped in place, then fell backward…

She hit a wall… bounced…

Fell.

Adam, who was closest to her, caught Taylor, his face looking both surprised at the weight of her and thoroughly uncomfortable to be touching her. "Help!" he shouted in a voice jittering on the raw edge of panic.

Clarice got there first, somehow. She helped ease Taylor to the floor, rolling her over. As she did, Taylor's other hand opened. Something made a small, dry *click* on the floor. God or the devil or whoever was in charge of the night must have had a wicked sense of humor, because the twirling light came to a stop, finally, illuminating what she had been holding: the empty needle she must have used on herself.

Mary was reaching for Taylor now, but Ken stopped her. "Give her room," he shouted as Mary started clawing at him. "Clarice is her best shot at help."

That seemed to sink in. Then a terrible darkness came over Mary, and Paul saw her face contort in the most terrible expression he had ever seen. She turned on Bella, who was peering at it all like a looky-loo at a traffic accident. No connection on her face to the tragedy that was playing out. Just idle, shallow curiosity.

"You!" Mary shouted. "*You* did this to her!"

Mary moved fast. In an eyeblink she was in front of Bella, shoving her hard, knocking her down.

Bella took a few swipes as Mary loomed over her, trying to hit the woman who had metamorphosed from simple terminal employee to outraged mama bear. Paul heard himself shout in anticipated pain, knowing that there was no way someone as good and gentle as Mary –

He drew up short, shocked as Mary batted away Bella's attack. She did it casually, easily as someone who'd been in a thousand fights. Like someone who knew the ins and outs of pain – and not just from the receiving end.

Mary shoved Bella flat, then dropped on top of her. One knee planted on either side of the smaller girl, straddling her stomach, Mary began raining down blows on Bella's face with the precision of a career MMA fighter. "You stay away from my daughter, you hear? Stay away from her you… *little… BITCH!*"

Bella screamed and tried to roll away. Mary aimed a straight punch into Bella's left breast, then followed that up with a devastating left hook into the side of the girl's head. "Maybe next time you'll *think* about what you're doing. Every… time… you look… in the mirror, you'll remember…"

Bella's face had turned to a misshapen, lumpy mass of blood and bruising. Her cheek had a strange divot to it that made Paul suspect she was going to be disfigured for life.

No one tried to stop her. No one moved at all, and Paul could see the shock on their faces as everyone realized how much they had underestimated the potential strength and ferocity of the kind woman at the ticket window.

Paul was no less shocked than they, but he felt himself moving, pulling Mary off Bella. It wasn't because it was the cop thing to do, or even maybe the right one. But he couldn't let her go on. Couldn't let her do this to someone else.

Mary fought him like a rabid creature. She cursed and screamed, flailing at him, raking at his eyes. Other hands joined in: Adam. The kid was pulling at her, too, trying to pin Mary's arms to her sides.

It took all their strength to pull Mary away from the now-sobbing Bella. And still she struggled, until Paul managed to get his lips close to her ear. In a funereal whisper, he said, "Mary, go to her."

The fight went out of Mary as she looked toward her daughter. She pulled away from Paul, all the grace and physical self-possession she had just demonstrated fleeing in an instant as she stumbled toward her daughter. She fell at the side of her girl.

Taylor didn't notice. Her face moved, but only because it was bouncing up and down minutely with each chest compression Clarice gave her. Taylor's eyes were open. They stared up, and saw nothing.

Paul saw the eyes of that kid who had taken a shot at him. He saw himself kneeling beside her after he shot her, pushing against the sucking wounds he had given her.

The worst thing that had ever happened to him, and now it was happening to Mary. Worse, even, because at least Paul hadn't known that poor girl from so long ago, let alone birthed her and watched her grow up.

"Don't you do this, Taylor," Mary was sobbing. She took her daughter's hand. "Stay with me, baby."

Clarice tilted Taylor's chin upward. A few puffs. Taylor's chest rose and fell as the breath was pushed into her and leaked out again. There was no movement behind the movement. No motion from Taylor, just physics pushing air into an empty vessel.

"You're getting out of this place, Taylor. Getting out of this town, out of all this..." Mary was looking down, but Paul could tell she was seeing nothing of this place. Just the same darkness Paul had seen as that girl died in his arms.

Clarice finally sat back. She shook her head, and wiped at the tears that had been dropping down on Taylor's face and chest for some time. Ken touched her shoulder and she grabbed his hand so tightly he gasped.

Mary sat silently. Paul didn't know what to do for her. There was nothing *to* do. Just wait. Watch.

Mary leaned forward. She crossed Taylor's hands across her chest. She kissed her daughter on the forehead.

She stood.

She turned.

She began walking toward Bella.

Paul moved between them. "Don't," he said. A rushing sound seemed to envelope him. He was in the middle of a moment that would be an earthquake to his life. It would define the new landscape of his universe, for however long that lasted.

He would not let that earthquake blast Mary.

"I have to –" Mary began.

The earthquake roared in his ears, in his mind. "You don't," he said. Then the earthquake stilled. Silence everywhere as he turned to Bella and said, "Because I'm going to do it for you."

One of Bella's eyes was a swollen purple plum of a thing, bubbling grotesquely out of her flesh from the top of her now-ruined cheek to her hairline. It didn't even look like she had an eyebrow on that side, the skin was stretched so taut.

There was no way she could see anything out of that ruined eye. But the other eye was whole. It rolled back in its socket, but flopped forward in time to see Paul striding toward her. She began screaming. Batted at him with hands and fists even more pitiful than when she had tried the same thing with Mary.

Paul punched her. Hard. Right in the middle of the face. As her head lolled, he grabbed her shirt and began dragging her. "Let go of me," said Bella. At least, he thought that was what she said; the actual sounds were closer to a bubbling, loose, "Leggoahmuh."

He laughed. Kept dragging her.

Bella's eye must have been working enough to see where he was dragging her. What was coming next. "No!" she shouted ("Nuh!") and then again, "No no no!" ("Nuh-nuh-uh!") as he yanked her forward.

Beside him, Paul saw Ken take a few steps, as though he was going to try and stop what was happening. Mary shoved Ken hard enough that Paul heard the man's teeth clack together. "She killed my baby," she hissed.

"This isn't the right way –" Ken shouted, as Clarice, still kneeling beside Taylor's body, screamed, "Stop, please stop!"

Ken took a small step toward Paul, who had dragged Taylor far enough that he was now standing beside the headless corpse of Jeremy Cutter. He stepped over the body, dragging Bella along so she bounced and rolled over the headless thing. She twisted in Paul's grip and he let her, just enough to turn over and flop face-first into headless stump of a neck. She screamed as her own face flopped into what was left of the man who had promised her the world.

Paul would give her that. He would give her the *real* world as they now knew it.

He got to the entry doors. They slid open. No apparent power in the terminal, other than the countdown on the wall. But they opened nonetheless, because that was what The Other wanted.

Paul picked up Bella. Held her upright and looked at the one untouched eye that sat like an interloper in the ruined landscape of her face. "You shouldn't have," he whispered.

"Please," sobbed Bella ("Pweeeese").

The line of fog waited outside the terminal, hanging where it was without moving in. Paul looked into it, seeing nothing but the fog. Nothing but that ghostly, ghastly gray.

For a moment, he wondered what he was doing; what he was *about* to do. For a moment, he thought about letting Bella drop safely inside. Dragging her back and waiting until the glass doors closed on the mist and The Other.

Then a single, thin tendril reached into the terminal. The rushing sound came back to his ears, only now it was centered on his hip. Frowning, Paul felt there. Felt the vibration. Pulled out his phone. It stopped buzzing as he did, the screen glowing bright, the words clear:

The Other: do it

Paul still heard the rushing in his ears. He looked at Bella, and wondered if he could if he would if he *should*.

He looked at Mary, who nodded. He looked at Clarice and Ken, who looked pointedly away. He looked at Jesús, who laughed. When he looked at Adam, the kid looked more relieved and at peace than he had in hours. "It makes sense," whispered Adam.

Paul nodded. "It sure does," he said. Then looked back at Bella and smiled as he threw her out of the terminal and into the world of The Other.

Bella screamed as she flew out into the mist. She tripped off the curb behind her, and Paul heard her shriek as she hit the ground, no doubt losing even more skin to the rough asphalt of the parking slips.

Paul felt more than saw the others come to stand beside him. Watching the form in the mist.

The doors slid shut in front of them. They severed the single reaching tendril of mist that had entered to call Bella into itself. The tendril puffed and disappeared.

Bella did not. She managed to stand and ran for the doors. She hammered her fists into them, screaming wordlessly. The doors didn't open. Paul and the others, save Jesús, who was still on the floor far back, laughing more and more weakly, stared at her.

"Pweeeeeassssse," she slurred. Blood flecked the glass as she forced the word out of a ruined mouth.

Something surged behind her. The mist grew at the same time, becoming so dense that there was no way to see what was happening. But Bella's hands flew forward and down as her feet flew forward and up. They nearly touched, so completely did she fold in half as something yanked her into the mist.

Then she was gone.

A few minutes later, the fog outside the glass cleared… just enough to show the new, huge, bloody patch on the sidewalk a few feet away.

Mary fell into Paul then, weeping, "My baby, my baby."

Paul held her.

He watched the mist.

It was all he could do.

Interlude

Inside the terminal, panic reigns supreme.

The Watchers have seen this many times. They know, now, that there are two different branches of panic. The first instigates movement without thought: rapid motion that tries to subsume terror in action – useless, thoughtless action.

The second kind creates the opposite effect: no movement, no mania. Thought is subsumed, but this time in inertness so total the panicked creature looks more corpse than living being.

The people in the terminal are experiencing the second variety, at least for now.

When the youngest female dies, the Watchers note it. They expected it to happen. They *allowed* it to happen, as they allowed all this night to exist in the first place. Pushing the people in all the right ways, from turning off the power to allowing the young male's game to continue working. It is all calculated. It is all part of the plan.

They take note.

They are almost surprised when, instead of further stupor, the objects of their attention directly act against one of their own, well ahead of projected responses.

Up until now, everything has been standard: the fog, the introduction of the previous Cycle, the isolation as computers and cell phones are cut off from the outside world.

But this is new. Things have become interesting.

The Watchers communicate with the Engineers. The Engineers, in turn, send messages to the various communication devices belonging to the captives in the terminal.

The Watchers, the Engineers. Together they are *not* The Other. But they act for The Other, and that means they are powerful.

The one whom the men and women of the terminal deem at fault is ejected from the terminal.

The Watchers do nothing. For this part, there is another group. The ones that neither Watchers nor Engineers acknowledge. They are called for several times each Cycle, as the various objects of interest test the rules.

The Killers sweep forward. They take Bella Ricci, and they destroy her.

She screams, as she realizes at least some small part of what is happening to her. She sees the Killers, and understands a bit – *no one* fully grasps what is happening, even when it is happening to them – then she screams louder as the Killers begin their work.

Then she screams no more. She has been removed from the Cycle.

The Watchers attend the process. They watch her final moments. A few watch the terminal.

The Killers finish with the woman. The Watchers analyze everything, for that is their purpose here. To watch, to see, to understand.

When the Killers are done, the Watchers turn back toward the terminal.

The end is begun. The final countdown has started, and the ensuing panic should be interesting.

They know much more than do the ones left inside the terminal. They have watched, and seen, and understood. They know who is alive, who is dead – of course they do, for that is one of the things they watch closest. They know all things that happen in the terminal, many of which the subjects there do not know. Yet.

The Watchers are curious, one and all, which of the things the subjects will discover, which of the surprises they will manage to ferret out. This group is much cleverer than most have been. They have lasted farther into the Cycle than any other subject group.

That is interesting, the Watchers agree among themselves.

Then they all – Watchers, Engineers, and Killers – grow silent as the final moments begin.

The time has come for final voting.

The Other has deemed it so.

PART FOUR: All In Favor

1. Eres tú

There was a lot going on – Mary knew that.

A lot was about to happen – the clock on the wall, which had come down to 18:26 (…25… 24…) testified to that fact. But the one thing that kept dancing in Mary's head was this: her daughter was dead. Taylor was gone.

Paul held Mary for a moment after he threw Bella to The Other. She was surprised that she let him do that, and even more surprised that it felt good.

She sat with Taylor. The headless corpse of Jeremy Cutter lay on her other side, close enough to touch. She didn't care. She saw Taylor. Occasionally Taylor seemed to disappear, replaced by the man with the wrecked face, killed by Big J all those years ago. Once she thought she saw Big J himself, a Kool hanging from his lower lip as he grinned through his own bullet-ruined smile.

She knew they were not really here. Just like she knew Taylor was no longer here. The body was not her daughter. The body held none of the soul or brightness or the hope that Mary had invested in her child.

Clarice knelt beside her at one point. Mary tensed, expecting some kind of sympathy. She did not want that.

But Clarice only examined Taylor –

(Taylor's body*)*

– and then moved away, muttering to herself.

A few moments later, Paul took up a position next to Mary, hands folded in front of him, head bowed.

The gesture surprised her. She heard his words to her, over and over: what he had seen, his reasons for being here.

Most of all, she saw him holding her back, telling her she wasn't going to do anything to Bella, because *he* would do it. It was the kind of thing a loving father might do. The kind of thing Big J would *never* have done. He might have killed someone for profit, or to make a point, or because he felt disrespected. Rarely for vengeance, though… and even when vengeance *was* the endgame, it was always rooted in one of those three other reasons: profit, making a point, dealing with disrespect.

Never because of love lost.

Mary glanced at Paul, wondering what her life might have been like if she had had him as a father. She even wondered, for a moment, how *he* would have turned out if he had had her for a child.

She thought things would have been different. She suspected neither of them would have been here, in this desperate place on this most desperate of nights.

"I hope you're happy," said Clarice.

Mary looked at the woman. "What?" Mary said. Her voice sounded wooden, inert.

"That girl didn't kill your daughter," Clarice said, pointing out the window where, if you tried very hard, you could still make out a bloody patch through the mist. She waited, and as Mary's understanding swam upward, clawing its way back from the darkness of Taylor's death, Clarice jerked a thumb in Jesús' direction. "And he's probably going to die now, too. Because unless I miss my guess, your daughter OD'd taking his insulin."

Mary looked at Jesús. The *Mara Salvatrucha* gang member was slumped against the wall. His head had slipped to the side, and he mumbled to himself. His eyes were glassy, his sight far beyond the terminal.

"I don't understand," said Mary in the same heavy tones.

Clarice's expression softened. "Someone switched whatever..." She gestured at Taylor, lost her voice, swallowed, and started again. "Someone switched what she was taking for his meds."

Mary saw Adam stand and look out into the mist. "Do you think it was The Other?" he said.

Ken took up position behind Clarice, looking over her head into the same mist that Adam watched. Ken shook his head. "It's only killed people who went outside," he said.

"The leading hypothesis was that they *have* intruded in here," Adam reminded them.

"Sure," said Clarice. "To move things around and shake us up. To send us messages and provide power at the worst possible moments," she added, holding up a dark cell phone and nodding at the same time at the sliding glass exit doors. "But that's different than *killing* someone," Clarice continued. "They seem to want one or all of us to be the ones who get our hands dirty that way."

"But we've been together for the whole time," said Paul. "We would have seen –"

"No," said Ken softly. "We wouldn't. Just like we didn't see Shelly kill herself, or Taylor go into the bathroom."

Clarice turned and did an odd half-crawl toward Jesús. She stopped a good ten feet away, well out of reach of any final lunges with the knife he still clenched in his fist. She bent down further, bringing her head level with his. "Did you see anyone near your bag?" she asked.

Paul snapped his fingers. "The thief," he said.

"What?" asked Clarice, turning a bit to look at him.

Mary felt the world spinning. Everything flattening.

And Taylor is dead.

Taylor is dead.

My baby is dead.

"The voices said one of us was a thief. But that guy," said Paul, pointing at Jeremy's headless corpse, "was already dead. So maybe the thief is still here. Maybe whoever it is took the bags and switched out a needle full of heroin for a needle full of insulin."

Mary glanced at Taylor, then turned toward Clarice. "That's the kind of thing a nurse would know how to do, isn't it?" she in a low tone. "Maybe one who wanted to be last one standing?"

Clarice paled and moved back a step. She seemed to realize that she was now getting closer to Jesús, and stopped. "Why would I kill your daughter and then let you know that the person you thought did it was innocent?" she asked quietly.

Ken moved toward his wife. Mary hated the look on his face. Why should he have the thing he loved, and not her?

"Easier to stay on the island if people like you," said Paul. He moved forward, and Mary saw a bit of the dangerous glint in his eye that she knew must surely be shining from her own. "Doesn't mean –"

"I know who the thief is," said Jesús. He chuckled quietly, forcing himself to sit up as everyone oriented on him.

"It's *her*," said Mary, pointing at Clarice, not knowing if it was because she actually believed that or just because she needed someone to blame, someone to hurt the way Big J hurt people sometimes. She understood that now. Taylor was gone, so what purpose was there in pretending otherwise?

"No," Jesús was shaking his head. "Not her."

"Then *who*?" demanded Paul. "Spit it out."

Jesús smiled. His mouth was a black pit, nothing behind it but pain and impending death.

He nodded at Ken. "I will only tell him," he said.

Ken appeared confused. He looked at Jesús. It was obvious he wanted to hear what Jesús would say. Just as obvious he was afraid of the man.

Jesús sank even farther down than before. His body seemed to deflate before Mary's eyes. He was going. But he managed a weak wave toward Ken.

Ken stepped forward.

Another step...

Passing Clarice, who reached for him without making contact...

He knelt beside Jesús.

Jesús grabbed Ken. Even in this, his last few moments, he was fast. He took Ken's hand in a literal death grip, jerking himself upright and whispering, loudly enough to be heard by everyone, "The thief... *eres tú, amigo*. It's you."

2. No more than she deserved

Clarice didn't speak Spanish, but she knew, somehow, what Jesús' words meant. Even before he repeated them in English, she knew from Ken's face. Something was wrong. Something *had* been wrong for a while – and not just the problems caused by The Other. She had counted it as wedding jitters, but…

Ken's hands flailed at Jesús, trying to get him to let go. "That's ridiculous, ridiculous," he said, a mantra of denial.

Jesús grinned at Ken, then grinned even wider at Clarice. "You remember our talk about shortcuts? Your husband took his when he agreed to launder money for a client. He stepped further off the path when he started stealing from that man."

"No!" Ken shouted. He looked around wildly. "Help me!"

No one but Clarice moved. She was still on her knees, and shuffled forward a few inches, then stopped as Jesús shook Ken hard. "Stealing from him… enough to pay for a lifestyle beyond your means, enough to buy a diamond ring you had to lie about."

Clarice felt the sharp edges of the diamond wedding ring as she twisted it around her finger. Around, around, around… "Ken?" she said.

"He's lying," Ken insisted.

But he wasn't, she could tell. "Holy hell," muttered Kingsley, and Clarice could tell from the sound of his voice that he knew it, too. So did Mary. Even Adam's non-expression had darkened a bit.

"The man he stole from was a low-level criminal," Jesús said, gasping a bit but the firmness of his grip obvious by Ken's failed attempts to escape. "But he worked for others. And those people – *my* people, my family – do not suffer thieves." He yanked Ken close, even as his voice started to slur. "I was supposed to make a long, painful example of you. But since time is short, I will have to settle for exposing what you are, and seeing you lose what matters most in the instant before you die."

Jesús pulled his knife back to kill Ken. Clarice lurched forward, a voice in her mind that she did not recognize as her own screaming, *"No it can't be true Ken wouldn't do this he's good and he's mine and…*

(… and he picked me. *What kind of person would do that? A* good *one?*

No.)

She would have pulled back if she could. Would have withdrawn from him, and from the world. Eventually, she would have turned the knives on herself again. She would have ended herself – but later.

As it was, "later" became "now." Her lunge took her forward so fast it surprised everyone. It even took the hitman in their midst by surprise, and the knife that he was jabbing forward slid – so softly, so easily, so *kindly* – into her throat.

Ken screamed, "Clarice!" and she felt his hands on her shoulders. She batted them away. Her eyes widened. With pain, yes, but also with betrayal, with the knowledge that this – all this – was what someone like her deserved.

Ken had been her hero. Her savior.

A liar

Ken put his hands on her throat. Part of Clarice's receding consciousness understood that he was probably trying to stop the bleeding, but that wasn't what it felt like. It felt like he was strangling her.

That was certainly no more than she deserved.

3. Small starts

It was all falling apart around Ken. First the fog – that damnable, ugly, empty fog! – then the people dying. Now Clarice: the one thing he hadn't managed to sully, to spoil.

But of course, that was a lie. He spoiled everything. That was what people like him *did*.

Clarice gasped and beat against Ken's hands, but the strikes came weaker and weaker until they were just the wings of a moth, flapping against his flesh in the darkness.

"No, no, no," he said. "Not you. Don't die."

He said the words, then shouted them, then *shrieked* them.

Clarice died anyway. Died and, at the last, looked away from him. Her eyes didn't slide up and away like he had seen in movies or read about in books, though. Clarice was just making sure his face wasn't the last thing she saw. She even turned her head a bit, sending one last gout of blood surging over his hands, arcing into his face.

She died, and her blood was on his skin. On his hands.

He flung himself back, not knowing what he was going to do before he did it. Then he was on top of Jesús, driving him into the ground. He punched Jesús, who smiled as his teeth broke under Ken's fists.

He heard screaming and didn't know if it was him or if it came from someone else. Maybe it wasn't real at all. Maybe it was just what he heard in his soul.

His skin split against Jesús' teeth, nose, jaw. His knuckles broke as he punched. Ken had never been in a fight like this, and he was bad at it. He wouldn't be able to move his hands after this.

He felt something bite his side and looked down to see Jesús slamming his knife into Ken's stomach, over and over in a motion as even and measured as a sewing machine. Only this needle wasn't there to stitch together, but to rend apart. Ken felt his stomach open, felt the blood sluice all around.

It's going to touch her. It's going to touch her blood and then she'll be unclean uncleeeeeeeeeeeeeeaaaaaaaaaaaan!

The shout dissolved even in the confines of his mind. He was barely aware of wresting the knife from Jesús fingers. The other man went loose, and Ken saw his assassin's eyes become blank. He was dead, as though the knife had been his only line to life and once he lost it he had no reason to continue.

Ken looked down. He saw the ragged ruin of himself. He saw the blood falling like rain, then like a waterfall.

He wouldn't die here. Not next to her. He couldn't.

He heard a voice, speaking a monotone. "This makes no sense," said Adam.

And below him, Jesús wasn't dead after all. "Nothing does," he said. Then he *did* die.

Ken saw the waterfall of red. It painted Jesús from top to bottom. That was fine. But not Clarice. He wouldn't spoil her in death as he had in life.

He managed to rise to his feet.

He stumbled past Clarice's beautiful, still form, giving it a wide berth. He stumbled past the other survivors, and they gave *him* a wide berth.

That was fine, too.

He stumbled toward the exit, noticing gobbets of himself, bits of flesh and gore, tumbling away from him. He had become nothing but rapidly-spoiling meat.

The sliding glass doors whispered open.

He wobbled, almost lost his balance. Steadied himself. Someone – he thought it was the ticket lady –

(what's her name i can't remember her name but it started with m like moth or murder or –)

– whispered, "Don't."

He turned. He knew he shouldn't; even his gaze would dirty her. But he had to look at her once more time, if only for an instant. "None of this was my fault," he said. "I just… I just wanted to take care of her, you know?" Something ripped inside him, and a fresh torrent of blood sluiced out of his center, followed by tumbling coils of thick, dark, bowel that burst against the tile at his feet. "It started so small," he said.

He stepped out, into the fog.

Stumbled forward.

The terminal disappeared behind him.

Blue flashes appeared.

Green trios of light.

They circled him as he fell.

Ken looked up, and saw what was in the mist. He hitched in a breath and whispered, "Why?"

But he got no answer as the darkness closed over him and he had nothing but blackness to hold and nothing but the feel of the fog like the wings of a moth across his cheek and then the feel of nothing at all.

4. Fewer is good

Adam S. Miles watches Jesús Flores kill Clarice Nishimura, then watches Ken Nishimura kill Jesús Flores, then watches Ken Nishimura kill himself by walking out.

And none of it – *none of it* – makes any sense at all.

Adam S. Miles starts tapping his forehead with the back of his hand. It is a nervous gesture, one he has not indulged in in years. He is high-functioning, but even someone without his particular gifts and curses would have trouble coping at this moment.

How can he *not* have trouble, when everything is falling apart like this?

But he slows the motion before it moves to the next phase, which is to slap himself on his head, both hands rattling against his skull and creating sensations that will drown out some of the noise that constantly assails him.

His hand stops moving. The back of his hand rests against his hair.

He is thinking.

This is something good: there are fewer of them. Fewer is good.

"All in favor," he whispers. He looks at the clock. There is barely any time left. "Thirteen minutes, twenty-one seconds," he whispers. "Twenty. Nineteen."

He counts to himself.

He wishes he had his GameBoy.

He doesn't, so he has to find something else, some way to make the world make *sense*.

"All in favor."

5. I tried

Paul didn't know what he was going to do, not really; only that he couldn't stop, couldn't give up. There were three of them left: him, Adam, and Mary.

And of the three, only one of them really mattered. Mary was going to make it out, he would see to that.

But how?

He acted without thought, grabbing Mary's hand and drawing her into his office. It was an action drilled into him over years of hiding, but he wasn't really hiding this time. He was thinking, and as he pulled her into the office an idea began to form.

He let go of Mary's hand and went to his desk. Mary drifted to the window that looked out on the parking lot before all this started and now looked only onto featureless gray. "It's actually kind of lovely," she said in the dreamy voice of a drug addict flying high on a world-class score.

Paul turned away from the desk. He got between Mary and the window, holding her shoulders as he said, "It. Is. No. Such. Thing." He shook her with every word, jarring her mind away from the spiral into which it had fallen. It worked, at least a little. Mary blinked a few times and looked at him. "Sorry," he said, "but don't you go thinking of a beautiful death, Mary. We're going to live. End of story."

Paul waited a moment. He had seen the countdown as he entered. Only a few minutes left. He had to hurry, but he had to make sure that Mary didn't fall prey to the fog – either that outside or the creeping, insidious kind that had made its way into Mary's mind.

She nodded at him, telling him she was here. She was present. Darkness outside, yes, but not *inside*. Not yet.

Paul nodded back, then let go of her and went back to his desk. The last of the booze he had found earlier was still there. He hoped it would be enough. "Something I found out when I was still a real cop," he said, grabbing Mary's hand and drawing her back toward the lobby, "was that the measure of a person is what they're like at their worst. You and Taylor fought all the time, but I think – even at the end, even at *her* worst – she loved you. And I know for a fact that you loved her."

Paul was out in the lobby now, still pulling Mary with him.

"I don't think –" Mary began.

"I'm jealous of that," Paul said, talking right over her. He wasn't trying to cut her off, but time was short, and things needed saying. "It probably made me act like an asshole toward both of you, which is stupid as hell considering that you were the only things that kept me going. I'm sorry for that."

He stopped walking. Holding Mary with one hand and the bottle with the other. Mary looked at the booze and said, "That stuff'll kill you."

Paul laughed at that. So did Mary. Adam moved closer to them, clutching his hands tightly as he looked at them both. He saw the bottle, too, and said, "Good idea."

Paul grinned at him. The kid was weird but bright. He'd intuited what Paul was going to do – or try.

"What is?" asked Mary. "What's a good idea?"

Adam started tossing the contents of the various bags they had emptied into a pile in the center of the lobby. Not everything, of course. Just clothing, some papers. Anything that would burn.

Paul joined in. "Go for height, not width," he told Adam. To Mary, he said, "We're going to start a fire."

"Your plan is to burn us to death?" Mary asked.

Paul nodded at the ceiling. Mary followed his gaze, and he knew she would see only darkness. But she'd worked here for years, too. She knew where everything was. She would be able to find her way from one end of the terminal to the other in the pitch darkness without tripping, she'd know where every handle and switch could be found… and she'd know where the fire sprinklers were.

"Pretty much everything in here other than the seats is concrete or metal," said Paul, "so the only thing that's going to burn is what we put on the pile."

He sprinkled the booze across the pile, then began searching the bags again. "Matches, matches," he said, realizing he didn't have the one thing he needed to actually *start* the fire. He sure wasn't going to Boy Scout a blaze into existence, so if they didn't find –

Adam held something out. A lighter. He pointed at one of Shelly's bags. "It was in her luggage," he said.

Paul chuckled. "A gal who knows her way around pills, booze, cigarettes." He whistled as he spun the lighter's wheel. *Snick, snick.* "Hidden depths to that gal."

The third spark caught on the gas, and a flame flitted to life above the lighter. He held it up, waving it in the general direction of the lockers as a salute to the dead woman

Mary was wringing her hands. "But there's no phones, no power. Other than giving us a chance to make s'mores in the next couple minutes, what exactly is this going to accomplish?"

The words were delivered in calm, even tones. Paul had never been interested in her romantically, but he *did* love her. She'd been a good mom, a hard worker. She had represented the things he most missed about life: family, doing a job well because it needed doing, the kindness so absent from his heart for so very long. She was the best thing in his world, and he felt like a father toward her, now more than ever.

He pushed the flame at the pile of paper and clothing, aiming for a dark spot where he'd poured a little extra whiskey. "Fire alarms in public facilities have their own separate power supply, and the alarm is hard-lined directly to the fire department."

Mary squinted at him. "Is that actually true?"

The flame caught. Paul moved the lighter to another spot, coaxing more fire to life. He grinned at Mary. "Sure hope so. It *sounds* good, right?" He jabbed the lighter into the pile again. "So here's to a spot of luck."

The flames soared. A moment later Paul had to move back as the heat of the flame soared as well.

They waited. He tried not to look at the clock. The countdown.

With a *pop*, the fire sprinkler above them activated.

Mary danced out of the way of the cone of water that fell at ten gallons per minute. "Why aren't the rest turning on?" she asked, worry on her face as she looked up at the ceiling, eyes roving to the spots where the rest of the fire sprinklers hung mute and inert.

"It's not like in the movies," said Paul. "They're each individually heat-activated and –"

A fire alarm began to whoop. "Finally," sighed Adam. "Something makes sense…"

"Now the cavalry comes," said Paul. He smiled. So did Adam. The kid's hands were clutched behind his back, obviously holding back nervousness, nearly writhing in place with pent-up energy.

Mary wasn't smiling. "How far away is the fire department?" she asked.

"Close," said Paul. "There's a station only about…" His voice drifted to nothing as Mary pointed at the timer.

10:52… 51…

"They won't get here in time, will they?" Mary whispered.

"They will," Paul insisted, what felt like a chunk of melting lead in his stomach.

"They won't."

"They *will.*"

"We have to choose," said Adam. His movements were even jerkier now, but his eyes were fixed on the countdown. "All in favor, we have to choose, all in favor, we have to choose *now.*"

"How can we possibly do that?" asked Mary.

"We can't," said Paul.

He saw that sink in. Saw Mary understand that they were going to die. And saw her confusion as he smiled at her. "I vote for you, Mary," he said. "Get out of here. Live."

"No," said Adam. "No! I am *not* in favor, and the decision to choose her makes no –"

Paul punched him in the face.

Adam stumbled back, pitching into the still-blazing pile of luggage. He screamed and rolled away, burning.

Paul grabbed the closest thing he thought would finish the job: Jeremy's laptop with its dark, blank screen. It was a heavy block of plastic and metal. He held the laptop high, ready to do what had to be done. Mary would live. She *would.*

Something slammed into him, knocking him away before he could bring the laptop down on the burning kid. The computer went flying, and Paul found himself on his back, fighting whatever had knocked him down. Had kept him from doing *what he had to do.*

Only… it was *Mary* who had slammed him away. She was astride him the same way she had been on top of Bella, and now Paul got to feel the force of her blows himself as she aimed a single, sharp punch that caught him on the side of the ear and sent his vision sideways by a good three inches. "Mary, don't," he said. "You can go. You can live. You can –"

He heaved, managing to shove Mary up and over, then rolling in the opposite direction as she flew off him. He stood but she was faster, rising to her feet and standing squarely between him and Adam. The kid was writhing, the flames spreading across his back and around his shirt. He batted at them with one panicked hand.

"We can't do this anymore," Mary said in a low, hissing voice. "If we do, then how are we any better than whatever's out there? You do this, or I let you do it, and we *deserve* to die."

Paul didn't know what he would have said in response to that. *Something*. Before he could, though, the speakers in the room all activated. The Other spoke, its many voices as different from one another as sun and moon and stars. But the one thing they all had in common: every voice, young and old, male and female, practically oozed with glee.

"Time's a-tickin'!" shouted The Other. "Tickety tock, the clock is almost done, and the three blind mice are gonna run run run!"

Paul reached for Mary. "Please, just let me –"

She stepped back. "No! Not like this!"

Pop. Another sprinkler activated, dousing Adam's body. He rolled in it, slamming into chairs, walls – even into the dead body of the *Mara Salvatrucha* gang member as the flames on his clothing gradually snuffed out.

Paul shook his head. "Sorry, Mary, but you have to live." He lurched to the right, then juked left and right again, managing to fake Mary out and eventually lunging right as she stumbled to his left.

He only got a few steps before he felt arms across his throat and felt Mary's weight come crashing down on him as she leaped to his shoulders. "No!" she screamed. "No!"

Paul gagged, stumbled, but kept moving toward Adam. "Gotta... be... you..." he managed, the words coming out as croaks and groans.

He was at Adam's side. He leaned down, knowing that there was nothing the kid would be able to do. Knowing that he himself would be able to do anything and everything to ensure that Mary got out.

His fingers closed on Adam's shirt. The burnt cloth flaked apart in his hand. The clock was ticking. Paul balled up his fist.

Adam lunged upward. Paul felt something odd. He looked down as Adam hacked Jesús blade from right to left. The thin, so-sharp blade cut through Paul's gut. Blood exploded from him.

Paul fell. Adam didn't let go of the knife. He twisted it, and bright flowers of agony bloomed inside Paul's center. The molten lead that he had felt in his stomach a moment before now felt like it was spilling over his waist and groin and sheeting his legs with warmth.

Then the block of lead was gone. A searing cold took its place.

Paul felt Mary's weight come off him. Heard her scream. He turned a bit, finding her eyes. He smiled wistfully. "Sorry," he managed. "Tried..."

He fell face down in a puddle of water and blood that had melded and become one. The last thing he saw was the countdown on the wall.

6. Into the fog

Adam S. Miles knows that the world is a difficult place. He never imagined it would be *this* difficult. He never imagined that he would have to kill a man. And not just that…

Mary the ticket lady stares at him as he stands. He wipes his hands against his shirt. They are sticky and soon his shirt is sticky too. He does not like it but there is no way to clean it off unless he wants to stand under the water streaming from two spots in the ceiling.

He does not want to do that. He is already messy. He is already a *wreck*. At least – and he knows this is an odd thought, even for him – his GameBoy is not where he left it. Wherever it is, it is not being doused by gallons and gallons of water. Wherever it is, hopefully it is not ruined.

He would like to play a GameBoy again. If not *his*, then *some* GameBoy.

Mary the ticket lady is looking at him. She glances at the countdown on the wall. "Seven minutes, twenty-two seconds," says Adam. "Twenty-one. Twenty…"

Mary the ticket lady seems to come to a decision. She reaches for him. "I vote –"

Adam S. Miles does not let her finish. Perhaps she is going to vote for him. Perhaps not. He is done being here. He is sticky and sweaty and wet and hurting and burnt and he is –

"DONE BEING HERE!" he shrieks. He leaps forward, and Mary the ticket lady's throat is suddenly in his hands. He does not like the feel of it. He does not like her face as she gags and her eyes bug out, so he closes his eyes.

That is a mistake. Mary the ticket lady does something and suddenly he falls and she is on top of him. He does not let go of her neck, though. She tries to pull his hands away. She gets one of them loose and gasps.

Adam S. Miles opens his eyes. He twists and bucks the way he saw Deputy Paul Kingsley do earlier. Mary the ticket lady flies off him and now he is on *her* back. He puts his arm around her throat and is whispering, "I'm sorry I'm sorry sorry sorry. It's the only thing that makes sense..."

Mary the ticket lady is scrabbling across the tile, dragging Adam S. Miles with her as she scrambles across the floor like some life is waiting at the end of the lobby.

That makes no sense.

Mary the ticket lady is on top of Deputy Paul Kingsley's body. Adam S. Miles lets up a little. Maybe she wants to die with the policeman. He glances at the clock and decides he has time to let her do that.

He looks back down in time to see what Mary the ticket lady is *really* doing. She pulls the knife that belonged to Jesús Flores out of Deputy Paul Kingsley's stomach and whips it backward. Adam S. Miles screams as the knife goes into his side.

But he does not let go.

This is the only thing that makes sense, but obviously Mary the ticket lady does not understand that so he explains it to her which is nice of him, he thinks. "You have no one, and nothing," he says. He feels the knife come out of him, then go in again. "Your future is past," he grunts, and steels himself for the next thrust of the knife. It does not come. "Your future is past," he says again as he pulls harder, tighter. He feels her body slacken beneath him but does not let go. She could be pretending. "Your future is past." He says it three more times, each time precisely ten seconds apart. She does not move, and he feels no pulse under his arm or breath coming in or out of her. "Your future is past," he says one last time as he lets go of her, "and mine is not."

Adam S. Miles takes Mary the ticket lady's hand and puts it in the hand of Deputy Paul Kingsley. He thinks that is nice of him, too.

He looks at the countdown.

"Five minutes, forty seconds," he says. "Thirty-nine."

He walks to the exit doors. They open for him. The fog hangs there, still a strange wall that should come inside but does not. He waits a moment, wondering if he is missing anything. He almost steps out, then remembers the most important thing. "I call this vote in session," he says, intoning the words as best he can, wondering if this is how they do it in Congress. It is how they did it once when he was in school and there was a student mock United Nations. He was picked to be Somalia, which he did not like because "Somalia" sounded odd in his mouth and everyone else laughed whenever he raised his hand to ask for something as "Somalia."

This vote will be different. No one here is laughing at him. They are not doing anything at all, Adam is alone, and that is how he likes it. "I vote for me," he said. "All in favor?" he looked around. "The 'ayes' have it."

He steps out of the terminal and into the fog.

7. On the other side of the glass

The fog billows around him. Adam S. Miles says again, to make sure The Other hears, "I choose me. I am all that is left. I am unanimous."

The fog seems to press in on him. He wonders how he will get out of it. But he knows he has to walk. He has to move or the fog will come in so close it will come into him and he will die.

That is against the rules.

He takes two steps…

… into…

…the fog…

And suddenly there are dark shapes all around him. Green lights wink into life on each shape. The eyes, strange and wrong and yet oddly familiar (has he grown to understand this all? *Is* there sense to this?) blink and dance as the things draw closer.

They surround him on all sides but one. The side that will allow him back into the terminal. Adam S. Miles feels like running there. But he should not have to. He played by the rules. Everything he did made sense.

The shapes come closer. Lights flash deeper in the fog.

"I am all in favor," he says. "Adam S. Miles votes yea."

They keep creeping closer, the black shapes. There are arms and legs, but either they are strange and terrifying in their shapes, or the fog *makes* them that way.

Adam S. Miles turns and runs back to the terminal. He does not want to be in there, but something is so dreadfully wrong out here. Everything made sense for a second, when he decided that it made the most sense for him to live, for *him* to be the one to make and accept the final vote.

But sense has fled once more. Things do not make sense again, and Adam can think of nowhere to go but back to where he was.

He runs, tripping over the curb that is right behind him. He stumbles, arms making big circles as he almost falls but manages to keep his feet under him.

He comes to the terminal. The glass doors that opened to allow him to leave do not open to allow him to enter.

They stay closed.

And Adam screams, because a corpse is standing on the other side of the glass.

Interlude

The Watchers see it happen, of course. They see all things in the Cycles. That is their job and, in this place, the sum of their existence. They knew what was planned when the trick was first put in motion, though they did not see it playing out exactly the way it did. That makes it better. The unexpected moments make the Cycle more exciting.

They watch now, as Adam stares at the woman he thought was dead. Shelly Sherman stands inside the terminal. She smiles grimly as Adam says, "No. This doesn't make sense. It doesn't –" Then he stops speaking. He whispers, "There is a way to make the vote unanimous for one person: if that person is the only one still alive." His eyes refocus on Shelly. "*You* said that, Shelly Sherman. You realized it first."

She nods. She draws the scarf away from her neck, which is gray and bloodless-seeming. But beneath the scarf that the Watchers saw her arrange so carefully in the overlapping plates of the baggage carousel, the skin is red and healthy.

Shelly begins wiping her face with the scarf. More pink, healthy skin appears as she wipes the gray makeup off her face.

"Let me tell you how that story ends," says Adam, mimicking the words spoken only a few hours before. The Watchers note this, knowing they will go back later to review both what he says now and what Shelly said then, wondering how perfectly Adam is reproducing her words. "The 'big-time producer' turns out to be a fraud. Mine was a lonely liar of a makeup artist who knew almost no one… At least I learned how to do makeup," he whispers. "And that's something, because sooner or later *everyone* gets wrinkles." His gaze locks directly onto Shelly's eyes. For the first time, he makes and holds eye contact. This, too, the Watchers note, just as they note as he says, "Sooner or later *everyone* needs to hide something."

Then Adam switches to different words by a different speaker. The Watchers will check this later, too, to see how close he comes to what Clarice actually said.

"Shelly Sherman… history of drug and alcohol abuse… incarcerations for resorting to illegal means of getting drugs including – Burglary and prostitution?" Adam's eyes wander back and forth from Shelly's face to the fog, from memory of the past to acknowledgment of the present. "You are the thief. Not Jeremy Cutter, *you,*" he says. "It was *all* you, wasn't it? You took my games, too didn't you?"

Shelly smiles and holds up the GameBoy and the cartridges. "My granddaughter will love these," she says.

"That's a lovely ring," says Adam, again parroting Clarice's words.

Shelly shrugs. "I haven't done the thieving thing full-time for a while. And I never enjoyed it. But old habits do die hard."

"You watched us," says Adam.

Shelly nods. "Thought I was blown at one point. I kept sneaking my eyes open a bit to see if there were any moments I could use. Like when I lifted Taylor's purse and switched her fix for Jesús' insulin." She sighs. "I really am sorry, for what it's worth. You seem like a sweet boy, but I have a life to live and a granddaughter to meet."

The Watchers note Adam's response. He does not rant or rave. He looks strangely at peace as he says, "You made all the blocks fit just right." He nods and again looks at Shelly. "It makes sense."

The Watchers nod. There is nothing more to wait for.

They signal for the Killers, who yank Adam away from the glass, away from Shelly, away from the terminal and into the mist and into *them*.

A spray of blood flecks the doors, splattering over Shelly Sherman's increasingly lively face.

She looks out but does not see those who took Adam. Hints and traces, yes. But they are the fog, the night. They only show as much as they wish to show, and no more than the Cycle demands. That is what The Other has ordered, and so must be what The Other receives.

The Other has nearly finished with this group. The Cycle is drawing to a close.

PART FIVE: End of Cycle

1. Into the mist

Shelly watched the mist close around Adam. She saw the lights flashing – the same ones she had seen throughout the night, those blue flashes, those green triplets of light.

She had watched so carefully. No job she'd ever pulled as a kid had given her quite the same challenge – and certainly not quite the same rush.

She had stolen for money in her life. She had stolen for drugs. She had stolen to keep herself alive. She had stolen for a million reasons, big and small, and come out on top every time. But never had she felt like this, watching from the shadows as the world and everyone around her fell apart.

It was scary. The worst moments had been the first ones, when they found her "body" and she had to hold her breath and hope they wouldn't look too close.

That was something many thieves understood: the best procedure for getting away clean was often hiding in plain sight, either making the lie into something the marks *wanted* to believe or by presenting a reality so uncomfortable that they were happy not to look too closely.

Shelly had done both: she had given them one less person to figure into the tally. And she had hidden in plain sight, but in a way that kept them from watching her.

Still, she *had* been caught. That one time Taylor saw her, a moment when Shelly had her eyes cracked open. Waiting for moments to steal something, to stir things up.

She hadn't really taken Adam's GameBoy for her granddaughter. She *would* give it to Michelle, because that would be a good first present. But mostly she'd taken it hoping Adam would freak out, then that would be a bit more conflict, maybe one or two of the group taking themselves out in the ruckus. That hadn't happened, but her plan switching Taylor's drugs out with Jesús' meds – that had been a good one.

She stared out at the mist. She was alone.

She looked at the countdown on the wall. She had expected it to stop – she'd won, hadn't she? – *but it was still going*. Twenty seconds and counting.

Panic seeped into her blood, turning it to ice that ran through every part of her. "What –" Then she realized what she still had to do. "I vote that I be the one who lives," she said.

16… 15…

"All in favor?"

14…

She raised her hand.

13…

Shelly looked around.

11…

The headless corpse of Jeremy.

10…

The maimed body of Bella.

9…

Clarice in her pool of blood, her throat torn and her eyes staring.

8…

The greasy, strung-out visage of Taylor.

7…

Mary.

6…

Deputy Kingsley.

5…

"It appears the vote is unanimous," she said.

The countdown froze. Four seconds to go.

The glass doors slid open. And was it her imagination, or was the fog already lifting a bit?

Shelly took a step toward the doors, then stopped. She glanced at the clock, worried it might have started again. But it was still hanging at five seconds. The time had appeared, too: five a.m. on the dot.

That meant that she had survived. That meant Michelle was waiting nearby. She was so close. But Shelly still had a bit to do.

She wasn't going to steal the wallets or purses of the dead. That would be stupid. Wasting time in a situation she still didn't fully understand, and it would leave obvious signs of the thefts that would lead back to her if anyone ever investigated whatever had happened at the terminal.

But there were a few things she could grab. The rest of Adam's games. The thick wad of cash she found in Taylor's purse – money for the girl's next fix. Shelly had ached to take it the first time she grabbed Taylor's purse, but had left it untouched. For Shelly's switcharoo to work, to kill the girl and Jesús, Taylor had to believe everything in her purse was as it had been, including the drugs. Taking the money then might have alerted her.

Now: no one was left to alert. Shelly grabbed the money and the other things she had noted.

She passed by Clarice's body, pausing long enough to lift the girl's hand and strip off the ring. "It really is beautiful," she said. "Not the story you hoped for, and that's sad, but it'll make a good dent in my granddaughter's college tuition, and *that's* a nice story, too, isn't it?"

Then she turned back to the doors, which still hung open, and stepped out into the mist.

2. The shadows kept pace

Shelly expected the mist to drift away. She expected it to dissipate and leave her alone in a world where she had won, and her granddaughter waited.

She stepped forward, walking confidently at first then a bit more tentatively

The mist, which had seemed for a moment to lighten, to drift away, now pressed on her even harder.

The lights began flashing. Blue flashes, green trios of brightness. Dark shapes that surged forward, then melted away.

This wasn't supposed to happen. It was supposed to be *over*.

"I played the game! I did what I was supposed to do! I get to leave!" she shouted.

The shadows encircled her. They drew closer, the green eyes flaring brighter and brighter.

Then, on one side, they withdrew.

"Thank you," Shelly breathed.

She ran.

But the shadows did not disappear. They left room for her to run, but only in one direction. Shelly ran, knowing she was being pushed somewhere new and awful, but not able to stop. So she ran and ran… and the shadows kept pace as she fled.

3. And the darkness surged

She didn't know how long she ran. She only knew that she ran, ran, ran; and the fog was everywhere and the only break in what she saw was the dark gap where The Other wanted her to run.

She heard, suddenly, Red's voice in her mind. A voice haunted and mad:

"They herded me. Moooooo…. Moooooooooooooo.They herded me. Mooooooooooooooooooooooooooo."

She knew now what was happening.

"I did what you asked," she shouted. "I *did what you asked!"*

The Other did not speak. It simply moved, and she knew that if it moved too close the game would be over. What had Red called it? The Cycle.

The Cycle was over. But another was beginning.

She ran.

She saw something in the mist. Lights that grew and coalesced into something so glorious and bright Shelly almost wept: signs. Not signs of alien life, not signs of doom, just good old fashioned neon lights. A gas station.

She ran closer, seeing a U-Haul at one pump, a small car at another.

She ran even closer, now seeing a snack shack beyond the cars and the pumps. A few people were inside: a night clerk. A middle-age man who looked so tired he was the one she knew belonged to the U-Haul.

And two others….

"No," she breathed.

She kept running.

Running. Not wanting to get closer, because then she might see even clearer, but not able to stop because *not* seeing would be even worse.

She got closer. She saw clearly. A few moments later she was close enough that she could even hear the people inside.

There was a table in the snack shack. An older woman, perhaps early sixties, sat at the table. "I don't think the candy bar is a good idea," she said. "You don't want to have a sick tummy when you see her."

And the little girl who sat across from her – a girl Shelly had only seen in photos, but whose face she would know anywhere – said, "*Pleeease,*" in that drawn-out way that sounded awful in adults but so endearing when a child did it.

The older lady stared at her. "Okay," said the little girl. She pushed the candy bar away. "You think she's going to like me?"

The older lady, obviously the social worker assigned for the travel and transfer, said, "Are you kidding? She can't *wait* to see you."

Shelly realized she was no longer running.

She stared at the thing she had come here to find.

She did not want to go there now. Not with what she was bringing along for the ride.

She stared at the shapes in the mist. Drawing closer. Moving in ways she almost recognized, but absolutely *knew* meant she had to keep moving.

In her pocket, something buzzed. She pulled out her phone. Read the text.

The Other: keep going
a new Cycle begins

Shelly looked at the shapes. She looked at the phone. She looked at her granddaughter.

She shook her head. "No. I refuse to play." The shapes moved closer. "Game over," she said.

And the darkness surged over her and Shelly could not regret her final choice.

EPILOGUE: the other

The Watchers stare at the body as it is taken away. They turn to the gas station. One of them is surprised to see a little girl looking out at them. "Mrs. Garret!" she shouts, her hands pressed against the window. "I saw something out there! Something in the fog."

Mrs. Garret presses her own hands against the glass. "I don't see anything."

The Watchers move closer. They know what the people inside *are* seeing:

They are seeing the fog. They are seeing shapes in the fog. They are seeing lights flashing.

They are seeing the beginning of the next Cycle.

One of the Watchers grunts. He breaks protocol, removing the night-vision/infrared goggles whose trio of lenses allow him to see through the fog. He rubs his eyes. "Those things give me a headache."

His phone flashes. It hangs in a holster at his side, and the flashes are visible to the other Watchers – and anyone else looking this way – as blurs in the mist.

He pulls his phone off his hip. Looks at it. He texts a simple message:

Watcher 1: First Cycle where everyone died.

The phone blinks. The Watcher does not expect much response. He never does. He knows very little. Only that he is to watch events unfold, make sure anyone who leaves each location chosen for a new Cycle dies until only one is left, and he is to then write a report at the end of his shift. He will be spelled by another Watcher who will take his phone, his gear, and will go by his designation for the duration of the following shift.

He doesn't think the Engineers know much, either. They know how to run the machine that manipulates the fog, and for a while – the first three Cycles or so – he figured they were the ones in charge. But none of them have answers about what they're studying, or why.

The Killers – of course, they know nothing at all, other than who they are supposed to kill when Watcher 1 or one of the other team leaders indicates.

His phone flashes again. That could mean he is to provide an update, as he just did. Or it could mean he is receiving new orders, which it now does.

The message is short and simple, as all the incoming messages have been:

The Other: begin the next Cycle

One of the other Watchers approaches. It is a woman, but Watcher 1 knows her only as Watcher 18. No one here has a name, just a designation. That's the way these things always work. Names leave a trail. Names make it easier for the people involved to be found. If found, they can be asked questions that the most powerful people would prefer not to answer: who authorized this study? Who was behind the idea? What else has this technology been used for? And the worst one, which the Watcher knows is absolutely to be avoided by the person or people behind it:

"And how long did you know about this, Congressman?" It could be that, or it could be Senator, or it could even be "Mr. President" at the end of the question.

Whoever it is in this case, he or she is being careful. Just going by The Other.

Watcher 18 stares into the gas station. "What *are* we studying here?" she asks.

Watcher 1 smiles, but he knows that he will report this query. Watcher 18 will likely disappear sometime during the next Cycle. Asking questions when things like this are going on is very bad for one's health.

But he smiles. For now. "Above my pay grade," he says. "And it really doesn't matter, does it? 'Ours is not to reason why…'"

Watcher 18 nods, though Watcher 1 doubts she knows the end of the stanza he just paraphrased. A poem he loves: Tennyson's "Charge of the Light Brigade."

Theirs not to reason why
Theirs but to do and die:
Into the valley of Death
Rode the six hundred.

Watcher 1 likes that poem. It makes him feel powerful.

"Let's get started," he said. He stares into the window of the gas station's snack shop. A smaller group in this Cycle, but no doubt that is part of the plan, too. Whatever the plan *is*.

His phone flashes.

Watcher 1 reads the message. He laughs.

This Cycle is going to be fun. Maybe the most fun of them all.

Author's note

Unlike *Terminal,* the government and private experiments and cruelties which Adam details are not fiction. They happened.

"And all people, good or bad, walk a path surrounded by shortcuts. Most of them take one – for a good cause, of course. But once taken, the shortcuts become the path."

Jesús is a vile character.

He's also right.

This story is, ultimately, one about people who have taken shortcuts – or tried to sidestep the choices completely – and have come to grief because of it. We as humans are capable of great cruelty. It is almost always a shortcut. It follows on the heels of misinformation, disinformation, and ignorance. It is a shorthand, or an excuse, or sometimes (worst of all) just a product of "because I can."

We as humans are also capable of caring, sympathy, love. That is almost always a longer path, and the harder one to take at times. But it is certainly the worthier of the two.

- Michaelbrent Collings

A REQUEST FROM THE AUTHOR:

If you loved this book, **I would really appreciate a short review on the page where you bought the book**. Ebook retailers factor reviews into account when deciding which books to push, so a review by you will ABSOLUTELY make a difference to this book, and help other people find it.

And that matters, since that's how I keep writing and (more important) take care of my family. So please drop a quick review – even "Book good. Me like words in book. More words!" is fine and dandy, if that's what's in your heart.

And thanks again!

*

HOW TO GET YOUR FREE BOOK:

As promised, here's a goodie for you: sign up for Michaelbrent's newsletter and you'll get a free book (or maybe more!) with nothing ever to do or buy. Just go to http://eepurl.com/VHuvX to sign up for your freebie, and you're good to go!

*

FOR WRITERS:

Michaelbrent has helped hundreds of people write, publish, and market their books through articles, audio, video, and online courses. For his online courses, check out http://michaelbrentcollings.thinkific.com

*

ABOUT THE AUTHOR

Michaelbrent is an internationally-bestselling author, produced screenwriter, and member of the Writers Guild of America, but his greatest jobs are being a husband and father. See a complete list of Michaelbrent's books at writteninsomnia.com.

*

FOLLOW MICHAELBRENT

Twitter: twitter.com/mbcollings

Facebook: facebook.com/MichaelbrentCollings

ACKNOWLEDGMENTS

"Thank you" is always hard. Not because I don't feel it, but because if I said it to everyone who deserved it, I'd never write another book. I owe so much to so many that thanking everyone properly would be a full-time job. So I'll have to settle for…

THANK YOU to my wife, my kids, and my extended family. You are the reason I a) am what I am, and b) am not facedown in a ditch somewhere.

THANK YOU to my readers. You make this continuing adventure possible.

THANK YOU to my awesome Street Team, who get the word out early, and well. Special thanks to Julie Castle-Smith, Nicole Canale, Stacey Nagy, Nicole Toscano, Kim Napolitano, Chris Forbes, Debbie Dillis, Nic Heaton-Harris, Michelle Enelen, Shelley Milligan, DeAnna Morgan, Stacy Butchart, Dan Hilton, Mina Roos, Kimberly Adler-Morelli, and all the others who caught errors in the ARC and without whose input I would look like a fool (or at least, a bigger one).

THANK YOU to anyone reading all the way to the end. You are amazing.

NOVELS BY MICHAELBRENT COLLINGS

PREDATORS
THE DARKLIGHTS
THE LONGEST CON
THE HOUSE THAT DEATH BUILT
THE DEEP
TWISTED
THIS DARKNESS LIGHT
CRIME SEEN
STRANGERS
DARKBOUND
BLOOD RELATIONS:
A GOOD MORMON GIRL MYSTERY
THE HAUNTED
APPARITION
THE LOON
MR. GRAY (aka THE MERIDIANS)
RUN
RISING FEARS

THE COLONY SAGA:
THE COLONY: GENESIS (THE COLONY, Vol. 1)
THE COLONY: RENEGADES (THE COLONY, Vol. 2)
THE COLONY: DESCENT (THE COLONY, VOL. 3)
THE COLONY: VELOCITY (THE COLONY, VOL. 4)
THE COLONY: SHIFT (THE COLONY, VOL. 5)
THE COLONY: BURIED (THE COLONY, VOL. 6)
THE COLONY: RECKONING (THE COLONY, VOL. 7)
THE COLONY OMNIBUS
THE COLONY OMNIBUS II
THE COMPLETE COLONY SAGA BOX SET

YOUNG ADULT AND
MIDDLE GRADE FICTION:

THE SWORD CHRONICLES
THE SWORD CHRONICLES: CHILD OF THE EMPIRE
THE SWORD CHRONICLES: CHILD OF SORROWS
THE SWORD CHRONICLES: CHILD OF ASH

THE RIDEALONG
PETER & WENDY: A TALE OF THE LOST
(aka HOOKED: A TRUE FAERIE TALE)
KILLING TIME

THE BILLY SAGA:
BILLY: MESSENGER OF POWERS (BOOK 1)
BILLY: SEEKER OF POWERS (BOOK 2)
BILLY: DESTROYER OF POWERS (BOOK 3)
THE COMPLETE BILLY SAGA (BOOKS 1-3)

PRAISE FOR THE WORK OF MICHAELBRENT COLLINGS

"Epic fantasy meets superheroes, with lots of action and great characters.... Collings is a great storyteller." - Larry Correia, New York Times bestselling author of *Monster Hunter International* and *Son of the Black Sword*

"... intense... one slice of action after another... a great book and what looks to be an interesting start of a series that could be amazing." - Game Industry News

"Collings is so proficient at what he does, he crooks his finger to get you inside his world and before you know it, you are along for the ride. You don't even see it coming; he is that good." – *Only Five Star Book Reviews*

"What a ride.... This is one you will not be able to put down and one you will remember for a long time to come. Very highly recommended." – *Midwest Book Review*

"I would be remiss if I didn't say he's done it again. Twists and turns, and an out-come that will leave one saying, 'I so did not see that coming.'" – *Audiobook Reviewer*

"His prose is brilliant, his writing is visceral and violent, dark and enthralling." – *InD'Tale Magazine*

"I literally found my heart racing as I zoomed through each chapter to get to the next page." – *Media Mikes*

Cover image element by Elti Meshau from Pexels
cover design by Michaelbrent Collings

website: http://www.michaelbrentcollings.com
email: info@michaelbrentcollings.com

For more information on Michaelbrent's books, including specials and sales; and for info about signings, appearances, and media,
check out his webpage,
Like his Facebook fanpage
or
Follow him on Twitter.

Made in the USA
Monee, IL
05 May 2020

29853903R00189